Savage Love

BAILEY HART

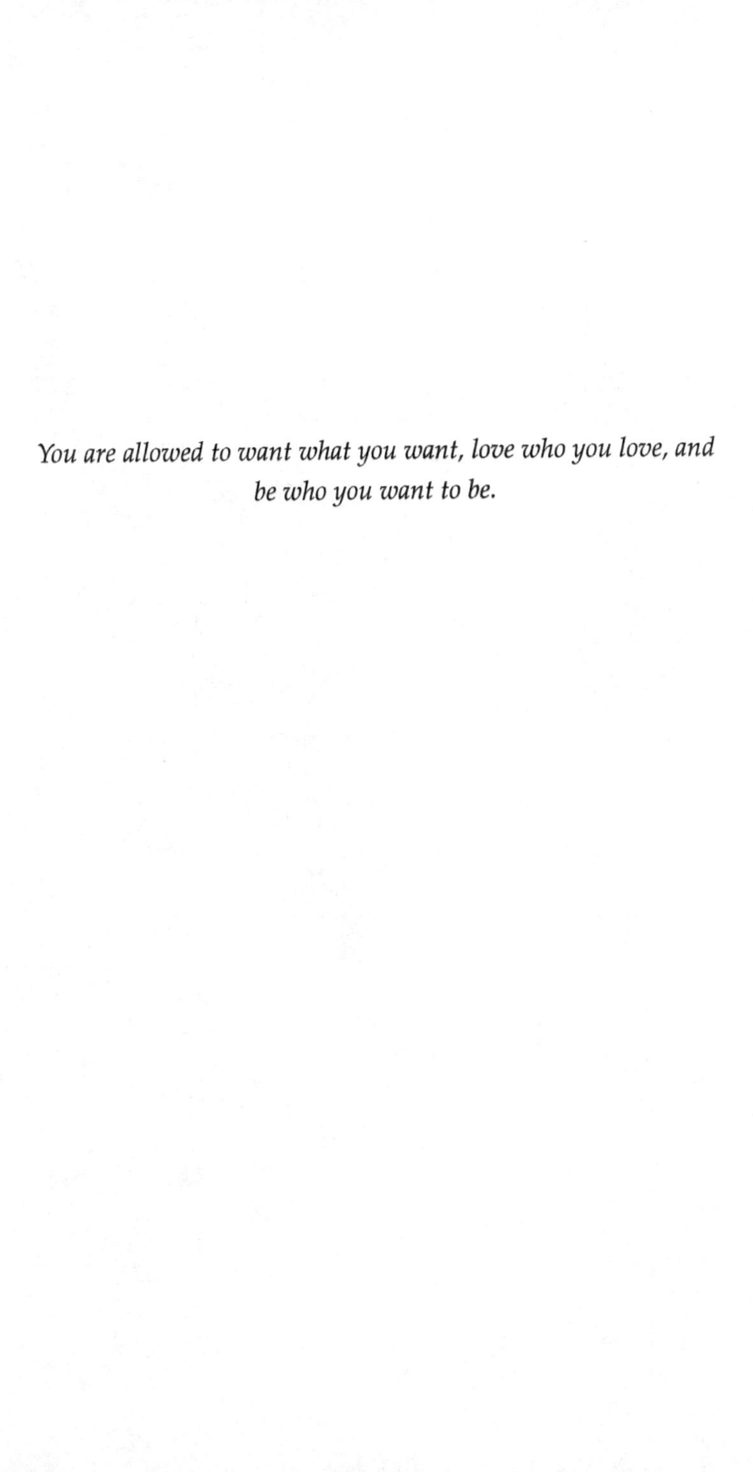

You are allowed to want what you want, love who you love, and be who you want to be.

Playlist

"Midnight Sky" — Miley Cyrus
"Yes, and?" — Ariana Grande
"Made You Look" — Meghan Traitor
"Fearless (Taylor's Version)" — Taylor Swift
"Put Your Head On My Shoulder" — Paul Anka
"Wicked Game" — Chris Isaac
"Watermelon Sugar" — Harry Styles
"Lover" — Taylor Swift
"Stay" — Rihanna, Mikky Elko
"I Will Always Love You" — Whitney Houston

Scan in app to listen:

Content Warning

This story contains topics that readers might find upsetting. I've done my best to handle them with grace and sensitivity.

Please visit www.baileyhartromance.com/svlcw or scan the QR CODE below for more details.

One

HANNAH

THIS IS the most important day of my life.

Fifty habanero peppers. Five contestants, and a crowd that's filled with so many familiar faces, my head swims. I can't afford to choke. I've been training for this for literal months.

"Welcome to Heatstroke's Twenty-Fifth Annual Hot Pepper Eating Contest!" The announcer, Richard Walton, is Heatstroke's favorite newscaster, and he's exactly what I imagined he'd be like. Elaborately-coiffed, overly friendly, with a thousand-watt smile and one of those combs tucked into the top pocket of his snazzy suit jacket.

It's easier to focus on his jacket than the way his gaze remains fixed on the TV camera below the makeshift stage in the Heatstroke Public Park.

The crowd cheers and claps.

"Let's go, Hannah!" June calls from somewhere in the masses.

I squeeze my eyes shut and exhale.

I am *so* not good with crowds. But I swore I would do

this, and I'm not backing out. The sky is peony blue, the grass in the park is lush, and the heat of the day is threatening, though it's barely past ten. And this is it. My shot.

"As y'all know, this year's contest is proudly sponsored by the Heatstroke Board of Better Businesses, a collection of local businesses, including the General Store, Beets and Yeets, Bagel's Bakery, the Heartstopper Diner, Longhorn's, and your very own News Channel Nine," Richard continues, in his professional announcer voice. "And get this folks, this year's prize is bigger than ever before, with the winner walking away with a grand prize of ten *thousand* dollars."

Gasps and cheers follow that, and I steel myself, trying not to be intimidated by the cameras, the mass of peppers on the plate, or Paul, who's last year's winner, standing next to me with his arms folded, and a look on his face that says, "Why did you even bother to show up?"

I'm here for two reasons.

First, because I want to show my family that "boring" little librarian Hannah can be just as crazy and adventurous as the rest of my siblings.

Second, the money.

With that kind of money, I can revamp the children's section of the library before I leave.

My stomach twists, and I glance toward Richard.

"—how it's going to work. In the first round, contestants will eat up to fifty habanero peppers. Those who survive will move on to the final round, in which they will eat as many Carolina Reaper peppers as they can handle. The last person standing wins."

Sweat beads on the back of my neck. The Carolina Reaper pepper is one of the hottest in the world at over 1.5

million Scoville units. In other words, hot enough to make a grown woman cry or eviscerate this particular woman's digestive system.

Why am I doing this again? The children. A parting gift. *You can do this.*

"Don't touch your eyes," I murmur. "Do *not* touch your eyes."

"Worried, sweetheart? You should drop out now," Paul says. "Save yourself the pain. We all know I'm going to win, and this ain't the amateur leagues."

"What's the matter, Paul?" I whisper. "Can't handle a little healthy competition?"

Paul's eyes widen, but before he can retort, the crowd bursts into cheers again.

"All right, folks," Richard says. "Let's get this pepper-eating show on the road! Contestants, come forward and stand behind your eating stations."

I tie my hair back in a high ponytail as I step forward. I grab the plastic bib that's been laid over the back of the chair at my station. Really, it's just a spot behind a long wooden table that might as well be an eating trough.

Hot peppers have a myriad of benefits. They decrease inflammation, for one. They—

"Take your seats," Richard says.

I sit down and stare at the hot pepper pile. My gaze lifts to the crowd, and I spot June and Cash out there. Cash is unmistakable, especially since he's taller than most of the other people, and he's wearing that "Hannah, what the heck are you doing" scowl. I'm grateful he's here. He turned down an invitation to host the event, and an interview about me, which would really have been about him.

That's the cross my famous brother has to bear, and he handles it so well.

I force a smile.

June waves frantically, bobbing up onto her tiptoes, and I wave back.

"At the ready," Richard says. "Let's count it down. Three."

The crowd joins in, clapping on the countdown.

"Two."

"One! Start eating," Richard yells.

Next to me, Paul fists five peppers, stem and all, and rams them into his mouth. He chews like a man blessed by Çhicomecoatl, the Mexican goddess of fire and fertility herself.

"Go, Hannah!" June screams above the crowd. If Marci wasn't on her honeymoon, she'd be here too.

I grab the first three peppers on my plate and shove them into my mouth. And the world becomes fiery pain. My diaphragm contracts, and I start hiccuping so hard it's a struggle to swallow one pepper, let alone three.

Maybe if I swallow them whole?

My eyes and nose stream.

Paul's making grunting noises and chewing through habaneros at a rate that's inhuman.

Eat past the pain. Remember why you're doing this. Tears trickle down my cheeks, and I shove another pepper into my mouth and then another. I blink, my vision blurry, and try seeking out June in the crowd for moral support, and that's when it happens.

That's when I see *him*.

Carter Savage, striding toward Cash, the crowd parting in front of him effortlessly. My brother's best friend, who doesn't know I exist as anything other than Cash's hopeless little sister.

Carter's gorgeous, even through tears with his rough, well-kept beard streaked with gray, tattoos that arc up his muscular neck, tan skin and those dark, devilish eyes. A gray T-shirt strains against the muscles that make up this man's body.

I can't help staring or the butterflies in my stomach or the fact that I gasp when his gaze wanders to the stage and lands on me.

Thanks to Savage, I've conveniently forgotten that I have a mouth full of hot peppers. And now, chunks of them are lodged in my throat.

I can't breathe. The realization hits me, and I try to inhale again. I gag and smack my hands down on the table. I slap Paul on the arm for help, but he ignores me and keeps deep-throating peppers.

Help me. Help me.

I'm choking on national television. I'm choking in front of the entirety of Heatstroke.

I scramble to my feet.

I'm choking in front of Savage.

I stumble on the stage, heading toward Richard, pointing at my throat. Panic has my mind in an iron grip.

You're going to die. You're going to die in front of all these people.

I gag and sputter.

Richard gives me a smile, blissfully unaware. Or maybe he just thinks this is what peppers do to people. "Looks like we've got our first tap out, folks. Hannah Taylor is—"

I pull on Richard's arm and fall to my knees, trying to drag him down with me, to make him realize.

Please. Help. Anyone. Anyone.

Strong arms wrap around my middle and lift me into the air. The scent of cedar and smoke envelops me, but I barely have a second to register them, because those muscular arms tighten and thrust upward into my abdomen. A rush of air bursts from my lungs, sending chunks of pepper splattering across the front of Richard's suit.

I suck in air and fire, doubling over, but I'm held upright by my savior.

He sets my feet down on the stage. "Are you all right?" he asks, and his voice is gravelly and impossibly deep.

No. No, no. No. Nope. This isn't happening.

I turn around and stare up into Savage's dark eyes, streaked amber by the morning sunlight, and hate my life. He releases me, a frown wrinkling his brow, and holds his arms around me in a protective circle without touching me.

Because why would he want to touch me? I'm the geeky younger sister who just choked on a pepper in front of *everyone.*

"I'm fine," I manage, even though my throat is raw, and I am mentally not okay.

I want out of here. The competition is over for me because the rules are simple—leave your station and you're out.

Savage scans my face, searching me for I have no idea what, and then he finally gives a nod. His gaze shifts over my head and darkens into something beastly. "You," he says, and then he moves past me.

He walks up to Richard and grabs him by the front of his pepper-spritzed jacket. He lifts him off the stage so that his fancy loafers dangle and kick. Richard's jaw drops. The reporter's face is dotted with bits of orange pepper and habanero seeds. He's lucky he didn't get any in the eyes.

The crowd shouts, the cameraman is getting every second of the altercation and loving it, and most of the other contestants have stopped their pepper-eating, unsure of whether the contest is still on or not. Except for Paul, of course, who is just about done with his first plate.

"You didn't realize she was choking? Are you fucking dumb?" Savage growls, giving Richard a shake. "Where are the medics?"

"M-Medics?" Richard manages.

"You don't have a medical team on standby at this event?" Savage's words are deathly. "What kind of idiot are you?"

"Hey, man, I'm just the host," Richard says, his tone reedy. "Listen, I—"

"Do safety standards mean nothing to you people?" Savage drops him, towering over him.

It's too much. The choking, Savage saving me. The mortification and the loss. I turn and run down the stage steps as fast as my legs will carry me.

The most important day of my life? Try the worst day of my life. I can't get out of Heatstroke fast enough.

Two

SAVAGE

I'M PLAYING with fire by coming here, but I can't *not* check on her. And I have an excuse.

The Harley burbles as I direct it toward the Heatstroke Public Library. It's been a day since Hannah choked on a hot pepper, and I've spent every minute thinking about what happened.

I haven't been angry enough to lose control in years. Not since before I moved to Heatstroke, but yesterday, I nearly lost it. That fucking dumbass. It still makes me boil with anger—the sight of Hannah red in the face, dragging on that reporter's arm, dropping to her knees in front of him while he gave her a vacant "TV-friendly" smile and announced she was out of the contest.

What kind of man was he to let that happen?

What kind of man are you?

I park the Harley in a spot outside the library, take off my helmet, hang it over my handlebar, and snap the helmet lock into place. I grab the book on horticulture from my saddlebag and head up the stone steps toward the open front doors.

Turn around.

But I won't or I can't.

I made a promise to look out for her. And another promise I try not to think about, and the two parts of my brain are warring. I manage to convince myself that I'm being a good friend to Cash by the time I enter the library.

Hannah's not at the glossy front counter, the wood worn from years of use, so I tuck the book under my arm and head between the stacks. I nod to the elderly woman behind the counter, and she purses her lips. Maybe because she was there for my loss of temper yesterday. Or maybe it's the permanent frown I wear.

The library smells like every library on the planet. Books, a hint of dust, and old wood. The quiet in here is a comfort, but it doesn't stop me from pacing up and down the rows of books with my features twisted into a scowl.

Shouldn't be here. This is a bad fucking idea.

But I can't forget it. My arms wrapped around her middle, the soft scent of her floral perfume, hints of roses and something else I couldn't place. Her blue eyes staring up at me, wide, shining, innocent.

You're sick. You're a sick, sick man. This is my best friend's little sister. She is ten years younger than me, for fuck's sake.

I pace back to the front of the library, the book under my arm, and stop near the romance section, my gaze tracing the spines of the books.

"There you are, Hannah," the librarian at the counter says.

"Sorry, Irma, I had to use the bathroom," Hannah replies, her voice sweet and soft.

Normal. Her voice is normal. Her voice is almost childlike. But I can't convince myself of that, because it's not. It's a tempting voice from a twenty-eight-year-old woman.

"Again?" Irma asks.

"Yeah, let's just say habaneros and I do *not* get along."

The corners of my lips twitch, and I stroke my beard, staying behind the shelf and out of line of sight.

"It's such a pity that happened yesterday," Irma says, and she doesn't sound upset enough in my humble opinion. "You vomited all over Richard Walton, you know. People are not going to forget that any time soon. Goodness, I'm surprised you decided to come into work today. I wouldn't dare show my face after that."

Hannah clears her throat. "I didn't *vomit* on him."

"Well, what on earth would you call it? He was covered in pieces of pepper. I heard *The Heatstroke Hit Piece* is going to interview him about the ordeal. I'm surprised they haven't been in contact."

"My official comment is that I have no comment," Hannah says. "And what I'd call it, Irma, is nearly choking to death on a mouthful of peppers. Or 'the incident.'" She lets out a sigh that makes me grit my teeth. "I just want to put the whole darn thing behind me. I want to put this town behind me, now that we're talking about it."

"You're still going to do it then, dear?" Irma asks.

"Yeah. I've saved up enough money. I just have to book the tickets. Work up the courage to tell my family."

My fists ball up and release. She's leaving?

"We're going to miss you," Irma says. "But maybe it's for the best. Give the town some time to cool off after what happened yesterday. People were shocked, especially when Carter Savage accosted poor Mr. Walton."

"He was trying to help," Hannah says.

"I've never seen him behave that way. Like an animal. I heard he was getting up to all sorts of strange things out on that ranch, but—"

"He's running a self-defense camp," Hannah cuts in. "He's an ex-Navy SEAL so he was probably just worried about the safety standards or something."

I wish that was why. Fuck, I'm not entirely sure why I blew my lid like that. I don't want to believe it's because of Hannah.

The conversation between the women dies down as another person enters the library and returns their books. I grab a book off the shelf in front of me, then head over to the counter where Hannah's working.

She is *beautiful*. Beyond compare.

Her dark hair falls loose around her shoulders today, and she's wearing those black cat's eye glasses on the tip of her button nose as she peers down at the computer screen. It's summer, and Hannah's camisole is tight across her chest, showing off perky tits and an expanse of tan cleavage that reminds me how bad of a choice this was to come here today.

Irma gives me a sideways glance but continues helping the man at her side of the counter.

I place the books down.

Hannah gives a benign smile and tears her gaze away from the screen. "Hi—oh," she says, and her smile disappears the minute our eyes meet.

"Returning." I tap the book on horticulture. "Checking out." I tap the book I grabbed off the shelf. I haven't even read its title. It's just an excuse to check on her.

But you already did. You don't need to be here.

Hannah's lips part, and she gnaws on her bottom lip. "Oh. Right." She glances down. "Right. Yeah. Okay, so you're returning a book on horticulture, huh?" Her voice squeaks. "That's great. Are you learning how to… horticult?" Two pink spots appear on her cheeks. "I mean, uh, grow things? You're learning how to grow. Plants. Not you. Ha." She lifts a hand to her forehead and then drops it again. "It's been a long day, sorry, you know, after and the whole… pepper-spewing incident yesterday? I've, uh, been meaning to thank you for that. So, thank you. It was the most horrifying moment of my life, but at least I'm alive to experience the shame and humiliation, right?"

"You're welcome." I place my library card on the counter.

Her throat works as she swallows, those gorgeous lips part again and she wets them. "Well, that's great. Thanks! I was just about to ask for your library lard." She squeezes her eyes shut and shakes her head. "Card."

She is so fucking adorable it makes me angry. "Can you hurry it up?"

"Right!" She scans my card and taps away on the computer with the tips of her cute pink nails. Her hands are artistic, her fingers long, and I picture them doing things that I shouldn't. Running over her breasts, grasping them, sliding over the plane of her tan stomach, toward the hem of a lacy—

"No fines, so that's good." She sucks in a breath and nearly chokes on it. She makes a grab for the book, just as I lower my gaze to the cover.

And the couple on the cover, caught in a romantic embrace. The guy has Fabio hair and a bare chest, and the woman is swooning in his arms, wearing a cotton shift that hides nothing.

The title, *Riding the Wind,* is printed across the cover in sweeping lettering, and I'm regretting the fact that I did *not* check what I picked off the shelf before coming over. I'm more of an "enemies-to-lovers" man.

"Oh," Hannah says. "Oh, well, I… Wow. No horticulting tonight, I guess." She shifts her glasses up her nose. "Sorry, I don't know what's wrong with me."

Nothing at all, Princess.

She hurriedly stamps the book for me, scans my card, and slides both of them back. "There you go."

"Thanks."

"You're welcome, of course."

I tuck the book under my arm and study her. "You good?" The memory of that reporter ignoring her has my jaw clenched tight.

"Yes," she says, and glances sideways, clearly uncomfortable. "Are you?"

I grunt, and then I turn and walk off.

"Have a nice day!" she calls out.

The only way my day is going to be "nice" is if I manage to forget the way she smells, moves, and talks. Which is not going to happen, because there's a potluck at Ganny Taylor's house tonight, and I'm attending.

I don't date women. I don't even think about touching women any more. But Hannah Taylor has and always will make me question everything. And that's exactly why I'll never get too close.

Three

HANNAH

"WHEN I TELL you I painted the man orange, I am not exaggerating," I say, my phone pinned to my ear as I hunt for my earrings in my apartment above the bakery. I frown, one hand on my hip, and scan my bedroom.

"Orange?" Marci laughs on the other end of the line. "I thought peppers were red or green."

"No, these were those orange habaneros," I say, then get down on all fours and look under the bed. Nothing. I scoot my hand over the carpet and feel around anyway, then sigh and sit up. "And everyone is talking about it."

"It's Heatstroke," Marci replies. "You know they're going to talk about the dumbest shit imaginable. Don't worry about it. You, Hannah Taylor, are a superstar. Heatstroke's answer to… What's the opposite of Jackson Pollock?"

"I don't know, but the way I've spent half of my day in the bathroom, I might be able to give him a run for his money."

"Eugh."

"Yeah," I say. "The worst part is Paul won the grand prize, and I don't have any money to donate to the library."

"I would think the worst part would be choking half-to-death."

"Yeah, well, given that the person who saved me was Carter friggin' Savage, I am pretty much maxed out on all of the parts." I push myself up and sit down on the edge of my single bed, the duvet cover white and speckled with bluebells. Flowers are my favorite thing. Apart from books. And kids. "I really wanted to get that reader group up and running, get kids reading again. I had a plan, Marci. I had a plan and now, I'm just—"

"What, honey?"

"I don't know. I just don't know."

"Look, Han, this sucks big fat sweaty balls," Marci says.

"There's an image."

"But you have plenty of time to revamp and rework your plan, right? It might be slow progress, but maybe you can approach the town council for help? You've got a great cause."

I don't have time. But I couldn't say it out loud yet. I wasn't sure how long I'd be gone for, and as much as I adored Marci, she would want to fly back from Rome if I told her I was leaving. And that I couldn't allow. My bestie had been waiting an eternity for the right man, though she hadn't realized that, and I wasn't going to ruin that for her.

"Han?"

"I'm here," I say. "Just thinking."

"About?"

"How you're totally right. I'm not going to give up on

this. I'll find a way to make it work, even if I have to approach the principal of the middle school myself." I'll have to be quick, though, if I want to do it before I leave. The last time we had a reading at the library, it was pretty successful.

"That's the spirit!"

"Anyway, I'm being super selfish," I say. "My gosh, you and my brother are in Italy. What's that like? Tell me everything!"

"It's all pasta, parmigiano reggiano, and sex. So much—"

"Oooooh-kay. Let's not with that last part. He's my brother."

"Right, right. But we saw the Colosseum."

"What was that like?" I ask.

"We had sex in it."

"Please."

"I'm kidding!"

Marci tells me about their sightseeing while I listen and move through my apartment. I enter my bathroom and grimace at my reflection in the mirror over my sink. *There she is. The pepper-spewer. The epic choker.*

I grab cute silver rosebud earrings from the sink and put them in my ears while I listen. "That sounds amazing, Marce."

"It is amazing. But we miss Mr. Skitters like crazy. We've been face-timing with him every night."

"Aww. I bet June's taking great care of him."

"She is," Marci says. "I'm half-convinced Skits is falling in love with her."

"I heard that!" Jesse's voice is a muffled shout in the background.

"Jesse's too jealous for his own good," Marci says, and then she lets out a shriek. "Jesse, what are you—?"

"Han?" Jesse's voice replaces Marci's.

"Hey, bro."

"Enjoy the potluck tonight," he says. "Be careful."

"Jesse, I'm a grown woman."

"Yeah, but you never know how many hot peppers there might be at Ganny's tonight. You gotta watch out."

"You ass."

He guffaws. "Love ya! Byeeeee." And then he hangs up.

I smile at the phone. It's so good to hear both my best friend and my brother happy. It's the kind of happiness I've never experienced. I never *will* experience.

The last guy who I dated was an unmitigated disaster. He was into me until he found out I'm probably not able to have kids thanks to my Premature Ovarian Insufficiency.

I grab my handbag off my living room sofa, fetch the tiramisu that is my contribution, and then I'm on my way out of the door, and onto the fire exit I use instead of the stairs that lead down into the bakery. My white tennis shoe comes down on something soft, and I yelp and step back, my heart pounding.

A crushed white rose lies on the grating.

It's the second one this week, but this time, it doesn't have a card attached.

I lift the rose by the bottom of its stem, grimacing, and march down the grated steps. I toss the flower into the dumpster and wipe off my hands on my jeans, then snap a picture of said flower and send it to Franklin.

> STOP SENDING ME FLOWERS.

> **Franklin**
> I'll keep sending them until you let me
> sweep you off your feet.

> Not interested. What don't you get?

> Consider them an apology. I'm going to
> send you bouquets every day.

> Blocked.

Franklin is a guy I met on a dating site. I never met him in person because he gave off too many red flags. He insulted me, tried to convince me that I was crazy when I got offended, and then found my number and has been texting me ever since.

Cash wants to rip his throat out. The police can't do anything about it—apparently, sending flowers and texting is not enough grounds for a restraining order. And Dad is convinced that I should just move into Ganny's house and stay with them.

I block Franklin's number, even though I'm pretty sure he'll message me from another one by tomorrow. Blocking one is like lopping the head off a snake that keeps growing heads.

I grab my pepper spray out of my purse and head out of the alleyway and over to my car, nerves building. Nerves that have nothing to do with my weird pseudo-flower-stalker and everything to do with telling my family about my plans to skip town.

I take the drive at a furious pace, because I love driving

and it makes me feel adventurous and free, and screech to a halt in front of Ganny's house.

Savage's Harley is parked out front, shimmering in the afternoon sun, and my heart pounds in my throat.

Forget about it. Just forget about it.

I've had a crush on Savage since he'd first rolled into town, and I'd embarrassed myself so many times in front of him. I should've been immune at this point, but the pepper-choking had taken the cake for *most* humiliating moment in front of Savage of all time.

The second good reason for taking an extended "vacation"? I'll hopefully get over my Savage crush and move on with my life.

I enter the house and am greeted by the burst of sound I associate with my family. Fireball the Chihuahua chases Alex around the house. She's in her teens, but she still loves playing with the dog and does so every Sunday.

"Hey, Aunt Hannah," she says, stopping for a quick hug.

"Hey, Alex. Nice shoes." She's wearing glitter-spangled black tennis shoes painted with unicorns.

"Thanks!" And then she's gone, racing off with purple ribbons fluttering in her hair.

I enter the living room and stop dead, grasping the tiramisu in both hands.

Savage is alone in here, staring out the front window, frowning. He's always frowning. Why? Why is he always—?

"Hannah!" Ganny enters the living room. "There you are, honey pie."

"Hey, Ganny." I kiss her soft rosy cheeks. "I missed you."

"I missed you two, sweetheart."

Cash follows her in and reaches out to ruffle my hair, but I dodge him and head into the hall for the open kitchen doorway. I drop off the tiramisu on the counter next to a collection of dishes. The interior is filled with the scent of baking lasagna and pies. I turn to find my brother filling the doorway, arms folded.

"You haven't been answering my calls," he says, his blue eyes laser-focused on me.

"Cash, I'm fine."

"You almost died this week." His usually surly expression, the one that only shifts when he's looking at June or Alex, is filled with concern. "And what's going on with that Fucklin dude? You haven't updated us."

"Fucklin? Nice."

"I came up with it myself," he says.

"Proud of you," I reply. "Nothing's happening."

"I heard you turned down Dad's offer to move into Ganny's?" He says it like I'm out of my mind.

"I'm fine, Cash. But I do need to talk to you. And Dad, and everybody. Kind of?"

"What's going on?" Cash asks.

Here goes nothing.

Four

SAVAGE

"ABSO-FUCKING-LUTELY NOT," Cash says, from where he's sandwiched between his grandmother and Mr. Taylor, his hands on his knees.

June stands next to Hannah, her arm around her shoulders. "Han, are you sure about this?"

I'm standing in the kitchen, my back braced against the counter, my arms folded. I'm part of the family as far as Cash is concerned, but I refuse to be in the living room for this conversation. The minute Cash called for everyone to gather around, I bowed out. I figured what this was about after overhearing Hannah in the library, and I'm fucking knotted up about it.

Hannah leaving.

"I'm sure," Hannah says, after a beat. "Look, this is important to me. I need to be free. I—All of you have left Heatstroke, you've lived your lives, and I want to be my own person. I want to leave this place. I want to—"

"Nope," Cash says. "Nope. You went to college. That was far enough away."

"Cash," June says. "She's her own woman. You can't tell her what to do."

"You can't baby me forever," Hannah says. "I'm not sick any more, Cash. We're not kids. And I love you guys, but I'm doing this no matter what you think." And then she slips out of June's grasp and heads into the hall. She doesn't meet my eyes as she moves out of sight and to the back door. The screen door slams and an awkward silence spreads through the living room.

Fuck.

Fuck.

Fuck.

She's going through with it.

Which is a good thing. Because that fucked up temptation will be gone. She's not the only one who's going to be free.

The Taylors disperse. June pulls Cash aside to talk to him, but he's scowling like only he can. He kisses her on the cheek, whispers something in her ear, then makes a beeline for me.

"Savage."

I nod toward him. "You good?"

"No," Cash says. "This whole thing is fucked."

"I don't see how you can stop her. She's going on a vacation," I say. "That's a pretty normal thing for an adult woman to do."

"You don't know the full story."

I arch an eyebrow.

"Let's talk in the study."

Apparently, this is that serious. Cash's grandfather's study is stuffy, full of dark wood and old pictures, and the faint smell of cigar smoke. It's like the spirit of the man inhabits the place, staring down on anyone who enters with disapproval. He reminds me of a drill sergeant, even in pictures with his family.

Cash opens the curtains and allows in light that show off motes of dust. "Ganny keeps it like it was when he was alive."

I nod. "What did you want to talk to me about?"

"I need your help."

"What do you need?" I'll always help Cash. He's been my best friend since the day I arrived in Heatstroke. He saved my life, and I owe him a debt that runs so deep, there's no denying a request.

During my time in the SEALs, I had brothers. Cash didn't serve with me, but I consider him as close as those men because of what he's done to help me.

Cash pinches the bridge of his nose and stares out of the window at the slatted fence that rings the yard.

"What is it?" I ask.

"She's got a stalker."

Heat travels through my body at the speed of fucking light. I hold my breath and release it slowly. "What?"

"Hannah has a stalker. Some fuckhead out in Houston who met her on a dating site. He keeps texting her, calling her, that kind of thing. He seems like a limp dick, but I'm not willing to take any chances," Cash says. "Dad's been trying to get her to move in here, but she says no. He went as far as to get movers to go over to her apartment, but she refused. And the messages are increasing in frequency. It's only a matter of time until this guy shows up, and if he can find her here, he can find her when she's away from Heatstroke. When she's vulnerable. The most she'll do is arm herself, or so she says."

"She has a gun?"

"No. Pepper spray."

"That would be first prize," I say. "A gun. She learns how to shoot. What about the cops?"

"You know they won't do a damn thing," Cash replies. "My hands have been tied, but you—"

"Me, what?" I ask.

"You are the only man I trust around her."

That's a kick to the stomach, both because it's a reminder and because it sends my guilt to new heights.

"Savage," Cash says. "I need you to be her bodyguard."

"Say what now?"

"Her bodyguard. At least while she's still in town, until —" Cash's gaze flickers from left to right, desperate. "Fuck. Okay, I get that you can't uproot your whole life and follow her across the country—"

"You'd be right there. I can't leave the camp."

"You haven't hosted a camp yet, right?" he asks. "You're still getting it set up?"

"Yes," I say.

"That's good, that's actually good," Cash says. "You've been teaching women self-defense. That's great. You can teach her, and keep her safe while you're doing it."

"Whoa, whoa, what the fuck are you talking about?"

Cash clicks his fingers. "I've got it. June and Hannah can come out to the ranch and try out a trial run of your self-defense class. You can look out for Hannah, be her bodyguard while she's there in case this psycho shows up, and I'll do what I can to hunt this guy down."

"Wouldn't it be better if I hunt the guy down and you keep her safe?" I ask, because there is no fucking chance I want Hannah on my property for an extended period of time. Even a few minutes is torture.

"No," Cash says. "I want to find him myself, and Dad, he can help me. Leo's heads so far up his ass, he can't do shit, but whatever."

"What's he got to do with it?" I haven't seen Cash's other brother in years.

"He called yesterday and said he's coming back to town," Cash says, and waves away the question like it's unimportant. "This is it, Savage."

"What exactly are you going to do?" I ask. "It's not like you can hurt the guy. That's going to make headline news. In case you've forgotten, Taylor, you're kind of a big deal." I could picture the headlines. Cash's face splashed across the front of the tabloids. *Country Music Star, Cash Taylor, Loses Control.*

"Just let me handle that," Cash says. "You take care of Hannah. She won't listen to me, but she *will* listen to you."

"How do you figure that?"

"Because she wants to learn to fight," Cash says. "She likes that kind of thing."

My pulse notches upward. "She does?"

"Yeah," Cash says. "I think this might be the one thing I could convince her to do."

"So, you're asking me to train her," I say.

"And be her bodyguard while you're training her. Keep her with you until I get back," Cash says.

"This is fucking crazy, Cash. You have no idea where this guy lives or what he's capable of," I say. "It's a bad idea."

"I'm gonna do it anyway," he says. "She's my sister, man. There's nothing more important to me than family."

The sensation of a knife twisting in my gut follows his words, and I keep my features blank.

"Fuck. Sorry." Cash squeezes my shoulder.

I stare down at him. He's a little shorter than me, but not by much. I inhale through my nose and brace myself for what I'm about to say, because I hate this. Hate that I will have to be around her, whether June is there or not. I hate that my solitude on the ranch will be broken. Hate that I won't be left alone, and that when I am, it's with thoughts that torture me.

"Please?" Cash prompts.

"Fine."

Five

HANNAH

I SIT in a booth in Longhorn's with a glass of sweet rosé, my nerves shot. Each sip helps me feel a little better, and June's company does too. Our table flanks the dancefloor, which is surprisingly full for a Sunday night. Lights flash, the warm thump of bass moves through the back of my seat, and I exhale through my nose.

At least I told them. And nobody threw a tantrum. Unless you counted Cash's man tantrum, or mantrum as I like to call it.

"It's going to be fun," June says, leaning in and catching my attention, her smile bright. "I can't wait." She swivels her wine glass slowly by the stem then drinks from it.

"I can," I mumble. "I can't believe I let you guys talk me into this."

Cash and Savage are over at the bar, and I glare at the back of my brother's head. Mostly because it keeps me from looking at Savage, or thinking about how embarrassed I am on so many levels.

"You've always wanted to learn self-defense, right?"

"I wanted to learn boxing," I say, after a beat. "But Dad never let me when I was a kid." And then when I hit adulthood, it felt like there were more important things to do. Like study or manage things at the library or help keep our family together after Mom died.

My throat tightens, and I give June a wobbly smile. "I just can't stand the thought of it," I say.

June takes my hand and squeezes. "What, Han?"

She's older than me, Marci is too, but they're both my best friends now. "Being around *him*. I thought I would be over this by now. There's nothing to get over. It's so pathetic."

The girls know about my inappropriate crush. I can't hide the way I feel from them, and June is sworn to secrecy. She won't tell Cash anything I say because we're all about girl code.

"It is *not* pathetic. The heart wants what it wants. And don't worry, I'm going to be there," June says. "I'll act as an awkwardness buffer or whatever you want to call it. I've got your back."

"You're the best."

June and I clink our glasses together and take a drink.

"Ugh, I wish Marci was here," I say. "Or Belle. I miss her so much." Belle studied with me during college, which was the *only* time I ever left Heatstroke.

"I miss her too," June says. "She was so much fun. Have you heard from Lily? She's gone super quiet in the group chat."

"No," I say. "But I think it's got something to do with her big secret. The show."

"You think it's a show?"

"I mean, probably. It makes sense. She is a reality TV star," I say. "And knowing my luck, I am too. Just for all the wrong reasons."

"I'm sure they're not going to air you spraying Richard Walton with pepper bits."

I laugh at myself. "Mortifying. But you know what, it'll make a good story to tell Alex's kids one day."

The music changes, and a shadow falls across our table. We look up, and June pulls a face at the sight of Seth Deveraux, his hair cut short, and his eyes sparkling. His gaze slides from June to me.

"Enjoying your evening, ladies?" he asks.

"What's it to you, Deveraux?" I counter.

My brother hates this guy for buying our dad's bar, but I think that low-key saved him. If Dad had reopened Chuckles, I doubt he would've wound up getting clean. I don't hate Deveraux, but I don't trust him either. Then again, I trust a sum total of five men.

Deveraux's sleeves are rolled up and show off his tattooed forearms. He's clean-shaven, tall and lean, and good-looking. He knows it, too. "Given that it's my establishment, I thought I'd check."

"Your establishment?" June's jaw drops. "What about Missy?"

"Missy opted to take her much overdue retirement," Deveraux says. "She's currently on a cruise to the Bahamas."

"You can't just pay everybody off," I say, taking a sip of wine. I'm feeling brave thanks to the alcohol, which is probably a bad thing, but what the hell. After the pepper fiasco, I've pretty much hit rock bottom.

"Can't I?" he asks. "Money makes the world go around."

"What about love?" I raise my chin.

"How old are you?" Deveraux frowns at me.

"Old enough to know an ass when I see one," I reply. "And you, sir, are a donkey of the finest kind."

"There a problem here?" Cash appears behind Deveraux on the left. Savage on the right.

"Just wishing these ladies a good evening," Seth says, and then mock strums a guitar at Cash before walking off.

"That guy is a giant dingus," I say.

"Dingus?" Cash asks, as he slides in beside June, tucking her against his side.

And it hits me like a ton of bricks that if Cash is sitting next to June, then Savage has nowhere to sit but beside me, and I'm going to be trapped beside him while I die inside thinking about his arms around me, the way he smells and—

"I gotta go to the ladies' room." I slide out of the booth and hoof it across the dance floor.

I don't look back. The fact that Savage didn't immediately slide into the seat beside me tells me everything I need to know.

In the bathroom, I slip my phone out of my pocket and check my messages. Blessedly, there aren't any from Franklin. Belle's left text messages in the group chat, and I read them, smiling to myself, happy about the distraction.

> **BELLE**
> Kill me now. Kill me now.

> Helloooo??? Where are you bitches? I need you. Like yesterday.

> Belle? What's wrong?

BELLE
Everything.

> You've always had a flair for the dramatic.

BELLE
I got an emergency message from my boss. Apparently, I'm about to meet my worst nightmare made flesh. Some hot shot rugby player who needs a babysitter. Pray for me.

> You'll be fine. You're the consummate professional.

I splash water on my face to freshen up, then head for the bathroom door. I push it open an inch but stop at the familiar rumble of Savage's voice, floating above the thump of music from the dancefloor.

"… stay away from her."

I frown and peek out.

Savage's back is to me, his shirt stretched over taut muscles, and he's glaring down at Seth Deveraux, who has his hand on the men's room door. His gaze flickers past Savage's shoulder and lands on my face, and a smile twists his lips.

"Why should I? Is she your woman or something?" Seth asks.

"No," Savage says, and he stands stiff, like he's ready to spring into action at a moment's notice.

"Then I don't see what the problem is here. We were just talking."

"Don't talk to her. She's off-limits." Savage's tone is

deathly serious, and I can barely believe what I'm hearing. My heart flutters.

Is he interested in me?

"Off-limits? How so? It's a free country, and I can talk to whoever I like. So, unless you've got a reason for threatening me like a fucking Neanderthal—"

Savage stiffens. "I'm her bodyguard," he says. "I'm doing my job."

Oh. My. God.

Heat rushes to my cheeks, and it feels as if I'm being sucked into the floor.

Seth's gaze collides with mine again, and he's wearing a frown. "Your job? She hired you to be her bodyguard? What for?"

"She didn't hire me, and it's none of your business why," Savage says. "Just stay the fuck away from her."

Seth reaches up and loosens his tie. "I have no interest in harming Hannah Taylor. So, you can relax, beefcake." He pats Savage on the arm and then enters the men's room. The door swings shut behind him.

Savage turns around, and I'm too slow and too stunned to close the door before he sees me. He freezes, and those dark eyes deepen with an emotion I can't place.

My body heats from head to toe, and an itch crawls up my spine. "Bodyguard?" I ask, stepping out to meet him.

Savage stares down at me, frowning. He's a huge man, and usually his presence overwhelms me, but tonight, I've had just enough wine and heard enough to make me so angry that I don't care any more. It's not like Savage and I are friends. We don't have long conversations, though we've known each other for years.

He avoids me, and I do my best to avoid him because of my "feelings".

"Bodyguard?" I repeat it, because the tension hasn't snapped, and he hasn't moved a muscle. "What the hell is that about?"

"Your brother hired me to look out for you," he says. "He's concerned for your safety, given that you have a stalker."

And let's add that to the layers of humiliation. Savage knows about Franklin. "I don't need a bodyguard."

Savage shrugs.

"Listen, I don't care what Cash wants, I don't need—"

"No."

"Huh?"

Savage's chest expands as he takes in a breath. "You need protection. I've been asked to watch out for you, and I will. If you have a problem with that, take it up with your brother."

"Listen, buddy," I say, stepping up to him, trying to ignore the immediate sizzling desire that slides over my skin at the proximity. "You don't presume to tell me what to do. I'm my own person."

"Then do what you want," Savage says, his gaze firmly on mine. He takes me in, looks at my lips. He is glued to me. So much eye contact it makes goosebumps rise on my skin.

"I will."

"But you can expect me watching your back while you do."

How dare Cash do this to me? Well-meaning or not, my brother can't just—

"This is for your safety," Savage says, his words are

level, almost monotone. Like he doesn't care about me, like I'm just a job to him, and it makes this so much worse.

"You said you'll be watching my back, right?"

Savage doesn't even nod, he keeps that unflinching eye contact.

"So watch it while I walk away." And then I spin on my heel and start down the hall.

I'm so pissed, I don't even want to see my brother right now. I'm going to cause a scene in this bar if I have to discuss this with Cash.

He could have asked about the bodyguard thing. It's not like I'm an unreasonable person. When June and Cash suggested the self-defense training, I was into it, even though it's going to put me in close proximity with Savage. But this is a waking nightmare.

Having Savage around me all the time? I can barely handle being at potluck dinners with him. I find it difficult not to act awkward, especially after *that night*.

No, no, no. We are not going there.

I want my goddamn independence, and I'm going to get it.

Six

SAVAGE

I **DO WATCH** her while she walks away, and I hate myself during every second of it.

Cash doesn't want Hannah to know I'm her makeshift fucking bodyguard because she'll react exactly like this, and I don't blame her. I'd lose my shit if someone tried to watch over me. But I'm also qualified to protect myself.

I follow Hannah through the bar, but she doesn't head back to the table where June and Cash have their heads together. She's moving toward the exit, fast, and I can't let her out of my sight.

Fuck, a part of me wants to go over to Cash and tell him this is not going to happen. She doesn't want a bodyguard, she doesn't even want to stay in this town, but the other part, the one that takes over whenever she's close by, is nudging me relentlessly.

I war with myself as I stride out of Longhorn's and into the parking lot.

The sea salt on the air is punctuated by the wash of

waves on the beach, the thump of music from the bar. My senses take it in, but I home in on her.

Hannah stands near the road, her phone in hand, shaking her head. "Unbelievable," she mutters. "What an ass."

I walk up behind her. "Talking to yourself?"

Hannah screams and throws up her hands, her phone flips end over end and lands in the dirt. She glares back at me, her blue eyes flashing hot, and then picks up her phone.

"You all right?"

"You mean, apart from you scaring the pants off me?"

I scan her body, and grit my teeth.

She takes a step back, eyes widening, her heel hits the tarmac on the street, and I grab her by the elbow and pull her out of harm's way.

Her skin is soft, and I fucking despise how my body reacts. A grinding heat that works its way up my arms, through my chest, and travels straight to my dick.

I release her and wipe my hand on my jeans.

She stares at the spot I wiped and makes a noise in her throat. "Right," she says. "Right. I'm leaving."

"I'll give you a ride."

"No, I'm leaving," she says. "And you're staying here with my brother and June. We both know you have no desire to be my bodyguard, and I don't want a bodyguard either, so let's just stop the friggin' madness and move on with our lives."

I fold my arms.

She tilts her head, her glossy dark locks chasing over her cheek, resting against her throat. I picture brushing them away and kissing that soft, supple, delicate neck.

Closing my hand around it, pressing her against a wall, dominating her.

She is ten years younger than you. She is your best friend's sister. You swore.

"What?" she asks. "Why do you always look like that? Like you're about to rip somebody's head off."

"I made a promise to your brother," I say.

"And you just do everything my brother says?"

"I'll take you home. You can't drive."

"And you can?"

"Yes," I say. "I haven't had anything to drink."

She bites her bottom lip, and she's killing me.

"You know what?" Hannah lifts her phone and starts tapping away on the screen. "I think I'll just call Todd. I'll come by and get my car tomorrow, because I can't deal with Cash right now, and I certainly don't want to deal with *this*." She shakes her hand toward me. "And, ugh. Just ugh."

"What's the problem? Your brother cares about you. He wants you to be safe."

"And that's exactly why I'm doing your one-day crash course, the self-defense thing. I can get behind that. That's great, but the bodyguard thing? No. Hell no. Sorry." And then she starts walking off.

I catch her by the arm and turn her around. "No."

"No?" Her gaze drops to where my hand rests on her tan skin.

I pull away, wiping my hand on my jeans again. "No. If you call Todd, I'll be taking a ride with him too. And once we get to your apartment, I'll be posted outside your door all night."

Her jaw drops.

"It will be more comfortable for me if I get to spend the night in my SUV, rather than on the steps of your apartment."

"SUV?"

I point toward my SUV with blacked-out windows. It's a new acquisition, and it has my logo "Savage Self-Defense" printed across the side. Looking at it makes me sweat. I like my privacy, and setting up the camp and the classes is working on my nerves, but it's something I *have* to do. I've been running a few courses, but never a full-on camp.

"You can't follow me."

"It doesn't matter what you think," I say. "I will be following you. Closely. So either I take you home or Todd does, but we're both going to your apartment tonight."

She lets out a tiny breath, her lips parted.

I stare at them, and the seconds tick by, the tension bands across my chest.

"Fine," she says. "Fine. Whatever. But tomorrow, you two, you and Cash, you're going to pay for this." And she goes as far as to poke me in the chest, right on my pec. She snatches her finger back. "Wow. That is... That's hard." And then she blushes and practically runs for my SUV.

Adorable.

I follow her and unlock it with a click of a button. She's standing at the back door, but I walk to the front passenger door and open it for her. "In."

Hannah blinks.

"I'm not an Uber driver. Get in the front seat."

She walks over and grabs the door handle. I take her elbow and help feed her into the car safely, then let go like

I've been burned, because I have. I have been burned by Hannah Taylor, not that I'll let her know it.

I shut her door, then head over to my side and get in, starting the engine in silence.

Hannah puts on her seatbelt and stares out the window, which suits me fine. We don't have to talk and make this worse, but I keep glancing at her, whenever I can, taking in her side profile, her cute nose, the glasses that are slipping down and that she keeps pushing back into place.

"I live above the bakery on—"

"I know."

Her head whips around.

"We've been going to the same potluck dinner for years," I say. "Did you think I wouldn't know where you stayed?"

She shrugs. "I didn't think you cared."

I don't step on that landmine.

I park in front of Bagel's Bakery. "Stay in the car," I say.

"But—"

I get out and slam the door, then head around the side of the brick building to assess the alleyway and the grated steps that lead up to the apartment. The alleyway ends in a chain link fence that would be easy to climb. It's dark, the light from the lampposts barely reaching the first step. There are two green dumpsters that are shut.

I don't like it one fucking bit.

There are plenty of places to hide, an escape route over that fence, and it's dark. This will have to be remedied.

I open the dumpsters, check around them, jog up the stairs and back down them, and make sure the area is clear.

I walk back to the car and open her door.

"What are—?

"You're going to listen to me," I say, "and you're not going to talk. Understand?"

She glares, her beautiful eyes narrowed almost to slits. My cock throbs in my jeans, and I want to punch a hole through a wall because of it.

"Understand?" I repeat.

"I'm confused," Hannah says, "do you want me to talk or not?"

"Just say you understand."

"Fine." She sweeps a hand through the air. "I understand."

I grunt. "The entrance to your building isn't safe. From now on, I will be escorting you in and out of it. I don't want to hear any complaints. You'll move quickly and do as I say. If I say get down, you get down. If I say run, you run. Got it?"

She presses her lips into a thin line.

"Confirm that you got it."

"But that would be breaking rule number one," she says. "No talking. Because I'm a mute woman who needs to be cared for by a big strong man."

"I don't like it any more than you do," I say.

Her expression shifts, a drawing downward of her brows, a widening of her eyes, and then she shakes her head. "Yeah."

I hate this shit.

I'm aware that Hannah has a crush on me. Or she did. Seems like she hates me tonight.

Either way, it's *never going to happen*. I won't allow it.

I exhale. "There could be a fucking psycho with a knife

in your dumpster, or waiting at the top of the stairs, and until that issue has been resolved, you're going to do what I say."

"How is the issue going to be resolved?" she asks.

Big foot in my big mouth.

Cash wouldn't want his sister in on this shit.

"You said you were leaving town, didn't you?" I ask, deadpan.

"Right."

She slips out of the car, handbag over her shoulder, phone in hand.

"Follow me, and move fast."

I lead her toward the entrance and up the stairs. Once we hit them, I walk behind her, creating a protective barrier between her and the stairs, my gaze fixed on the empty landing.

Hannah pauses on the steps and looks around. "This is crazy. You and Cash are out of your minds, I swear."

"You have a stalker."

She doesn't argue but gets her keys out of her purse and inserts them into the lock. She turns it and opens the door, and I step through.

"Hey, I didn't even invite you in," she cries, but I'm already moving through her house, checking the closet, under the bed, anywhere a man could hide. I force down the memory of the last time I was in here.

Thankfully, it's a small apartment, so the search goes quickly.

I find her standing in the living room, hugging herself, her purse on the coffee table. "I hate this," she says.

"Good night, Hannah. Lock the door behind me." And then I walk for the exit, because the scent of her perfume is on the air, and being in her personal space is doing things to me I don't want to think about.

Even if Hannah Taylor wasn't off-limits, even if she wasn't younger than me, I don't have enough pieces of a heart to give to any woman, let alone Hannah. Hannah who deserves a life of joy, a man who can love her.

I pause at the door. "Keep it locked," I repeat.

"Okay." She stands there, painfully pretty, her nipples plucking at the front of her camisole, her bottom lip caught between her lips. "Goodnight."

I slam the door shut and wait for her to lock it, then jog down the stairs and get into my SUV. I punch the dashboard so hard it cracks.

Seven

HANNAH

SAVAGE KNOWS I have a crush on him, and he avoids me like I'm carrying the plague. And that's why Cash forcing him to be my bodyguard is the worst. First, because it's degrading and second, because I *know* Savage doesn't want to spend time around me.

He touches me and then wipes his hand off on his jeans. He gets angry when he looks at me.

I sit on my living room sofa, frozen, my mind traveling back to that night, the scent of his cedar and smoke cologne trapped in my nose.

It wasn't that long ago. Just a couple of weeks.

Marci was upset and I took her to Longhorn's for some girly day drinking. Jesse took her home, and he called Savage to fetch me. And after tequilas and enough cock-tails to tranquilize a horse, you would think I *wouldn't* remember it in painful detail.

But I do.

Oh my God, do I remember it. I cover my eyes, my cheeks heating.

———

Savage feeds me into the back of his SUV and leans across me, clipping on the seatbelt. I smile up at him, because, what the fuck? Why not?

He might hate me, but he's so gorgeous, and I am so *tired* of holding back. So tired of wanting a man who doesn't want me.

Why is it that the only guys who are interested in me are people like Franklin? Ugh. Men who are walking red flags, who see me as an object?

Savage peers at me. "You good?"

"You have pretty eyes," I say, fluttering my eyelashes at him.

Savage makes a noise that might be a laugh, and his dark eyes pinch at the corners. "Tell me if you need me to stop the car. Lie down if you need to."

"Okay." And then I flop sideways with a sigh.

Savage gets into the car, and the engine purrs to life. I drift in and out, the SUV spinning around me, as I stare at his muscular arms, hands on the wheel of the car, his beard, the tattoos inked along his strong neck.

A while later, we park, and an influx of cool air tells me that the door is open. "We're here," he says, and then gentle hands lift me upright.

"Thanks," I manage, as he unclips my seatbelt and lifts me out of the back of the SUV into his strong arms.

I loop my arms around his neck and snuggle in close, pressing my nose to his neck, inhaling deeply.

He stiffens.

But I can't help myself. This is the closest I've ever been

to him, and hell, it's probably the last time I'll ever get to feel his arms on my body.

This is wrong.

Or maybe it's right. Maybe Savage likes me?

It's a tequila-addled thought, but I don't care.

The door slams shut, and I'm carried upward. I stare up at the side of his face, and my finger moves to his beard. "This is nice," I say. "Your beard. I like the way it looks on you."

His breaths come quickly. I'm not imagining it, right?

"Your keys," he says.

"Oh, they're in my purse." I struggle, trying to get it off my shoulder where I hooked it at some point during the night. I don't remember when.

"I've got it." He takes the purse from me, and gets the keys out of it. He opens my apartment door one-handed then carries me inside, tucking a hand over the back of my head to keep it safe.

Lights flare, and I blink and shut one eye. I catch a glimpse of my living room before I'm carried through to the bedroom and set down on the bed.

"Can you sit up?" he asks.

"Yeah, I think so." I struggle upright, and he guides me. I sit on the bed, bracing my hands on the floral sheets, and watch as Savage carefully removes my shoes, his fingers brushing over the sensitive skin on my ankles and feet.

It's obscene, this huge man bowed before me, removing my shoes, and it makes my heart thrum in my chest, and a terrible, naughty idea forms in my mind.

He's so caring with me. So gentle. Surely that means

something? It can't just be because I'm part of the Taylor family or because I'm Cash's sister, right?

"Savage?" I whisper.

He's just removed my second shoe and set it aside. He frowns and looks up at me. His thighs are encased in jeans, and they look as if they barely fit, as if they're so strong he might just burst out of his clothes. God, I wish that would happen.

No, I wish he would take them off for me.

"Can you help me with my clothes?" I ask.

"Hannah."

"Please," I say. "I don't want to sleep in jeans and a sweater."

His jaw works, and his pupils dilate.

"Please," I repeat it sweetly.

He gets up and then he takes my hands and stands me upright. He holds me in place with one arm looped around my middle while he unbuttons my jeans and strips them down my legs. He lifts one foot and removes a pants leg, and then does the same with the other.

The cool air brushes against my skin. I struggle to remember which underwear I chose today. The pink lace? Please, let it be the pink lace.

Savage stands and keeps his gaze fixed on a spot on the wall.

"My sweater," I say.

His strong, callused fingers brush over my stomach, and I inhale.

"That feels nice," I whisper.

"Hannah." It's a warning.

"Please," I murmur. "I'll be good."

Savage's nostrils flare, but he takes the hem of my

sweater and pulls up. He helps me get it off. I rest my hands on his chest to keep my balance, and his gaze snaps to my face then down an inch to my chest.

I look down too, and I am, indeed, wearing the pink lacy bra.

Yes.

He grinds his teeth audibly.

"Savage," I whisper softly, and move my arms, loop them around his neck, my gaze imploring. "Can you help me into bed?"

His hands are at his sides, and I don't like it. I want him so bad, I ache for him. I don't care if it's pathetic, or if it's one night that I'll regret for the rest of my life, because I just know that touching Savage will ruin me.

I run my hands up the back of his neck and into his dark hair.

His gaze doesn't flinch. His hands come up and he loops one arm around my waist. He lowers me onto the bed carefully, but he's not coming down with me.

I pull on him, tipping us backward so that he lands, arms on either side of my body, his hot weight held above mine. His gaze tracks over my face and down to my body, and I swear desire flares in that look. Or maybe I'm lying to myself.

"Hannah, what are you doing?"

"I want you," I say. "Okay? I want you. Please."

"Hannah."

"I want you so bad I can't think straight," I whisper. "I want you inside me."

"No."

"No?"

He shakes his head firmly. "No. You and I will *never*

happen," he says. The last two words are sharp and harsh. "Never." And then he pushes off the bed and looks away. "Get under the covers."

My insides boil with shame, and I crawl under the duvet and drag it up to my chin. Tears prick at the sides of my eyes, and I turn my back on him. Hating that I tried, hating that I want him.

He switches off the light. "Goodnight, Hannah."

———

THE MEMORY RUNS on repeat through my mind, and it's so clear, the pain, the shame, Savage's expression when he told me he would never want me, that it's like I'm reliving it for the fiftieth time. I keep torturing myself with that memory, and it makes me angry.

Why? What's wrong with me?

Because I'm Cash's sister? Because he doesn't find me attractive?

Either way, he's made it clear that he doesn't want me. And I've made it clear that I want him. And now, it's awkward, and I simply cannot be trapped with him watching my every move.

I can't even be in the same town as him. How am I going to survive him being around me constantly?

I forced myself onto him. I made a fool of myself. I upset him.

And I'm never getting drunk in front of him ever again. Not only did I lose my dignity, but I lost my mother's bracelet and my favorite lipstick that night.

"You're okay, this is fine," I say, into my empty living room. "He's out there, and you're in here, and you are never going to act the fool around him ever again. You are never going to tell him you want him again. You're going to leave. Simple. It's only a couple of weeks until you go, so…"

And now, I was talking to myself like a crazy person.

I force myself off my sofa and get ready for bed. I shower, brush my teeth and put on my comfiest PJs—pink cotton shorts and a cotton strappy top—and then I shut off the lights and lie in my bed, staring at the ceiling.

"No. You and I will never happen." The words, rumbled in his deep voice, come back to me again and again.

"Ugh. Stop it. Stop."

What is he even doing out there? Just sitting in his car? Sitting in his car and staring at my apartment against his will? It's bad enough that I threw myself at him, now he's out there when he doesn't want to be. God, the only saving grace in this situation is that it doesn't seem like he told Cash about what happened. If he had, I would've dissolved into a librarian-shaped puddle of goo.

I get out of bed in the dark and walk through to the living room. I twitch the curtains back and peer down at the sliver of the street I can see from my front window.

Savage leans against the front of his SUV, his arms folded, and his head tilted back, staring directly up at me.

I almost flinch back, but I stop myself.

This is my apartment. I don't even want him out there. Why shouldn't I look out of the window? Embarrassed or not, he knows I don't want him here, but he stayed, so if Savage doesn't like me looking out my own damn front window, he can leave.

He keeps staring up at me, and I fold my arms and stare right back down at him.

It's like we're playing chicken. First person to look away is the loser, except I'm already the loser thanks to the whole "pink lace incident". And the pepper-spewing. Oh God, the pepper-spewing.

I'm about to pull back when Savage pushes off the front of his SUV, and I grin. He's going to leave. I win.

But Savage doesn't circle around his car. Instead, he walks toward the stairs, watching me like I'm a deer, and he's the hunter.

Eight

SAVAGE

I AM A FOOL.

I knock on her front door.

A fucking fool.

She doesn't answer. I knock again.

Finally, the latch scrapes and she appears, fucking breath-taking as always. Hannah narrows her eyes at me, still standing in the darkness in her apartment, the door only half open.

"What's up?" she asks.

"What's wrong with your power?"

"What kind of power are we talking about?" Hannah asks, covering her breasts with both arms, and my God, am I grateful that she does, because she is wearing punishment in clothing form. "Like my power over my mind, my power as a woman? Because there is nothing wrong with that. My power over my gag reflex, however—" She cuts off, her eyes widening. "I need to stop talking. Oh my God, why do I have a mouth?"

And why isn't it on mine?

"Your lights are out," I say.

"Huh?"

"You were standing in the dark at the window. Your lights are out."

"*That's* why you came up here?" Hannah asks, her eyebrows climbing. "Of course. Of course, that's why you came up here. You were worried that I was alone in the dark with a stalker. Because you're my bodyguard now. Because that's a wonderful thing that's happened in the past couple of hours. And I'm doing it again." She gives a tight smile and rams her lips together.

"It would be much easier to look after you from inside your apartment."

"Say what now?"

I clear my throat and take a single step inside.

She releases her door and backs up, her eyelids fluttering. "You can't just—"

"What?"

"You can't just come in without asking."

"All right," I say. "May I come in?"

"You're already in."

We stare at each other in the slanting moonlight from outside. I'm close. So close to her, I could reach out and take her in my arms, walk her back and press her into the wall.

"Savage?" she murmurs, tipping her chin up so she can look me in the eye.

I'm aware that I'm an intimidating guy, and I like that Hannah never acts like she's afraid of me. Even though she fucking should be.

I shut the door behind me, plunging us both into darkness. She makes a tiny noise, one of those delicious noises I want to swallow, and I reach over and flick on the lights in the living room.

Hannah stares at me, her one knee tipped in toward the other, the heel of her left foot lifted and even that's fucking cute.

I step closer, and she's barely breathing, her chest rising and falling so rapidly, she might hyperventilate.

And I want to make her lose her breath. I want it so bad, my fists ball up again.

I walk past her to the window where she was standing a couple of minutes ago and draw the curtains shut. "I told your brother I would be your bodyguard until you leave town."

Hannah lets out a breath. "We've been over that whole fiasco already. But forgive me, I'd rather not be in the same apartment as you while I'm—" She shakes her head rapidly. "I'm not going there. Oh my God, this is so messed up. Look, Savage. Carter."

I freeze. I haven't been called Carter in years. Nobody calls me Carter. "Savage is fine," I grunt.

"Savage," she says. "I get that I made a total fool of myself with you, several times, and that you probably despise being around me, but I—"

"I don't despise being around you," I say, before I can stop my idiot fool fucking mouth.

"You don't?" She scratches her forehead.

I don't blame her for being confused after what happened a couple of weeks ago, but I'm not going to set her straight, at least not completely. I told her we could never be together, and I never told her why. Because it would give her hope if she knew how much I wanted her, and how terrible it would be for both of us if I followed through.

"I don't feel anything toward you," I say, and bring myself to new level of self-loathing.

She claps her hands. "Right. Of course, you do. I mean, don't."

"And that is exactly why I'm equipped to make sure that you're kept safe. I can remain impassive where your brother clearly can't," I say.

"You're not wrong there." Hannah gives a small smile.

"You don't like this," I say. "Neither do I. But it's going to get your brother off your back, and it would be more comfortable for me to be on your couch than in my SUV."

I tip my head to the side and trace my gaze down her body. My eyes haven't caught the memo about not wanting her. Fuck, my entire body hasn't. She's tan and tall, her lean legs a temptation in those short pink cotton PJs.

Hannah clears her throat. "I don't like to share my apartment with anyone." She circles her couch and stands behind it, putting space between us.

"And if you don't want to share it with your stalker, you should probably have someone around who can protect you."

"I have pepper spray," she says.

"Do you have your escape route planned out?" I ask.

"My what?"

"Your escape route. If you need to run, you have to plan it out, and know that route so well, you could run it in the dark."

"I—"

"Let's say you're woken in the night by the sound of glass breaking. What are you going to do?"

"I… don't. I mean, probably get out of bed, I would assume."

"Assuming will get you killed. You need to be prepared."

"What are you, Ross from *Friends*? You going to tell me about unagi next?"

"Isn't that an eel?"

"That's literally the joke from the show." She flips her palm out. "And this is the most I've heard you talk, like, ever."

"I give a shit about this."

She freezes. "About… About what?"

"Self-defense. Keeping people safe. It's what I do." Until I failed at it.

"I might not have an escape route planned out, but I've been fine up until now."

"You haven't had a stalker up until now, correct?"

"Technically," she says, pressing a hand to her chest. "But hey, I don't know that for sure. None of us do. There could be somebody stalking me right now."

"That's the point."

"Darn," she whispers. "That made way more sense in my head." She points at me. "I'm still mad. But, fine. Whatever. Sleep on the couch. I'm not going to be the girl who lets you sleep in an SUV because of… Anyway, doesn't matter. Do you need a pillow and a blanket?"

"That would be nice," I say.

Hannah stares at me for a second, then walks off and stops. She turns back around, fists on her hips. "I don't like this either," she says. "I want you to know that. I—I don't like it either. This isn't fun for me."

"I understand."

"No, you really don't," she says. "And I—" Hannah makes a zipping motion over her lips. "I really don't know you well enough to be blabbing about this."

"We'll keep it that way."

She huffs and throws her hands up before walking down the hall. She stops at the closet next to her bedroom and opens the concertina, slatted door. She mumbles under her breath for a bit then returns with a pillow and a comforter.

I go to take them from her, but she hurriedly plops them on the couch before I can get there. "Are we sure you're going to fit on this thing?"

"I'm sure I'll manage."

"Right, you were in the Navy. You probably slept on cots and bunk beds and in bushes and stuff."

"Yeah, something like that."

Hannah gnaws on the corner of her lip. "I wasn't that drunk tonight. I had, like, two glasses of wine."

I let the silence brew. What am I supposed to say to her? I don't care how much she drinks or when, only that she's safe. And that there are no men gawking at her, hovering nearby. *Asshole.*

Hannah puffs out her lips on an exhale. "Right. Goodnight, Savage."

"Goodnight." *Princess.*

And then she walks off to her bedroom and shuts the door. Her bedsprings creak and then she's still. I walk through the living room and check everything's locked up tight. Finally, I strip off my shirt and hang it over the back of a stool that flanks her kitchen counter, and cut the lights.

I lay down on the sofa that's way too small for me, my legs and calves hanging over the edge, my arms behind my head, and wait for my mind to still. Except it won't.

Because Hannah is right down the hall.

Nine

SAVAGE

SLEEP WON'T COME.

I don't try to force it any more. When I was on active duty, sleeping wasn't a problem. I could've slept standing up if it was necessary to get the energy needed to complete the mission, but now? My thoughts aren't as easily silenced.

And for once, they're not torturing me with images of the past, the mistakes I've made, the people I've lost, and —the rest.

Tonight, it's Hannah caught in my mind. She's tiptoeing through it, in those pink PJs, talking too much, saying too little, and telling me everything I need to know without words. She wants me. But she doesn't actually want me. She wants my body, she wants the thought of me, rather than the reality of what I am.

I check the time on my watch.

It's past three in the morning, and it's been hours since I got here.

Lying here isn't achieving anything. So I push myself up

and walk through to the kitchen, keeping quiet so as to not wake Hannah. I pour myself a glass of water and drink it, then make my way to the bathroom but stop.

A noise. Imagined?

No. I trust my instincts.

That was something, but what was it?

Soft and—

A tiny, muffled moan penetrates the quiet.

My hands ball into fists. *What the fuck?*

Another moan. Coming from Hannah's bedroom.

This can't be happening, but it is. I'm inches away from the door to her room, which is right across from the bathroom, but I can't move.

Because she is in there, and she is moaning. And I swear to fucking God, it is like every part of me is on high alert, like I'm living for the next sound.

I take a step toward the room and stop myself.

She wants you.

You can't.

I won't.

This could be anything. This could be her having an inappropriate dream, and she doesn't need me hanging out around her bedroom listening in on her private—

"Yes." Her voice is laden with desire, muffled, so quiet, that I definitely wouldn't have heard it if not for the fact that I had gotten up. "Savage, please."

Fuck. Oh my God. Holy fuck.

I'm in front of her door, my hands at my sides, staring at it like I can see through the wood. Like I haven't pictured her touching herself, touching me, a million fucking times in the last couple of years.

"Savage," she whispers, and her moan is punctuated by the wet sounds of her playing with herself.

My cock is hard as rock, and I bite the back of my fist to keep myself from kicking that fucking door down and taking her.

Hannah's breathy little moans, accompanied by those forbidden fucking sounds, are driving me to the brink. I press both my fists to the doorjamb, either side of her bedroom door and hang my head, staring directly at the wood.

You can't. You won't.

You can't. You won't.

The words reverberate through my mind, as she pleasures herself, and in that moment I feel so fucking connected to her, I can almost taste her. I can just about picture being the one to give her the pleasure she's wringing from her body.

Her pace grows frantic. "Oh God, Savage, yes." The last moan is a little louder than the others, like she can't hold back, but it's still muffled, and I picture her, pressing her face into her floral pillow, crying out, her hand down the front of those shorts.

Yes, Princess. Come hard.

There's silence afterward, and I stand there for a few minutes, trying to bring myself back down to earth. She is Hannah Taylor.

I am me.

Nothing will ever happen.

She can come and dream about me, but I can't—

The door opens, and Hannah steps out and right into my chest. She lets out a horrified scream and starts banging on my chest like my pecs are bongo drums. It would be hilarious if I wasn't harder than a fucking granite dildo.

I take her by the shoulders and hold her out. "It's me," I say.

Hannah's screams die slowly. "S-Savage?" She peers up at me with those sapphire blue eyes. "Savage? What the hell are you—?" And then it dawns on her. I witness the realization flashing across her face, that I'm out here, and she was just touching herself in there, whispering my name. Moaning it. She gulps. "You... What...? You were...? Huh?"

"I was getting some water," I say.

"Water?" She turns her head in the direction of the kitchen.

"And then I was heading to the bathroom."

"Bathroom." Her head swivels toward the bathroom.

"Yeah. You opened your door just as I was heading in." It's a blatant fucking lie, but if she can tell, she doesn't call me on it. I keep her away from my body, away from the evidence of my arousal for her.

Hannah sucks her bottom lip between her teeth, then pops it free, and my resolve is weakening so fast, it's criminal. I'm no better than this stalker, standing outside her door and listening to her make herself come.

Moaning my name.

"You good?" I ask.

"Y-Yeah."

"This is why you need an escape route," I say. "Banging on your attacker's chest is not the best defense mechanism."

"I was just going to use the bathroom."

Hannah's not hearing me, even though I'm trying to

taunt her and get her to fight back. To forget about what happened so I can too.

I purposefully keep my focus on her face and *don't* let it wander lower.

"Go ahead," I say, stepping back and gesturing toward the door.

Hannah hesitates. She stares at my bare chest, eyes wide. "Goodnight."

I nod, and Hannah darts into the bathroom. I head back to the living room to wait for my dick to calm the fuck down. I plump the pillow she gave me, resisting the urge to break something.

This is a fucking recipe for disaster, us being around each other, but now that I've agreed to help, I can't go back. I'm going to bury this memory deep fucking down and never touch it again. Hopefully, Hannah will do the same.

The toilet flushes, and Hannah's bedroom door shuts a couple of seconds later. I wait a while then get up and use the bathroom myself, staring at myself in the mirror of the sink, at the gray streaks in my beard, the tattoos. A lifetime stares back at me.

No matter what, I can't fuck this up. I won't break Cash's trust in me. I won't lose another person I care about.

Who? Hannah or Cash?

I go back to staring at the living room ceiling.

Ten

HANNAH

HE DIDN'T HEAR ME. There's no way he heard me. No way.

I've been going back and forth on that all day, from when I woke up and found Savage was gone, to when I spilled coffee over my shirt at the kitchen sink, to now, in the library listening to Irma grumble about unpaid late fees and how the youth of today have no respect.

"You would think," Irma says, "that they would understand what it means when we say have the book back by a certain date. But nooooo. They just don't get it." She taps away on the keys at the computer, using the index fingers of either hand to type. "No, they just cannot fathom what it means to return a book on time. There are other people who want to take out those books."

"Yuh-huh." I nod and stare out of the open doors of the library.

It's a strangely blustery day outside. The clouds rolled in this morning, accompanied by the occasional gust of wind or a roll of thunder. There's this strange tension in the air, like the world's holding its breath and waiting for something to happen.

Or maybe that's my nerves talking. This afternoon, I'm heading out to Savage's ranch for a one-day self-defense crash course. Thank God June will be there, because I can't be alone with him after last night.

He didn't hear you.

But he was *right there.* Right outside the door.

And I ran into him.

It was late. I was sure he wouldn't be awake, and I'd woken up from the most erotic dream ever, featuring Savage, of course, and well, a girl has to do what a girl has to do. It wasn't like I was out there in the living room, flicking the bean, as Marci would call it.

I was in the privacy of my own bedroom, and I was quiet about it.

Wasn't I?

Oh God, what if I wasn't quiet enough?

What if he's currently so revolted about what he heard that he's avoiding me?

That's a good thing. That's what you want. Savage probably heard me and decided to tender his resignation as my bodyguard as a result.

Kill me now.

"—storm rolling in, we can be sure that those books will be late too."

"Yeah," I say, patting Irma on the shoulder. "You know what, I'll print out another notice about late books and stick it up in the library. Will that help?"

Irma sniffs. "Your guess is as good as mine. It's the least you can do, since you're abandoning us."

"That's six weeks away. And it's just for a few months," I say.

"Let's hope your job is still here when you get back," Irma replies, waspishly.

Her bark is worse than her bite, and I'm used to it by now. Irma likes verbal jousting, but if you show her that she bothers you, she'll never let it go. Besides, if you get upset about everything a person says, you'll never have enough time to look after yourself.

And if Taylor Swift has taught me anything, it's that karma is my friend.

"Aren't you leaving?" Irma asks. "You're done for the day."

"Yeah," I say, and then take a step out from behind the counter. I stop, shaking my head, and go back and grab my purse before heading out. This is it. I'm supposed to go home, pack an overnight bag, and drive out to Savage's ranch. June's meeting me there after she's run a few errands, so I'll be fine. I'll be totally fine.

He so didn't hear you orgasm while screaming his name.

At this point, it's yet another chapter of mortification to add to the book that is my life story. It's not even a chapter, it's a tiny scene compared to the litany of embarrassing events that revolve around Carter Savage. Oops, just Savage. Can't call him Carter, not even in my head, because, you know, he doesn't like that. We're not close enough.

I get into my car and drive home, park out front then stop and peer down the side alley of the bakery.

Bagel's is plenty busy today with a line stretching out the open doors—if Franklin is hiding out behind a dumpster, he won't take me in front of these people. I like to think the Heatstrokers will step in.

I head upstairs, my heels clanking on the grated steps, and a gust of wind blasts me to the side. I catch myself on the wall. "What the heck?" I look up at the bruising sky.

It's the middle of summer, but we get thunderstorms in Heatstroke. The kind that blow through town and tear things up before leaving as fast as they came. Great. This means we'll likely be training indoors.

It'll be fun. It'll be great.

I'll finally learn how to fight, which will be super fun. I don't want to kick anyone's ass, but having the capability to do so would be cool.

I think about that instead of Savage's bare chest, rippling with muscles in the dark, with just the right amount of chest hair, while I pack my bag. And I purpose-fully don't pack the lacy pink underwear.

Ten minutes later, I'm on my way, the radio blasting, my window rolled down. One of Cash's songs is on the radio, and I sing along to it, tapping my fingers on the steering wheel. I'm mad at him, but damn, he's a good songwriter.

"And that was *Soaring Hearts* by Cash Taylor, Heat-stroke's very own. Gotta love him, right Jill?"

"Right you are, Jack," Jill says, in her best radio presenter voice. "Folks, this is Radio Heat, bringing you the hottest hits as we get 'em. It's right about that time for the five-o-clock news update, and boy, do we have a doozy of a report today."

Radio Heat's "serious" news jingle plays, and Jack takes over. "This is the five-o-clock update, with Jack

Barnes. Residents of Wait County have been encouraged to batten down the hatches and prepare for what climatologists are calling, 'The Storm of the Century'." Earlier today, we caught up with Davey Prink, Channel Nine's meteorologist, and he had this to say."

"Folks, y'all are going to want to lock up tight and stay indoors. We're talking a Severe Thunderstorm Warning and a Flood Advisory. At this time, we are not expecting those winds to sweep in from farther up the coast, but be on the lookout for updates. The weather service will issue them as they come in, and here at Channel Nine, we'll do our best to keep you updated on developments as they happen. This means you're likely going to see a lot of rain that might take out roads in and around our county. So, as of six this evening, stay off the roads and stay indoors. Keep your devices charged, and ensure you have enough fresh drinking water and food for the next couple of days."

A weather warning? Gosh, I've been so far up my own behind today, I didn't check the weather. And I haven't been listening to Irma most of the day.

"You heard it, folks," Jack continues. "You stay safe out there. In other news, Sheriff Oakes has issued a—"

I turn the radio down as I turn onto the dirt road that leads toward Savage's ranch. It's on the opposite side of town to Cash's place, and the road is overgrown, trees hanging over on either side, their leaves and branches scratching the top of the car. I bump along, gritting my teeth, and slowing the car to a crawl.

This is not good. A weather warning?

I should turn back, go to the apartment while I still can,

but a quick glance at the clock on my dash shows me that it's ten minutes until six.

I lean forward and peer up at the sky. A lightning bolt splits it, almost as if on cue, and rain pelts down on the windshield.

"Crap!" I hurriedly close my windows.

I slow down even more and switch on my windshield wipers, watching as they sluice the water across the glass. This is bad. This is so bad.

I direct the car down the long road. I've never been out to Savage's ranch, but Cash sent me directions that I scribbled down on a piece of paper. I keep the engine running but stop the car, grappling the directions out of my purse.

I smooth the paper and read them.

Drive straight until you see the sign for Lost Hope Ranch then take a right.

Seems pretty straightforward. I start driving again, squinting through the rain and hunched over the steering wheel. It's twenty minutes before I see the sign on my right, and I let out a breath and take the turn off, praying that June's already here.

I wouldn't want her driving in this. It's crazy! But knowing my brother, he made sure she got here right on time so she'd be safe.

The road that leads up to the ranch is a little more smooth, but it winds around a bend, between trees, and it's only after another five minutes that the lights of the ranch house, blurred by the downpour, come into view.

I park the car in front of it, my heart pounding in my chest, partly because of the storm and also because I'm here. It's getting dark fast, and the rain pelts down on the car's roof, drumming furiously.

"You can do this. This is fine. It's fine." I scramble my purse off the passenger seat, then turn and try to grab my bag. My seatbelt jerks me back into place. "That's fine. That's just fine—" I unclip it and turn, then yelp.

A dark figure stands next to my door. Knuckles rap on the window.

Savage.

I unlock the car doors, and Savage jerks the back door open and grabs my bag. I get out into the mud and rain, and cold water slides down the back of my shirt.

"I've got it," I say, shutting my door, and holding out a hand for the bag.

Savage takes me by the elbow. "Let's go, Prin—" Thunder cuts out the last of his sentence, and I don't get a chance to ask what he said, because we're sprinting toward the front of his house.

I slip in the mud, and he catches me and helps me up.

We barrel up the front steps of the porch together and into the warmth of the house. Savage shuts the door and locks it, and the roar of the rain dims.

"Thanks," I say, "but I was fine."

He grunts, and I'm suddenly aware of how close we're standing, and how wet his shirt is. So wet, it clings to every inch of his chest, outlining what I felt last night in the dark. He runs a hand over his neck, and shakes out his hair, and I'm mesmerized.

He places my bag on the floor next to an end table. "You want to shower?"

"Yes, please," I squeak. "I mean, yeah, uh, yeah." Which is, of course, way better than "yes, please" in a mouse voice.

Savage looks as if he wants to smile. "This way." He

leads me down the hall, and I can't help peeking around at everything I pass by. This is my only glimpse into Savage's psyche, since he barely talks to me, and when he does talk to me, the sound of his voice and the way his lips move tends to distract me. Apparently, I'm a horny teenager.

The house is small. Much smaller than I expected, but not in a bad way. It's cozy, and there's an open plan living room with a fireplace. We're past the entrance to the kitchen too quickly for me to take much stock of what's in it.

"This is the bedroom," Savage says. "There's an en suite bathroom. You can shower and get changed in there."

"The bedroom," I say. "Wait, *the* bedroom?"

"That's right."

"There's only one bedroom? You don't have a guest bedroom?"

"I don't like to entertain," he says.

"You're kidding," I reply. "You? You're the regular life of the party."

His lips twitch.

Does Savage think I'm funny? "But, sorry, give me a second here. How are we, June and I, going to stay over for the night if there's no guest bedroom?"

"You'll be staying in my bed. I'll be on the couch."

"The couch," I say. "Aren't there like—Uh, you're running a camp, right?"

"I'm going to. Once the bungalows are finished being built."

"They're not done now?"

"No."

I press my lips together, mulling this particular development over. I thought coming out here meant June and I would have our own cute little camp spot or bungalow to ourselves, and we'd see Savage during "training" or whatever. But this is not that.

This is me, trapped in a cabin with my crush during a storm.

"More questions?" Savage asks.

"Where's June?"

"Not here." And then he turns and walks off.

"What do you mean, not here?" I call after him. "Where is she?"

No answer.

Great. Well, that is just friggin' perfect. June isn't here yet. She isn't here, and she's either going to be late or not arrive. This is a nightmare.

"You're dripping on the floor," Savage says.

"Oh, now he has a voice," I mutter, and enter his bedroom.

I stop after a few feet, swallowing nerves.

His bed is huge. King-sized, with white sheets and pillows, and a deep navy throw rug in front of it, a rustic wooden chest that's probably full of "man stuff". The bedside table on the right is empty except for a stack of books and a bedside lamp, and there are no pictures on the wall. Not a single one. But there are huge windows on either side of the bed that provide a view of the trees outside, the rain pouring down already flooding the backyard. It's beautiful.

I am in Carter Savage's bedroom. I've fantasized about being here more times than I remember, in the most pathetic ways, and now that I'm here, I'm woozy. It smells like him, that special brand of smoke and cedar and man.

I walk over to the bedside table and stare down at it. The book he borrowed from the library, the man chest romance, is on the top of the pile, a bookmark poking out from inside.

My curiosity gets the better of me, and I lift it off the table and open it.

"Please, I can't take it any more, Georgio, I need you now. I must have you."

"Anything for you, Kitten. I will fulfill your greatest desires." He ran his hands over her bosoms, licking his lips and—

"Trouble finding the bathroom?" Savage's breath is hot on my neck.

I jump and drop the book on the table. The bookmark flutters down to the ground, and I bend to grab it, my ass brushing against Savage.

Oh. Oh, no. What am I doing?

I spin around and hold up my hands and the bookmark. "I am so sorry," I say. "I didn't mean to rub, uh, to brush. No. Not those words. I didn't mean to do that." I swallow.

He's still soaked through, and he stares down at me, those dark eyes eating up the distance between us, which is not much. Savage's body heat is *a lot.* I bite down on the corner of my lip.

"The bathroom is through there." He points to the left. "I'm going to need to use it once you're done."

"Yeah, of course. Sorry."

"Stop apologizing."

"Sorry. I mean, yeah. Ha. I'm so wet right now, so I should probably—" I clamp my lips together.

"Just. Shower."

"Shower."

His voice is a low, hot rumble. "Stop. Talking. Shower. Now." And then he turns and walks off, and I'm left clutching the soggy bookmark and what's left of my dignity. Which is like a shred of it, at this point.

HANNAH

Where the hell are you? Are you kidding me with this? I'm sitting in Savage's living room alone. Like fully alone. You're not here.

JUNE
Honey, I am so sorry. I was on my way out of the door when Alex started throwing up. She's come down with a really bad case of the flu. I had to check on her. I was about to call you!

This is a nightmare. I am in a nightmare.

Are you guys safe out there?

I think so, yeah. I mean the house is cozy, so that part's fine. But June…

I know, Han, but you're going to make it through this, okay? It's just a couple of nights.

Try one.

They say the storm is going to last a
couple of days.

I'm choosing not to believe that.

BECAUSE THAT MEANT a couple of days with
Savage. Alone. And that was so not happening.

A door slams in the hall, and I tuck my phone back into
my purse and try to arrange myself in a way that looks
natural and not like I'm having a mini-heart attack. I place
my hands on my lap and sit up straighter. This is how
people sit, right?

He heard you. He totally heard you.

Nope, not today Satan-brain.

I am not going there right now!

Savage enters the living room wearing a pair of gray
sweatpants and a tight white T-shirt, his hair still damp
from the shower, and then it hits me. The universe hates
me. It actually hates me, because I can see *everything*.

Savage's sweatpants leave nothing to the imagination.
There are ridges. There are shapes. Very large shapes.

He clears his throat, and I lift my gaze to his face. "You
want something to eat?"

Is that a trick question?

"Eat?"

"Sure. It's getting late. I was going to run through some
moves with you guys before dinner, but the storm fucked
that idea."

"Uh, yeah! That would be great. Thanks." I get up and
wipe my hands on my yoga pants. I figured we'd spend
most of the day training, so I'd only need the yoga pants,

underwear, PJs, shirts, that kind of thing. "Do you need any help?"

Savage's gaze wanders to my legs, then back to my face. "No."

"I believe you mean, 'no, thank you.'"

"I mean, no. No. Stay on the sofa. Where you are. That is what I mean."

"Wow. Look, you don't want to do this any more than I do, but there's no need to be rude," I say.

"I'm not being rude. I'm being practical," he says. "Stay out of the kitchen."

"You worried I'm going to cut myself, and you'll have to report back to my brother?"

He sweeps that hot brown gaze over me again. "That is the *least* of my worries." And then he walks into the kitchen and starts opening cupboards and slamming pots around.

What do I do?

I open my purse and root around inside until I find my eReader, then I bring it out and switch it on, tucking my legs underneath myself.

But reading only makes me think of what Savage is reading, and his gray sweatpants, and the way he doesn't want me near him. I'm spiraling so hard I can barely breathe.

"Would you like a glass of wine?" Savage asks.

"That would be nice, thank you." I don't look up from my book, even though I've read the same line like fifty times over. "You know, the storm won't last that long. I can be out of here before you know it."

"Doesn't make a difference to me."

"Sure it doesn't. I'm sure you want me crowding up

your ranch house with my Hannah-ness." I gesture toward myself and turn around. My heart flips at the sight of him pouring wine into two glasses.

"This is the safest place for you to be."

Right. Bodyguard. Of course. "Where were you this morning?" I ask. "If you're supposed to be watching my back at all hours of the night and day on Cash's command, then how come you weren't at my apartment?"

"I had to set up a couple of important things for your safety. I had a friend watching over you while I was busy."

"What does that mean?"

Savage comes over with the wine and gives it to me. Our fingers brush as I take the glass, and I moan.

I actually… moan.

Is this real life?

Savage's eyes widen.

I pretend to cough. "Sorry, something caught in my throat." *It's my shame.* "Thanks." I take a sip of wine and almost choke on it, then smile at him. "Yum. White wine."

"You don't like white? I don't have anything else."

"It's great!"

Savage stands there and watches me.

"Are you sure you don't need my help making dinner?" I ask.

"I should give you a tour."

"Huh?"

"Of the house."

"Uh, okay, that's kind of sudden. Weren't you in the middle of making—"

He takes my hand and electricity streaks up my arm and through my body. My nipples pucker at his touch, and it's such an intense reaction to him, I lose my breath. But I am not moaning, and that's a step up from a few seconds ago, so I'm counting it as a win.

Savage releases my hand then gestures to the leather sofa, the flatscreen TV, and then to the glistening kitchen with its granite tops and dark wood counters. There's one of those kitchen islands with a rack of copper pots and pans hanging over it. "This is the living room and the kitchen."

"You don't say."

"This way." He points to the hall.

I walk out ahead of him, my skin prickling at the proximity. I take a sip of my wine for sustenance then grimace. The last time I had too much to drink—

Nope. Nope. Not going there.

Savage stops in the hall and points to one of the doors. "That's your bedroom." He shifts his hand over to the door on the far left. "That's a room you won't enter." Then points to the back door. "And you never leave the ranch house through that door."

"What?"

He takes a sip of wine. "Tour complete." And then he goes back to the living room.

"You should never have told me that," I call out. "About the rooms and doors, I'm not supposed to use. That's going to make me want to go through them even more."

"Do you always say everything that pops into your head?" Savage asks.

I enter the living room and sit down, tucking my feet underneath myself. "Yeah, you should try it sometime. It's freeing."

Savage keeps chopping and cooking. He doesn't ask what I want or if I'm allergic to anything, but I don't care, because I've got a front row ticket to his thick, muscular forearms working as he makes things. For me. To eat.

Never going to happen.

Those words are so painful, but I have to remind myself of them. Lightning cracks outside, illuminating the curtains that hang over Savage's front windows, and I jump a little at the sound that follows. The rush of rain grows stronger. "This is serious, isn't it?" I ask.

"What?"

"The storm." I bring my phone up and tap on the screen. No cell signal.

"I've heard that about weather warnings," Savage says. "That they're serious."

I snort then cover my mouth and nose, but Savage doesn't look up. He's smiling though, the tiniest smile, and it makes my insides twist. I hate that I can't have him, and that I want him in the first place. I hate everything about this situation. And most of all, I hate how stupidly handsome he is, how caring, even if he's gruff. How I don't know him that well, and I never will.

And that is exactly why I'm going to put on my track shoes and run the minute this rain stops. Run away from this town.

"Almost done," Savage says.

I bring my gaze up to his face. "Do you like to cook?"

"Don't usually do much cooking unless I have a guest," he says.

"I thought you don't like to entertain."

"I don't." And he scowls at me.

What the hell? "Are you angry at me?"

"No."

"I mean, you could have fooled me," I say. "You keep frowning at me."

He shrugs and continues cooking.

"Great talk."

I sigh, and lay back on the sofa. It puts him out of my line of sight, which is a good thing, since I'm tired of wanting what I can't have and loathing myself for it. Delicious smells drift from the kitchen, lemon zest and melted butter. My mouth waters.

"The last time I cooked for someone was sixteen years ago." Savage's gruff voice is audible just above the sizzle of whatever he's frying in the pan.

I sit up and open my mouth to reply, but no words come out.

His gaze remains on the stovetop.

"Sixteen years?"

"Yes."

"For a woman?"

Savage's jaw tightens, his face hardens so fast, it's scary. "Yes."

I swallow, scanning him. "I'm sorry."

"For what?"

"For whatever happened," I say. "If something did happen. Or—"

"Dinner's almost ready." The words are full of restraint.

"Great. Thanks for making dinner. I could have helped, you know, I really don't mind."

"No."

"Right." I sit back and watch him, my heart pounding. Did Savage just open up to me a little? Did we just have a tiny shred of a conversation that wasn't something to do with me or Cash, or this town?

He doesn't want you, remember? He said nothing will ever happen.

But he didn't say that he doesn't find me attractive.

Savage is the kind of man who relies on actions, and his actions have been flawless over the past ten years. He's tried to help my family, he's been there for Cash and even Jesse through every struggle, he's kind to Alex, and he loves animals. And even though he doesn't seem to like being around me, he still helps me.

He's a good person. He's just not *my* person. And I'm not going to beg for him. I'm going to leave.

Simple.

The storm continues, the lights flicker overhead, and finally, Savage plates up the food. He walks over and offers me a hand again, but I don't take it, because I'd prefer not to spontaneously orgasm when he touches me.

I brush past him, and he makes a low noise that rumbles through the living room. I can't tell what it means.

"I'm starving," I say. "Thank you for—" My gaze falls to the plate and my jaw drops. "Wow. Is this chicken piccata?"

"Yes."

"That's crazy. I love spicy food, but nothing beats that lemony bite and the butter and the capers. Chicken piccata is my favorite meal."

Savage sits down at the kitchen island with me and cuts into his chicken. "I know."

"You know?"

"I heard you mention it at a potluck dinner."

I scratch my head. "When?"

"Five years ago," he says.

I drop my fork with a clatter.

"Too much lemon?" he asks, tensing.

I shake my head, mute, and stare down at my plate.

Savage keeps on eating like he didn't just shake me to my core.

"You—You remembered that I mentioned I like chicken piccata five years ago?"

"You said you saw it in an episode of *Friends*, and you decided to try it out for yourself," Savage replies, and then eats another piece of chicken.

My stomach does something weird. A swooping sensation that travels up to my chest and clogs my throat with emotion.

Am I going to cry over chicken piccata?

"Food's getting cold."

And that's all he says. That's the only explanation for this. I'm caught between wondering if I'm reading too much into this gesture, or if Savage might not hate me. The latter seems impossible, but chicken piccata? After five years?

I take a bite of chicken, and it's perfect, because of course it is. It's the most perfect chicken I've ever tasted.

"Thank you," I say.

Savage spears me with that dark-eyed gaze and holds it. "Is it good? Are you happy?"

"Y-Yeah."

The tension bleeds out of his shoulders as he returns to his meal.

What the hell is going on?

Twelve

SAVAGE

SHE LIKES THE FOOD.

I made food that Hannah likes, and I'm the fool who can't stop smiling as I lay out a cushion and blanket on the sofa. It doesn't matter that she likes the damn food, or that I went out and bought the ingredients for chicken piccata before she arrived. I'm setting myself up for fucking disappointment here.

Hannah knocks on the doorjamb of the living room, and I slam that scowl back into place before I turn around.

She's wearing another pair of PJs which makes it difficult to concentrate. Strappy, baby blue silk top, matching shorts. Her hair falls in dark waves around her shoulders and bright blue eyes stare at me, full of concern. "Are you sure you're okay with me taking your bed?" she asks. "I could sleep on the sofa. It's not a problem."

"No."

Hannah hesitates. "That must be your favorite word."

"First word I ever said."

She snorts a laugh then blocks her mouth and nose

with a hand. I want to tug it away and make her giggle again. "Okay, if you're sure," she says, rubbing her hands over her arms.

"Do you want me to turn up the heat?" I ask.

"No, I'm fine. I'm sure I'll be good once I'm in your bed." Her eyes go wide. "The bed. The bed that's in your room, that I'm going to be spending the night in. Is what I mean."

I love when she does that, gets all flustered.

"I can turn it up."

"No, no. No. It's all good."

I frown at her.

She takes a step back. "Uh, I just wanted to say thank you for dinner. It was really tasty and super nice of you. It meant a—a regular amount to me." Hannah flashes me a quick smile, and I want to keep it. I want to see it every day.

You are a fucking delusional mess.

"Goodnight," she says.

"Goodnight."

Hannah pats the doorjamb once, then waves and disappears from view. The door to my bedroom clicks shut in the hall, and I force myself to exhale and not punch something.

It's a bad habit I have, breaking things when I can't have what I want. No, that's not true. I'm not two-years-old. I only break things when I can't have Hannah or when she's under threat.

I sit down on the sofa, rest my forearms on my knees and stare at my reflection on the black TV screen. I shake my head at myself. I've got to turn up the heat. Hannah might not want me to, but I've got to.

"Go to bed, Carter." I'm about to get up when the lights shut off.

Fuck. The storm has kicked the power, which means things are going to get a lot colder than they already were. Lightning flashes outside.

I'm halfway across the living room to go check on Hannah, when a high-pitched scream breaks the patter of the rain on the roof.

Adrenaline bursts through my body. I sprint down the hallway and kick open the bedroom door.

It's too dark to make anything out, but I grab my phone out of my pocket and switch on the flashlight. The beam cuts through the blackness.

Hannah's frozen next to the bed, her hands out at her sides, staring out of the window into the backyard.

I scan the room, but apart from her, it's empty.

"Hannah," I say.

She spins toward me, hands up, terror on her face, and I want to tear the world apart again.

"What's wrong?" I cross the distance between us. "What happened?"

"I—The power went out. The lightning. There's someone out there."

"Where?"

"There." She points out of the bedroom window. "I swear, there was someone standing there, looking in. I swear. I'm not imagining—"

I take her by the arms. "Take a breath. In through your nose, out through your mouth. Nice and slow and deep."

She nods and does what I tell her to.

I can't follow the advice because I'm already shaking with anger. I can't go out there and hunt this motherfucker down, because if I do, she'll be exposed. I don't have eyes on the threat. The house is secure, but I don't have a backup generator installed yet, so my cameras are out.

My laptop might have caught footage of whoever came up to the window before the cameras died, though.

I walk to the chest at the end of my bed then grab a taser from within. I hand it to Hannah. "Here," I say. "You used one of these before?"

"No."

I stand beside her, place my hand over hers, dwarfing her fingers with mine. "See this slide?" I click it back. "That's the safety. You pull it back, aim, and then you click this button here. You aim for center mass. Failing that, neck or groin."

"Groin?"

"Hit the fucker in the nutsack."

Her lips tip up the corners for a second.

Smile for me, Princess. Show me you're okay.

"You're not going to leave, are you?"

"No," I say. "I'm going to stay right here with you." I walk to the curtains and shut them. I find her phone on the bedside table and hand it to her.

Hannah unlocks the screen with trembling fingers, but she's freaking out so much she can't get the flashlight app to work.

I take the phone from her, switch on the flashlight, and then guide her to the bed. "Sit down. I'll be right back. I'm not leaving the house. Got it?"

"Okay."

I move through the darkened hall with my cell phone. I grab my laptop from the coffee table, the pillow and the blanket, and then I return to the room. I dump the blanket and pillow on the hardwood floor at the foot of the bed.

"What are you doing?" Hannah's got the taser in one hand and her phone in the other, and she's sitting upright on the bed, eyes wide.

"Stay out of line of the windows," I say, and lock the bedroom door. I lift the armchair from the corner of the room and place it in front of the bed, between the windows.

"Why?"

"Out of range of gunshots."

"Gunshots?" She gasps.

"Yes."

I sit in the armchair with my laptop, even though I want to tear through the window and rip out someone's throat with my bare hands. The key to being a good bodyguard is constant assessment, it's remaining calm under pressure, and I can't let my weird… whatever the fuck it is that I feel toward Hannah get in the way of keeping her safe.

"Savage?" she whispers. "What if there's someone out there? What do we do then?"

"You do nothing," I say. "I'll protect you."

Hannah doesn't answer, and I focus on my laptop screen. I don't have wifi thanks to the power outage, but I have a copy of the video footage leading up to the power outage—I make sure that the cloud downloads a backed up copy to my laptop every five minutes.

I open the video footage from the camera that's outside my bedroom and scroll through it rapidly.

No lights of approaching cars after Hannah arrived.

There. A guy in a hoodie approaching the window. I

can't make out his features, but he was there. I scan him, taking in what I can about potential height and weight. His hands are in his pockets. Baggy clothing. Could be armed.

It could also be a homeless person who was looking for help and who got spooked when Hannah screamed.

But I can't take that chance until I hear back from Cash. He left this morning, ahead of the storm, to get to Hannah's stalker.

"Savage? Was there actually a guy out there?"

"Yes." I shut the laptop lid and set it on the chest. I get up and lay the pillow and blanket out on the floor. It's already getting real fucking cold in here, real fast. "Do you need anything?" I ask. "Do you need a glass of water?"

"No, I'm fine," she whispers.

"Good. For your safety, I'm going to sleep on the floor over here."

Hannah swallows. "But—"

"I think it's for the best. You're safe with me."

Hannah presses her lips together and doesn't say anything more. She gets into bed and pulls the covers up to her chin, staring at the ceiling. She's shaking, and the rain and lightning continues, rumbling overhead.

Once the weather clears and the power is back on, I'll deal with the threat outside. Until then, I have to stay with her, in the same room, and it doesn't matter that it's pure torture. I will do anything to keep Hannah safe.

Thirteen

HANNAH

I **HOLD** the covers up to my chin and try not to shiver too loudly. Not that a person can shiver loudly or anything, but it is so friggin' cold in this room, and I'm spooked about what happened. Spooked isn't even the right word. I'm freaked out. Fully freaked out.

Because there was a guy out there.

Up until now, I figured this Franklin dude was creepy, but I didn't think he'd go through with coming all the way out here.

Cash was right. Damn it, I hate it when he's right.

And he'll never let me live it down, either. Assuming Franklin's not going to chainsaw me to death or something. *Eugh.*

It's been fifteen minutes since Savage lay down on the floor out of sight, and I can't stop thinking about him either.

He moves at the end of the bed, but doesn't get up.

"Savage?" I whisper. "Are you awake?"

"Yes," he says. "I will be for the rest of the night."

"What? Why?"

"Because there's a threat outside."

"Yeah, but you're lying on the floor," I say. "Surely you—"

"I'm keeping out of sight. And it's so *you* can sleep."

"You can't be comfortable."

"I've been in worse places before."

I fall silent and gnaw on my bottom lip.

"Savage?"

"Yeah."

"Do you want to lie in bed with me?"

Silence.

"Not in a weird way," I say, "I just mean that it will be more comfortable for you."

"I'm good."

Why would he want to lie in bed with me? He rejected me. How could I be *that* dumb? I take a breath. "Savage?"

"Yeah."

"It would make me feel a lot better if you were on the bed with me."

"It's not a good idea."

"Look," I say, slapping my hands down on the duvet. "I'm not going to touch you. I know you find me repulsive or whatever, but just lie on top of the covers. I'm not going to be able to sleep if you're down there, giving yourself a backache."

There's a moment of tension. I hold my breath.

Savage gets up and crosses to the other side of the bed. He lies down on top of the covers with his arms folded across his chest. I can barely make him out in the dark, but his presence sends a thrill through my body. *Pathetic.*

"I don't find you repulsive," he says. "There's not a man on this planet who could find you repulsive."

Oh. My. God. "You don't?"

"No."

"That's… something," I say.

"You think because I didn't want you when you were drunk that I find you unattractive?"

"I believe your exact words were, 'you and I are *never* going to happen.' So don't act like it was about consent."

"It can be about both," he says, in a gruff voice that's gravelly deep. He hasn't moved an inch since he lay down.

"Whatever." I turn my back on him and hug the duvet to my chest, my eyes narrow. "Anyway, after what happened the last time, even if you did want me, I'd make you beg for it." My insides squirm. It's a petty thing to say, but I don't care. I'm tired of having my ego chopped to shreds around this man.

His flashlight turns on, slicing through the pitch-black in the room. There's a moment where the only noise is the rain hammering on the roof. "Beg?"

"Yeah," I say, sitting up and lifting my chin with confidence I don't have. "Beg."

"You wouldn't have to make me beg," he says. "I'd already be on my knees for you."

I choke on thin air and stare at him, but those disastrously dark eyes are focused on me, and they are dead serious.

"What did you just say?"

"I would be on my knees for you."

"Oh," I say. "Okay, so that wasn't just in my head. Good. Good." And then I flop back down and stare at the ceiling wide-eyed because I have no idea what to do next. Or say next.

"Hannah," Savage says.

I can't look at him because I might melt into a puddle.

"Hannah, look at me."

Guess it's puddle time. I turn my head, trying not to embarrass myself by hyperventilating.

His Adam's apple bobs, his gaze drops to my lips, and his brows draw inward. "Any man who doesn't get on his knees for you isn't worthy of your time or energy."

I can't talk.

"You deserve to be treated like a princess," he continues. "Like a queen."

"But not by you," I manage, croaking it out.

"Not by me."

My chest squeezes, and I break eye contact with him. "Of course. Because that would be ridiculous. Why would you want me?"

"Hannah."

"No, no, it's totally fine. I'm used to this kind of thing. Every guy I've wanted has always seen me as a friend or not a woman, I guess. There's no future with me, ever."

"Hannah."

"Because I can't have kids."

Savage's silence is deafening this time.

Why did you tell him that? He really didn't need to know. It's not relevant.

"Most of the guys I meet," I say, because I never talk about this with anybody, not even my friends, so, of course, I'll discuss this with my not-so-secret crush who won't touch me with a ten-foot pole and thinks I'm pathetic. I clear my throat. "Most of the guys I meet either want sex, or if they don't, if they maybe think they could have a relationship with me, they drop me the minute they find out kids aren't in my future. So, trust me when I say, I get it. I get why you wouldn't want to—"

"Stop."

I squeeze my eyes shut, hot tears stinging them.

"Hannah, don't cry."

"Don't tell me what to do," I whisper. "I shouldn't have told you that. That was—Forget I said anything, okay?"

He shifts on the bed. "Open your eyes."

I open them, and I hate that I lose my breath.

He's hovering right above me, braced on one forearm, and he sweeps his gaze over my face. He brushes a finger down my cheek, drawing goosebumps. "None of what you said is part of the reason why we can't and won't happen."

"Oh yeah?"

"Yeah."

"First, you're ten years younger than me."

"Lame," I mutter.

His lips quirk at the corners. I can't handle it.

"It's not like I'm eighteen and you're thirty-eight. I'm twenty-eight. Age is a crappy excuse."

"You're Cash's little sister," he says.

I roll my eyes.

Savage's calloused hand cups my cheek, and my gaze snaps back to his face. "I am a broken shell of a man," he says. "I don't deserve a woman who shines like you, and I never will. And you, Hannah Taylor, deserve a man who can give you his whole heart, not just the shattered pieces of what's left of one."

It's the most I've heard him talk, and it's poetry. My heart beats a frantic pattern against the inside of my chest.

"I can't be with you, because with you, it could never be one night. And if it was longer than that, I couldn't give you what you deserve."

Tears streak down the sides of my face, and he catches them and wipes them away.

I don't know how to feel.

Savage leans in and brushes a kiss over my forehead, and it burns hot and painful when he lies down on his pillow. "Get some sleep."

Fourteen

SAVAGE

I SHOULD NEVER HAVE OPENED my mouth.

I shouldn't have told her any piece of the truth, because I'm playing with fire, but at that moment, when she was saying those things, I wanted to kiss her.

The truth seemed like a solid alternative.

We lie in the dark together while the rain beats down on the roof, and there's a canyon between us. Hannah's not crying any more, but I can tell she's not asleep because she's shivering nonstop. The temperature in the room has steadily dropped the later it's gotten, and I don't have a fireplace in here.

I haven't secured the rest of the house, so we're not going to hang out in the living room overnight.

And you like being in bed with her.

Hannah's teeth chatter next to me, and she tries to snuggle deeper under the covers.

"You good?"

"Y-Y-Yeah," she says. "J-J-Just dandy. B-B-Best n-n-night of my life." She exhales the last part of the sentence.

I get under the covers and make a snap decision. My hand closes on her upper arm, and she turns her head. "What are you—?"

"Come here." I pull her across the bed toward me, and she lets out a squeak. I wrap her against my side, her head resting on my bicep, but I stay on my back. If I try to spoon this woman, no amount of talking is going to bolster my willpower.

Hannah lies stiff as a board for a second, but the cold gets the better of her. Her hand sneaks across my chest and up to my neck, and she turns onto her side and nuzzles into me.

I place my hand on her back. "There," I say. "Now, get some sleep."

"I'll try." Her voice is shaking, but her body warms against mine.

She slides her leg up my thigh.

"Hannah."

"Hmm?"

"Stop moving." I'm already hard just lying next to her. Now that she's pressed up against my side, my dick is throbbing.

"Sorry, just trying to get warm and comfortable."

I grunt.

Her breathing evens out and slows, and I relax a little. I'm out of the danger zone now that she's dropped off, but the sweet floral scent of that perfume on her skin drives me crazy. I force myself to focus on my duties as a bodyguard.

I listen to the rain and the thunder. The ranch house creaks and groans around us, and the wind picks up, but

I'm listening for smaller sounds. Movements. Anything that can be a threat to her.

The thought of her in danger has me tense.

Hannah sighs in her sleep. She shifts her leg up my body to get more comfortable, and it brushes over my cock. I tense as she rests her thigh on top of my length.

Gently, I take her leg and move it down, hoping it won't wake her, but when I shift my gaze to her face, her eyes are open, glistening in the dark.

"Sleep," I say.

"Savage," she whispers.

"Sleep." I am fast losing control of this situation.

"I don't want to sleep," she whispers.

Fuck, this is bad. This is so fucking bad. "But you need to sleep, Princess."

"Princess?"

I clench my jaw.

Hannah shifts her leg over my cock, and it pulses in response to the contact. "You won't and can't touch me, is that right?"

I lie there, biting down so hard my teeth might crack.

"That's unfortunate," she whispers, pressing her nose against my throat and exhaling the words against me.

"Are you trying to torture me?" I grate it out.

"It would be nothing compared to what you've done to me over the years."

"What have I done to you, Hannah?"

"It's not so much what you've done," she whispers against my throat, her lips on my skin. Not a kiss. Just words. No rules broken. "It's how you've made me feel."

"I've never tried to make you—"

She shifts her body so quickly, I don't react in time. She's on top of me, straddling me.

Fuck. Hannah is straddling me, and she sits up in the dark, pressing the warmth of her pussy against my dick. We're both fully clothed. She's got those silk shorts, I've got my gray sweats, but I can still *feel* her, and she can feel me.

"Princess." The warning springs out of me, along with the word I shouldn't say.

"I like it when you call me that," she whispers, and moves in the dark. Her phone light flares, and she unlocks her screen, so that blue light illuminates her sitting astride me.

I tuck my hands to my sides. I swore I would not touch this woman.

She grinds against me a little, shifting this way and that. "This is how you made me feel, Savage," she whispers. "This is how torturous it is to be told you can't have something you desperately want. Someone you've wanted for so long, you can't even… think straight any more."

She stops moving, and I release a breath, trying to keep myself under control. If I move, I'm going to do something we'll both regret in the long run. "I won't hurt you," I snap.

"Then don't." Hannah takes the hem of her silk PJ top and lifts it up and over her head, exposing her full breasts to me, her nipples puckering in the cold. Her stomach is smooth, and she's got a tiny star tattooed underneath her left breast. "You know," she breathes, and there's a nervous hiccup to her words, "I heard that being naked is better for sharing body heat."

I do not have the capability to use my mouth. I stare at

her. She's more perfect than I imagined, than I fantasized about.

"And I meant what I said before," she says, as the light on her phone screen dies, hiding her gorgeous curves in the dark. She slips off me sideways and goes back to cuddling my side as if nothing happened. "I'm going to make you beg for it." This time, her voice is steady.

She drops off to sleep again, and I am left there, speechless and totally and utterly fucked.

Fifteen

HANNAH

I WAKE up to the salty smell of bacon and the patter of rain on the roof and windows. Dim light filters through the bedroom.

My eyes widen seconds after they open, and I grab the comforter, lift it up to my face and let out a muffled squeal. Savage doesn't hate me. Savage was *hard* for me. He wants me.

And I sat on top of him topless last night and taunted him. It's ridiculous, or maybe it's not, but I felt in control.

Already, my mind is spiraling.

What does this mean? Does he want me? I definitely want him, but it doesn't change anything. Savage doesn't take me seriously, and he "can't" give me what I want. And I can't stay in Heatstroke. If I do, I'm going to wind up doing what I've always done—plodding along, hoping things will change when they never do.

My family, while I love them, is a constant reminder of what I will never have. A husband and a child. A family of my own.

My excitement wanes, and I drop the comforter away from my face and stare at the ceiling, listening to the rain. It stops occasionally before starting up again.

Last night was a dream. A fantasy.

You are way overthinking this. It doesn't have to be a big deal.

If I'm going to be this newly independent, traveling woman, a rolling stone as it were, then I should probably stop obsessing about this. What will be, will be. That kind of thing.

Besides, I should be worried about the stalker freak standing outside the house last night, not how good it felt to press myself against Savage's side, or the expression on his face when I took off my shirt.

The bedroom door opens, and my intentions fly out of the window so fast, I'm surprised it doesn't spontaneously crack.

Savage enters the bedroom, wearing a thick woolen sweater, and stands at the end of the bed, holding a mug of coffee. "You're awake," he says.

"Hi." I sit upright, and the sheets fall away from my bare chest.

"Fuck." Savage actually jumps, and coffee splashes out of the mug and onto his hand. "Fuck."

"Oh my God, are you okay?" I grab the comforter and pull it up to my chest.

"Fine." It's a grunt instead of a word. "I'll be right back. Put some clothes on."

I lift my chin, but Savage is already on his way out of the room.

Put some clothes on? That's not what he said last night, but whatever.

I get out of bed and slip on my PJ top then wince. It's actually freezing, and I hurriedly rummage through my bag, searching for something warm to wear. But I've got nothing. I was in such a rush to leave, that I forgot anything long-sleeved—and I didn't pay attention to the weather.

"Darn," I mutter, fisting my hips.

"What's wrong?" Savage asks behind me.

My skin prickles, and I spin on the spot. *You're the one in control, remember? You're the independent, not clumsy, woman who straddled him last night.* "I forgot to bring a sweater or a hoodie or something. I didn't check the weather before I left."

Savage comes over to me in the half-light, his gaze fixed on my face.

The tension between us is exquisite, and my heart beats like crazy.

He stares. I stare.

I glance down at his lips and then back up at his eyes. He's so perfect, it should be criminal. Dark eyes, strong cheekbones, a nose that's definitely been broken before, his beard streaked through with gray, and the slight lines around his eyes. He looks like he's lived a million lives, and all of them are etched onto him like the tattoos that run up his neck.

I swallow.

"Hannah?"

"Huh?" I meet his gaze, and my plans to be the cool, independent woman who's never embarrassed evaporate. I blush, because he's watching me check him out. "Yeah? What's up?"

"I made you coffee." He lifts the mug.

"How? The power?"

"French press. Kettle on the gas stove."

"Thank you." I take the mug from him and sip from it. "Ooh, yum. Just enough sugar and cream."

He turns and walks over to the closet, opens it and enters. He comes out a second later with a sweater, then brings it over to me. "I don't think my pants will fit you."

I take the sweater from him, dying inside. "Thanks. This is great."

"Great."

We stand together in the quiet, me looking up at him. He stares over my head at the window. "I secured the perimeter while you were asleep. The power is still out, but the house is safe."

"There was a concern that the house wasn't safe?"

"I've made breakfast." And then he turns and walks out of the room. I stare at his butt in those punishing gray sweatpants.

He leaves the door open, but his footsteps retreat, and I take another sip of my coffee absently. He made me coffee. And breakfast. And he gave me his—

Get over yourself! It doesn't mean anything. Savage might be attracted to me, but he still doesn't want me.

I set down the coffee on the bedside table and then pull on his sweater. It's warm, and it smells of that smoky cedar cologne. I lift it to my nose and inhale. So unbelievably sexy. The sweater falls down past my thighs, oversized, just like Savage, and I squirm at the thought of him holding me. I put in my contacts instead of wearing my glasses.

Finally, I grab my coffee and head through to the living room.

Savage is bent over the fireplace, stoking it. He straightens, then directs me to the sofa. The coffee table, a polished wooden chest, carries a single yellow rose in a vase, two glasses of water, and two sets of silverware.

"This is—"

"I made eggs Benedict."

"You're kidding! That's one of my favorite breakfasts. But I don't like it with the ham, I like it with…"

He sets the plates down on the coffee table.

"…bacon," I finish.

And that's exactly what he's made.

Savage places the plate in his lap and starts eating.

I drink my coffee and stare at him. "This is really nice of you," I say. "I appreciate the—"

Savage gets off the couch and goes over to the leather armchair across from me. He sits down and continues eating, acting as if I don't exist.

"All right," I say. "Nice talk."

I lift the plate into my lap, cut into my breakfast and take a bite. I moan and roll my eyes. "Oh my God, Savage, this is just perfect."

His chewing slows as he watches me eat.

"Like unreal. You're a great cook. Where did you learn to—?"

"Road's out."

"You say what now?"

"The road is out. We're going to be stuck here for a while."

"Oh." I keep eating and frown. "Listen, about last night—"

"We're not going to talk about that."

"Why not?"

"Because I don't want to."

"You don't want to talk about me sitting on top of you, naked?" I sigh. "What an unexpected surprise. I can't believe you, Savage, chatterbox that you are, doesn't want to talk about it."

Silence. He eats his breakfast and occasionally glares at me over the table, frowning like I've offended him.

"So…" I take a sip of water and set the glass down on the coffee table. "What are we going to do today? It's not like I can leave."

"Spar."

"Huh?"

"I'm going to teach you how to defend yourself for the times when I am not around."

"Which will be soon, since I'm leaving," I say.

He takes another bite of food.

"Okay, that's great, actually. I've always wanted to learn to fight, but my father and Cash would never let me. They were afraid I was going to collapse or something."

"Why?"

"Uh, well, when I was a kid, I had cancer," I say. "So, I got really sick, and I was pretty frail for a while. They didn't really want me doing much after that, which I get, but, you know, it's been years now."

"You're fine?" Savage asks. "You went into remission?"

"Yes, thankfully," I say. "But I get tested once or twice a year, just to be safe."

"I'm sorry, Hannah. I didn't know."

"Not a lot of people do. I don't talk about it much, and it's why I kind of get that Cash is so overprotective. He is the oldest out of everyone, and he was probably the most conscious when it was happening. I think it was really scary for him."

"What about for you?"

I smile, dipping my gaze down to my knees. "It was bad, but I don't remember that much of it, thankfully. I don't know if that's a trauma response or if it's just because I was young, but I think about it a lot more these days." I take a sip of coffee. "I went through this huge, traumatic thing when I was a kid, right? And I… Well, I'm really lucky to be here. A lot of people aren't that lucky. I want to live my life bearing that in mind. I want to live it to the fullest, while I can, because if I did get tested one of these days, and I had to go through that again, and my family had to go through that again, I would want to have lived my life with no regrets."

The rain picks up. I continue eating, but Savage has stopped.

"What?" I ask, smiling.

"You are an amazing person." And then he gets up, grabs my empty coffee cup, and goes to refill it.

I'm too stunned to say a word.

Sixteen

SAVAGE

SHE'S TRYING to kill me. This woman is trying to kill me, either via a heart attack or because all the blood has spontaneously left my brain and rushed to my dick.

Hannah is *stretching* before we spar. In the middle of the living room.

We've just had a great breakfast, a talk that made my chest ache for her, and then she ran off to get changed for our self-defense class. The last thing I expected was to walk back into the room and find her bent over in the middle of it, her ass in the air, the perfect outline of her pussy on display.

I'm going to hell.

She's in downward dog, and the view is immaculate.

Hannah is never going to happen, and the reasons are mounting. Not only is she my fucking kryptonite, and not only do I have nothing to offer her, but she's been through enough. She deserves a full life, not one hidden out on a ranch, away from her hopes and dreams and future.

I will NOT touch her.

Hannah moans as she stretches her ass upward, and I've got to stop myself from punching the door jamb.

I clear my throat.

Hannah snaps upright. "Oh, hey. You ready to kick some ass?"

I frown.

"I mean, teach me to kick some ass?"

"Yes."

"That's the, uh, mild-mannered spirit, I guess?"

Mild-mannered? Is that what she thinks? I pull my shirt down so that my cock, which is tucked into the waistband of my sweatpants, isn't on display.

"So, what are we going to do?" she asks, clapping her hands together. "Teach me everything you know."

What's wrong with my brain? It's insistent on torturing me. Every word she says sounds dirty, and I've already fucked my hand to the image of her this morning. In my shower while she was asleep in the next room.

"We're going to start with the basics. Fighting stance, how to throw a punch, that kind of thing."

"Oh." Hannah wriggles her nose. "I thought you'd be teaching me how to break out of a chokehold or something like that. You know, since stalkers don't generally throw down their gloves and challenge you to a bout of fisticuffs."

"Fisticuffs?"

"Huzzah. Put up your dukes." She lifts her fists and pumps them back and forth.

I smile.

"Ha. Got you."

I frown.

"And we're back to our regular setting," she says.

"It's important to know how to throw a punch," I say. "We'll work on other self-defense techniques and exercises, but I want you to know how to sock a motherfucker in the face and break his nose."

"Mild-mannered, my ass," Hannah whispers.

"You good with blood?"

"I—Yeah. I think so?"

"You won't faint if you break someone's nose?"

"That's a scenario I've never been in before," Hannah says. "But I think I'll be fine. I mean, I've seen Cash and Jesse give each other bloody noses before, and Leo once broke his arm and there was a literal piece of bone sticking out, and I was okay. It was disgusting, but I didn't pass out."

"Good."

"He fell out of a tree when he was, like, five. It was before he started playing rugby. You know," Hannah says, tapping her chin and pouting those kissable lips, "I'm pretty sure he started playing rugby after that accident. Must have knocked something loose in his brain."

She keeps talking, and while I'm not one of those men who doesn't listen when a woman talks, I can't help admiring her.

Her dark hair is glossy and falls around her shoulders. While she talks, she scrapes it away from the fine column of her neck and into a ponytail. Her lips are full and slightly pink, and she's got beautiful blue eyes that shimmer gray in the right light. She's taken off my sweater and has on a T-shirt that's tight over her breasts but loose at the bottom, and those pink yoga pants are driving me crazy. The way they cling to her long, shapely legs is obscene.

"—throw a punch."

I snap my gaze to her face. "Yeah. Show me how you'd throw one."

"All right." She puts up her fists. "But are you sure you want me to do that? I don't want to hurt you or something."

I smirk.

"Hey, whatever," Hannah says. "Dynamite comes in small packages, remember?"

"Throw the punch."

She shoots out her fist, and I catch it in my palm. I release her, angry that I touched her.

"How was that?" she asks.

"Terrible."

"Wait, what? Why?"

"Because you tucked your thumb inside your fist, your wrist wasn't straight, and your stance is wrong."

"Well, damn," she says. "Don't hold back on the criticism or anything."

"You're right," I say. "Your punch was great."

"Thanks."

"If you want to break your wrist and possibly your hand."

"Ah," Hannah says. "Fine. So then, what do I do?"

I teach her, making sure she's got her weight adjusted and spread between her legs. I correct her form, talking her through how she should punch and where she should aim.

"Now, when you punch, the power isn't coming from your hand," I say. "It's not even coming from your arm. It's coming from your entire body. If you're aiming for the head, you want to push through the head."

"That's not possible."

"Picture that it is," I say. "And punch from the hip."

"I'll try," she says, and her uncertainty is so fucking adorable.

We move into the area between my sofa and armchair —I've already pushed the coffee table out of the way—and Hannah takes up her stance.

"From the hip," she says. "Okay. From the hip." She bounces on her feet, bobbling back and forth. "Straight wrist. The thumb is on the outside of the fist. Check. Check."

"Any day now."

"These hips don't lie," she yells, and throws a punch at me.

But she throws too much weight into it and stumbles right into my arms. I'm expecting a punch, not her entire body weight, and I lose my balance. We tumble to the floor together, but I catch her so that she doesn't get hurt.

She's on top of me again, her legs on either side of my body, her hot pussy pressing against the front of my sweatpants.

My cock hardens underneath her, and the smell of her soft, floral perfume fills my nostrils.

"Sorry," she says, sitting up. Her eyes widen as she rocks back onto my dick.

"Hannah." I grit my teeth. "You need to throw less of your weight into the punch."

She's frozen, sitting on top of me, and we stare at each other in the growing heat and silence. The fire cracks and spits. Hannah's breasts rise and fall. She falls forward onto my chest slowly. "Savage."

"Hannah."

She toys with my beard, then moves her fingers up toward my ear.

I cup the back of her head then roll her over onto the hardwood floor, and she lets out a yelp. I press my forehead against hers, and grind my cock against her warmth, picturing that this can happen. "You're trying to make me lose it, aren't you?" I hold her gaze with mine as I press my length against her heat.

Hannah's eyelashes flutter, she lets out a tiny, tight moan.

You swore!

I push myself upright, trying not to see how good she looks, lying down for me, or the wetness that's seeped through her yoga pants. "I need to check the perimeter." And then I leave the living room and slam out of the front door. I walk into the rain.

Seventeen

HANNAH

I'M SHAKING from the top of my head to the tips of my toes, and it's not from the cold.

He just—

Savage rubbed himself against me. Minus the clothes, he would've been…

Stop. Stop. He also just ran out of the room and into a storm to get away from you.

I've never been in a more frustrating and confusing situation. The man I thought despised me, or at least thought I was annoying and unattractive, wants me so badly, he can't stand to be in the same room as me.

And I'm the idiot who's lying here with ruined yoga pants, completely unfulfilled.

This is another memory I'll store away to keep for lonely nights.

That's not pathetic.

I get up and head for the master bedroom, then clean myself up in the bathroom and change my pants. I put on underwear this time, because panty-lines or not, I can't afford to ruin yet another pair of pants because of Savage. I only packed three.

I head out into the hall.

The fire crackles from the living room, and the front door is shut, probably locked from the outside to keep me safe. And Savage is out there in the rain, while I—

My gaze wanders to the other doors, and my heart skips a beat. One of the "forbidden" doors is open a crack.

I gnaw on the inside of my cheek.

"This is wrong," I murmur. "You're not doing this. You were told not to do this."

But I'm also tired of being told what not to do and when. My feet carry me toward the door, and I shiver, nervous about what I might find inside.

What is Savage hiding? Gosh, at this point, what isn't he hiding? The man is an enigma. All I know about him is that he was in the Navy, he doesn't like to talk, he cooks a mean chicken piccata, and he is seriously well-endowed. Scarily well-endowed. Like, I'm not even sure it will fit, well-endowed.

Ruining the pants, Hannah.

My curiosity gets the better of me, and I press my palm to the door. It opens on oiled hinges, and I gasp.

The room is hexagonal in shape, and the center is empty except for a few comfy-looking armchairs and a coffee table. The walls are dominated by bookshelves that groan under the weight of countless books. Books in every color and size, but neatly categorized so that it's beautifully aesthetic. The only spaces not occupied by the shelves are those that let in light from French windows. There's even a little nook beneath one of the windows that looks like it will get amazing sunlight.

"Wow," I breathe.

This is a librarian's fantasy. A beautiful home library filled with books? Unreal.

And Savage knows I'm a librarian, so why would he keep this from me?

I enter the room slowly and move along the bookshelves closest to me. They're not set up in alphabetical order. There's an entire bookcase dedicated to one author in particular. C. M. Casey.

I remove one of the books and turn it over. It's a middle grade fantasy adventure with a young girl on the front holding up her hand with a ball of fire above it. Gosh, these are exactly the types of books I wanted to get for the library before things fell through with the hot pepper-eating contest.

I've still got time. I can find donors for the revamp, talk to the—

"What are you doing?" Savage's voice rings through the space.

I swallow and turn toward him. "Sorry," I say, putting up a smile. "The door was open and once I saw what was in here I couldn't resist. This is an impressive collection. I mean, seriously. Are they all children's books?" I lift up the book in my hand.

His dark gaze flickers to it and then up to my face. "Put it back."

"What?"

"Put that back."

"Savage, look, I—"

"Put it back." It comes out as a bark that verges on a shout, and I jolt on the spot.

I grew up with brothers, so I've seen my fair share of

testosterone-fueled arguments, but it shocks me. I have seen Savage lose control once. And it was at the hot pepper eating contest after he saved my life.

"You don't need to raise your voice at me," I say, lifting my chin and glaring at him.

"I wasn't raising my voice."

"And now you're going to gaslight me too?"

"Hannah, put the book back. Please."

"No."

"What?"

I walk over to him and shove the book against his chest. "You put the book back. I wouldn't want to touch anything else in here in case you lose your friggin' mind." I push past him.

"I told you not to come in here," he says behind me.

I turn around and find him standing in the doorway, clutching the book in both hands. "I told you, this door and that door are off-limits." He nods to the far end of the hall.

"Yeah, well, unlike you, I don't care if somebody tells me something is off-limits."

"That's bullshit."

"No, you're bullshit. This whole situation is bullshit. Look, you didn't want me to go in there, and I get that what I did was wrong, but if you ever talk to me like that again, I will—" I lose my breath. What will I do? "I'll leave and never come back."

"I thought you were doing that anyway."

"Whatever. You think you're so smart, Savage. So smart and controlled. I can tell you think I'm, I don't know, less than you. Not worth your time."

"That must be why I made you chicken piccata for

dinner last night," he grunts. "Because you're not worth my time."

"No, you're right. You just... keep your distance and then randomly make me my favorite meal that you happened to hear me mention years ago," I say. "Without any explanation. You acted like you despised me for years. Watched me embarrass myself over and over again. And then you invite me out here, and next thing, you're telling me actually, you think I'm an amazing person, and here's your favorite breakfast, next to one of your favorite flowers, and by the way, let me grind my dick into you for a hot minute." I take a breath. "Do you have any idea how confusing this is? For me? For you? I don't know what the hell is going on half the time. So I am sorry. Truly. I'm sorry I entered your secret library. I just—I wanted to know you. And that was my mistake."

He grinds his teeth. Even when he does that, he's handsome, but I can't stand the sight of him.

"I'll just go to the bedroom and stay in there. That way you can protect me just like my brother wants you to, without you having to have me in your home."

"Hannah," he says, in that gruff tone. It's just below a shout.

My hair stands on end, and I march up to him. "What?"

"You—You have no idea why I asked you not to go in there," he says.

"And whose fault is that?" I ask.

We glare at each other for a moment. He takes a step toward me, but I put up my hands. "Don't come near me. I don't want to talk to you right now." And then I enter his bedroom and slam the door behind me.

It's ridiculous, but I well up instantly.

I walk to the bed and plop down.

It's not that Savage is upset I violated his privacy or his rules, or even that he got snappy with me about it. It's how frustrated I am.

How can one guy send this many mixed signals? And why? Why can't he just open up to me and tell me what he wants?

I lay back on the bed and let the tears come. Why is life so *messed up* at the moment?

Eighteen

SAVAGE

I'M AN ASSHOLE.

I shouldn't have told her not to go into the library. I should have kept the library door locked. Or locked it after my check of the perimeter and the interior of the house. But I didn't, and I snapped at her.

Fuck. You idiot.

I put the book back on the shelf carefully, then leave the room and shut it behind me.

You shouldn't care about this.

I'm meant to be keeping my distance. Hannah is meant to be a friend at best, a person who is learning from me, not a woman I care deeply about, but each passing moment I spend in her presence, I am losing control. And I will do anything to make this right.

I walk to my bedroom door and knock once.

No answer.

"Hannah?"

"Yeah?"

"May I come in?"

Quiet, and then her footsteps on the hardwood floor. She opens the door and narrows her eyes up at me. "You going to yell at me again?"

"I'm sorry."

She bites down on her bottom lip.

"I shouldn't have been a dick."

"It's okay," she says. "I shouldn't have gone in there when you didn't want me to. I just, I saw the door cracked open, and I was super curious, and then I when I saw the books…"

"You couldn't resist?"

"No," she says, and laughs. "I couldn't resist." She backs up then turns and sways her hips over to the bed. She sits down on it and hugs herself. She's wearing my sweater again, which I'm taking as a good sign.

The fact that I'm taking it as anything makes me an idiot.

"You can go into the library any time you like." It hurts to say that. It physically hurts. "Just don't expect me to spend a lot of time with you in there."

"Oh." And she bites that lip again. I can tell she wants to ask why, but I do not have it in me to tell her today.

"Forget I said that." And I beckon to her. "Come on. Let me give you a tour."

"Of the library?"

"Yeah." I hold out a hand.

Hannah stares at it a second before slipping off the bed and padding over. I take her hand and deeply regret it. It's soft and warm, it's delicate, and even now, I picture it wrapped around my cock. I need help.

I guide her down the hallway and open the library door. I grit my teeth but force myself to take a breath.

"You can read whatever you like in here."

"Thank you," she says. "I feel guilty, though. I—"

"I shouldn't have snapped at you. I'm not used to company. I like things done in a certain way, and I don't really like people being in my space most of the time." But she was fast becoming the exception to that rule, and one that I couldn't afford to make.

"Why is that?" she asks, walking toward the book-shelves opposite us. She strokes her fingers down the spines of the books with care, and I admire her fingers, the pink nail polish, the way she moves.

Fuck, I am so screwed. I'm getting a boner over the way she touches books.

"These are... uh, steamy," she says, lifting one of the novels from the contemporary romance section off the shelf. "Do you read any of these? Wait, silly question, there's that one you borrowed from the library."

"That was an accident."

"Is it also an accident that you bookmarked several pages?" she murmurs the question.

I stroke my beard to hide my smile. "I don't usually read historical romance," I say. "I prefer contemporary stuff."

Hannah clears her throat and puts the book back. "We have that in common."

An awkward silence drifts between us. She looks down at her feet, then shakes her head and turns back to the books. "This is really an amazing collection." She moves from one bookcase to the next, until she reaches the one I caught her in front of before. "Lots of middle-grade fiction and kids' books. Oh, cute, there's even a section for toddlers. You know, I've been hoping to revamp the kids section of the library."

"You have?"

"I wanted to start a whole reading initiative before I left. Get kids interested in books again. But I just don't have the funds for it. I've been thinking of approaching the local schools and seeing if they'd be interested in helping host a fundraising event."

"I'll help."

"W-What?" She spins toward me, eyes wide.

"I'll help you," I say.

What are you doing? You don't like people.

"I'll sponsor the event," I say. "Help you get some more people interested in taking part."

"You can't be serious," Hannah replies. "You'd do that?"

"If it would help," I say. "I like kids. Always thought I would…" I glance off toward one side and swallow. "I thought I would have one."

Hannah falls silent, and I can tell she's watching me. "Savage?"

"Yeah."

"Do you want to talk about it?" she asks.

"What?"

"Whatever it is that's making you upset."

"No." It's the easiest word for me. Shut it down. Shut her out. "I'll be in the living room when you're done. You can read whatever you want, but it's warmer in there if you want to sit on the sofa and read. I'm going to stoke the fire."

"Thank you," she says. "This is amazing."

"It's nothing."

But she comes over before I can walk away. She slides her arms around my waist and hugs me.

I freeze for a moment then hug her back, hesitant. She feels good in my arms, like she was meant to be there. I step out of her grasp, turn and walk away.

Nineteen

HANNAH

THE DAY HAS WORN ON. Savage has spent it on the leather armchair across from the sofa, his laptop on his lap while I read. Lunch was grilled cheese sandwiches paired with white wine, and the rain patters on. Not roaring like it was last night or even this morning, but a steady drum of noise.

He grunts under his breath and lifts his phone, using those large thumbs to type something out on the screen. His sweater tugs over his biceps, and I can't help staring at him. Or remembering the look on his face when he caught me in the library.

Not just anger, but a coldness.

Like a shutter had slammed shut over his emotions. Like he was looking through me at someone else.

I take a sip of my wine and try to focus on the page in my book, but I can't concentrate because of Savage.

His presence isn't just distracting, it makes me squirm. I'm constantly thinking of how he pressed into me earlier, how angry he got, and his words from last night. That he is a broken man.

"You want to play a drinking game?" I ask.

Savage lifts his gaze to meet mine. "I don't think that's a good idea."

"No, it's a terrible idea," I say. "But there's nothing else to do, and I can't concentrate on my book."

"Why?"

"Because it's giving me inappropriate thoughts," I say.

That gets his attention. He sets his laptop on the coffee table and sits up a little straighter. "What kind of drinking game?"

I grin at him. "It's easy to manipulate you into doing what I want, you know. All I have to do is mention anything related to sex, and you jump like somebody poked you in the ass."

"You don't have to manipulate me," he says. "You just have to ask."

"Yeah, right."

"What do you want?" he asks.

And I can almost picture him calling me princess again. I press my thighs together. "If I told you, do you promise to give it to me?"

He takes a sip of his wine.

"That's what I thought," I say. "You sir, are scared."

His lip quirks up at the corner, and my stomach rolls and flutters. I've never seen Savage afraid of anything. He's the picture of control, but this afternoon, when he rubbed himself against me like we were horny teens, I got a peek behind that mask.

I want more.

"What about truth or dare?"

"That's not a drinking game," he says.

"Okay, then never have I ever?"

Savage arches an eyebrow at me.

This is juvenile, but there's nothing else to do. Is it criminal that I want to know more about Savage? He's so shut off. He won't answer my questions or even hint at the truth about the library or about the fact that he knew my favorite food and made it for me. It might not seem like a big deal to someone else, but it *means* something to me.

"Never have I ever," I start, then bite my lip. "Wait, you know how this works, right? I say never have I ever and the thing, and then if you've done it, you have to drink."

"I'm familiar," Savage says. "I'm almost forty, not almost seventy."

"Fair enough," I laugh. "Okay, uh, never have I ever had sex in a public place."

Savage takes a sip of his drink. I don't.

"Revealing," I say, grinning at him. "Mr. Navy SEAL Bodyguard is a rule breaker."

Savage studies his glass, then looks up at me. "Never have I ever," he grumbles, "had a massage."

I drink, but he doesn't. "Boring," I call. "A massage? Seriously?"

"I don't like people touching me," he replies.

"That's not what you said last night."

He chokes on a little wine and dabs his beard.

I laugh, because it's fun that I can get under his skin. Painful, but fun. And it's given me an idea. "Never have I ever stripped for someone."

I take a sip of wine. He doesn't.

Savage glares at me over the rim of his glass. "Who did you strip for?"

"Huh?"

"Who the fuck did you strip for?"

"What does it matter?"

"Is it this Franklin idiot?"

"No," I say.

"The guy before that. What was his name?"

"Does it matter what his name is?" I ask.

"Yes. What's his name?" Savage leans forward, his eyes intense and focused on me.

"Savage, I didn't strip for him. But I did strip for you last night," I say, "if you recall. I took my shirt off while I was sitting in your lap."

He freezes. His jaw works, but no sound comes out.

So, I did make an impression.

"Enough of this game," he grunts, and sits back.

I hide my smile behind the rim of my glass. I can't help it. I've spent years feeling awkward and nervous around Savage, and now I'm making him feel the same way?

"You want to try truth or dare?" I ask.

"I do *not.*"

"Oh, come on, it will be fun," I say.

His expression is unreadable. The rain, the crackle of the fire, the wine. It couldn't be more romantic, but there's still a space between us, and I'm not sure that will change.

I've never been particularly forward. I don't want to come on too strong, but I want him so bad I keep crossing and uncrossing my legs, and looking for comfort I can't get.

Savage holds my gaze but doesn't talk, and my breathing hitches in my chest.

"Y-You know what I've never done?" I ask.

He raises an eyebrow.

"I've never taken a ride on the back of a motorcycle."

He nods. "Because your brother would have a heart attack."

"Probably. Cash has been mostly distracted by June this past while, so I could've gotten away with it if not for my meddling stalker," I say, with a cheesy grin. "What made you get, uh, a motorcycle?"

Savage stiffens incrementally, and for a second, I'm sure I've crossed yet another line. He releases a gruff breath. "Before I came out here, to Heatstroke, I lived in San Diego. I was part of a motorcycle club out there for a couple of years."

"A motorcycle club?"

"Yeah."

"What was that like?"

"It wasn't great," he says. "It was dangerous, and it led me down the wrong path pretty damn quick. I did some things I'm not proud of." He scratches his neck, and I can't help staring at the tattoos, how strong his hands are, the way he moves. "I wasn't part of the club for long."

"Why? What happened?" I sit forward, tucking my knees underneath my body, and setting the wine glass down on the table.

"A lot of shitty things," he says. "I was in a bad place when I joined the club. I was looking for revenge in the wrong places, and I thought they would help me get it."

My pulse races. "Revenge?"

He downs his wine in one swift motion and sets it aside. The glass looks ridiculous in his huge hands.

"Yes. Revenge. But the leader of that club, Davis, made promises to me that he couldn't keep. It was a trade. I did what he wanted, he was supposed to help me get what I wanted," he says.

I'm stuck on every word.

"But he didn't hold up his end of the bargain," Savage continues. "And I realized that the parts of me I liked were gone. And all that was left was anger. So I decided to leave."

I gnaw on my bottom lip. "You left? Is that a thing you can do?" Granted, my knowledge about motorcycle clubs comes solely from motorcycle club romance novels, but whatever.

"Not easily," Savage says.

"But you're fine now?"

"That depends on your definition of fine, Princess."

My stomach pirouettes. I love it when he calls me that. I shouldn't, because I'm half convinced it's a reference to how helpless I am and how everyone looks after me, but from his mouth… My God.

"You met Cash after you arrived in Heatstroke, right?"

"That's right," Savage says. "Your brother saved my life."

"Are you serious? I had no idea."

"It's how we met." Savage takes a breath.

I'm so nervous my palms are clammy. Before, all I had to go on was my raw physical attraction to Savage, but now that he's opening up to me, things are getting so much worse. He's fascinating. Mysterious. Strong.

"I arrived in Heatstroke late at night. You know the overlook on the bay?"

"Sure." There was a road that ran up the hill encircling the bay on the coastal road into Heatstroke

"I stopped there," Savage says. "And I was, uh, considering my options. I wanted to be rid of everything that had happened over the past couple of years. I was going to drive my motorcycle off the cliff and end it."

"Savage, I'm so sorry." I press my hand over my mouth.

"But your brother happened to arrive up there in time to stop me. He was practically a kid. He'd just brought Alex back to Heatstroke, and he was up there having a night off. He talked me down," Savage says. "I owe your brother my life."

"That's—"

"It is what it is," Savage says. "There's no amount of favors I could do for him that would repay what he's given me."

"Cash wouldn't want you to feel indebted to him," I say. "He's not like that."

Savage doesn't answer me, but the quiet in the room grows. He gets up and comes back a minute later with a battery-powered radio. Music drifts from its tinny speakers. Romantic music.

"What about you?" Savage asks.

"What about me?"

"What do you enjoy that excites you? Motorcycles did that for me. Still do when I get the chance to ride. What does it for you?"

"Uh." I swallow. *Don't say anything dumb.* "Books, listening to music, and travel. I would love to travel. I've always dreamed of visiting other countries. Honestly, I've always dreamed about experiencing the things I read about in books."

Savage's gaze darkens. The fire crackles and spits, the music sweeps through the room, and I'm caught up in the moment. In hoping that whatever Savage is thinking is as "bad" as what I'm thinking.

"What?"

"What kind of things?"

"Uh, all kinds of things," I whisper.

He gets up, crosses the room and stands over me. Savage is huge even when I'm standing, but sitting down, his presence is unbearable. "Show me," he says.

Oh. My. God.

"S-Show you?"

"Yeah." He puts out a hand.

I take it and stand up. "Are you—? You realize what I mean, right?"

He doesn't answer.

"Most of the books I read are romance novels. Or fantasy romance novels. Or romance novels that are fifty percent smut."

Savage smiles at me, and it's a stunning smile. It makes my toes curl. It's like the anger and grumpiness he usually carries with him is a facade, and it's gone. He's open. "I figured as much."

He figured… He figured as much. "Oh. I… Oh, well I…" I'm stammering like a fool. Gone is "Miss In Control Hannah."

My hand is still in his, and his fingers brush up the side of it to my wrist. He holds it tight and squeezes.

"Hannah, if I could, I would worship your body."

I inhale sharply, my gaze dancing to his.

He draws closer, so that his body heat is unbearable, and I look up at him. He runs his fingers from my wrist, up the side of my body to my throat and rests them there. "Your heart is beating fast."

I tremble.

Savage leans in, his lips against my ear. "You've enjoyed torturing me for the past couple of hours, haven't you?"

He rests his hand around my throat, squeezing gently.

"You've enjoyed making my cock hard."

I whimper.

"You've enjoyed knowing that I want you," he murmurs. "I can't touch you, Hannah. I can't bend you over the sofa and eat your pussy until you come so many times, you can't breathe. Until you scream so hard your throat hurts. Until your body is shaking and you can't remember what time of the day it is, what month it is, what year it is, or anything else other than my name."

I shut my eyes and breathe through my nose.

"You've been playing with fire all fucking day long," he says, his breath on my neck. "Now, you're going to be a good fucking girl, and say my name."

I moan. I swear, I'm going to spontaneously combust. Or even come without him having touched me.

This is crazy.

"That's it," Savage says. "But this time, moan while you say my name."

I'm hyperventilating. Getting dizzy.

His grip on my throat tightens, and it sends pulsing desire shooting through my core. He's completely in control. "Say my name, Hannah. Moan it."

"Savage," I whisper, and it does come out as a moan. A desperate moan.

"That's it, Princess. Just like that. I want you to do that again, but this time I want you to picture me fucking my hand and coming all over your face."

"Savage." The moan is obscene. It's out of control. I swear to God, I am going to pass out in a second.

He squeezes even tighter, and it's our only point of contact apart from his lips brushing against my ear, his beard tickling my skin. "And the last thing I want you to know, Hannah, is that I heard you coming for me the other night. And if you think your fantasies are good, they are nothing compared to the real thing."

I moan his name one last time.

Savage releases my throat, and I nearly collapse. He catches me halfway to the sofa. He eases me onto it, his lips inches from mine.

"Don't play with me again," he says. "The next time you do, I'm going to ruin you."

Twenty

SAVAGE

I'M SO FUCKING AROUSED, the inside of my sweats are wet. I keep my dick tucked into the waistband of my sweatpants, then grab my wine glass and Hannah's and move through to the kitchen.

She's a quivering mess on the sofa, and I haven't even touched her. It's nothing compared to how I've felt today.

I pour wine into our glasses and bring them back to the living room, setting hers on the coffee table. She stares up at me, her cheeks pink, her lips parted, and I have to restrain myself from picturing her mouth encircling the tip of my dick.

"Wine," I say, tapping my finger beside the glass on the table.

I return to my seat, then take a sip from my glass. It's a struggle to appear unaffected by her while my cock is tugging against my pants, and my mind is firmly stuck in the fucking gutter.

"You were going to tell me about what you've always wanted to do," I say.

She lets out a shaky breath, reaches up and pushes a few strands back from her forehead. "You're kidding, right?"

"I'm not much of a kidder."

"You don't say." She reaches for her wine, almost knocks over the glass, but catches it. She brings it to her lips and drinks, and I watch her throat working, the way her eyes are glazed with desire. Finally, she puts the glass back down and takes a breath. "I've always wanted to do something crazy."

I tilt my head and watch her.

She's trying so hard to bring her thoughts under control. I like it. I like the effect I have on her, I like that she's been pining for me, just the same as I've been denying myself what I want for fucking years. I like all of it. Even that it's wrong, and I'm going to regret talking to her like this.

"What crazy thing do you want to do, Hannah?"

She drinks more of her wine then puts down her glass with a clink. "I've always wanted to dance in the rain," she says. "Just because. I've never done that before."

"You have the opportunity to do that right now," I say.

"Are you serious?"

"Why not? I'm here to protect you in case your stalker appears." The frustrating lack of cell service has stopped me from confirming that it's him with Cash. "And you've always wanted to do it."

"But it's so out there. It's so crazy."

"It's not that crazy. It's not like you're asking to go skydiving during a tornado."

"Are you calling me boring?" she asks. "Just because I'm a librarian, doesn't make me boring."

"I'm not saying that, Princess."

"Can you not call me that?"

"Why?"

She opens her mouth and shuts it.

I get up again and walk over, hold out my hand. She stares at it.

"Come."

She sucks in a breath.

"Hannah," I say, "I meant come with me."

"Right, of course. Yeah. That's definitely…" She takes my hand, and I walk her out of the living room and down the hall toward the front door. She's barefoot, but I don't want to get spooked and run before she's done what she's always wanted to do.

Being scared is a mindset.

The first step to moving on from it, to becoming fearless, is facing your fears head-on.

I open the front door, and she hesitates on the threshold.

"What if we get hit by lightning?" Hannah blushes. "That was dumb, sorry."

I scoop her off her feet, and she shrieks a giggle. I run us both into the rain, sloshing across the waterlogged ground in front of my cabin. It's flooded, the water reaching the bottom of Hannah's car door. My truck is a little higher and safer from the rain.

Hannah laughs and tilts her head back so that the rain spatters down on her face.

She's beautiful and free, even in the cage of my arms.

"Put your legs around my waist," I say.

Hannah's eyes widen, but I shift her so that her arms are around my neck, and her legs wrapped around my middle. She clings to me, and the rain intensifies, pouring down from above, soaking us both through, but her feet are protected from the water, and she's got me.

And so we dance.

I sway her on the spot, and she presses her forehead against mine, our body heat mingling.

"Like this?" I ask. "Is this what you pictured?"

She shakes her head. "It's better." She shouts it over the rain, her lips inches from mine, droplets of water running down her nose, over the contours of her mouth.

The way I want to kiss her is unreal. It's almost overwhelming. She shivers against me, then tips her head back and lets out a whoop of joy, rising high against my body.

I carry her back inside and set her down in the hallway. We're both dripping wet as I run through the house, grab her a towel and guide her through to the living room. I stand her in front of the fire, and then give her the glass of wine before jogging back to the front door and making sure I locked it on the way in.

"You need to go shower and get warm," I say.

"But you're soaked through as well," she says.

"I'm fine. You shower first. Come on."

The song on the radio changes, and Hannah freezes halfway across the living room. "Oh my—"

"What?" I ask.

It's the first smooth notes of "Put Your Head on My Shoulder" by Paul Anka.

"I love this song," she says, with a pretty smile.

I take the wine glass from her hand and set it down.

"Savage?"

"Come here."

I take her in my arms, placing one around her waist

and bringing her close to my body, and then I sway her on the spot beside the fire. She rests her head against my chest, her hand in mine as we dance to the song. Slowly, quietly, beside the fire, where no one will ever see us. Where no one will ever find out.

The song is over too quickly, and afterward, I lead Hannah down the hall to the bathroom. She hesitates before she steps inside.

"Thank you," she says. "For everything."

Anything for you, Princess.

I grunt instead of saying it, then leave her to shower.

Twenty-One

HANNAH

I CUDDLE UP in front of the fire while I wait for Savage to get done showering. I'm deliciously mellow, even after running out into the rain, and my heart feels as if it's going to beat its way right out of my chest. It's the weirdest sensation—being warm, comfortable and relaxed but on edge.

I replay what Savage said to me, what he did to me, over and over again.

It feels as if we had sex, but he hasn't even touched me yet. Not in the way I want. We haven't even kissed.

Instead, he teased me relentlessly as payback for last night and this morning. And I ruined yet another pair of yoga pants.

"I'm going to ruin you." The words I will never forget.

And the reason why I'm not wearing underwear or a bra, and I've opted to put on *only* Savage's warm fuzzy sweater.

He thinks I'm playing with fire? Two can play at this game, and I don't care how badly he thinks he's going to ruin me. I want him. I want him more than I've ever wanted anyone in my entire life.

The shower shuts off down the hall, and I hurriedly arrange the blanket over my legs so he can't tell how naked I am.

A few minutes later, Savage enters the living room, and my mouth goes dry.

His hair is still damp from the shower. He's wearing a long-sleeved shirt that hugs his muscles, showing off his tapered waist, the bulk of his shoulders and chest, and his strong arms. He's wearing a different pair of sweatpants, but they leave nothing to the imagination.

"Warm?" I ask.

Savage nods. "Are you hungry?"

"Not at the moment. Why don't you come sit down?" I pat the sofa beside me.

Savage frowns.

Ugh. How am I this cringy? "Uh, I just meant that it would be nice to sit with you after—"

"Hannah," he says, "if you think I'm going to fool around with you on the sofa, you're sorely mistaken."

I blush. "Excuse you, but you were the one who just held me by the throat and made me moan your name repeatedly."

"That's because I can't touch you."

"Are you saying you want me to touch myself?" I ask.

His jaw drops.

"And why can't you touch me, exactly? You've sort of brushed over that part."

"I told you," Savage says, and sits down in his armchair instead of next to me. "I can't offer you what you deserve."

"Right. Right, your heart?"

He rests his arms on the chair, completely at ease.

"What if I don't want your heart?" I ask, and it's taking all of my newly-earned bravery to talk to him like this. "What if I just want you?"

"It would be wrong."

"I get it. You want to live here, alone. And I want to leave Heatstroke. I never planned on staying here my entire life, it just kind of happened, and I don't want that to be the case. I want to find new places and friends and new people."

"What kind of people?" His eyes narrow.

"Jealous?"

"Don't change the subject," he says.

"I want to be free. I don't know, visit the South of France."

"Specifically the South of France?"

"Yeah," I continue. "And I can't do that if I stay here. So, trust me when I say that in about six weeks, after I've managed to get the kid's section stocked up, and I've created a program that will get more children reading, I'm going to leave."

"That's a lot to do in a couple of weeks."

"Now, you're changing the subject," I say. "Look, what I'm trying to get across to you is that I don't expect you to fall in love with me. I want you." And my cheeks can't burn any hotter than they already are. "I want to know what it's like to be with you."

Savage is speechless.

"It seems complicated," I say. "But it doesn't have to be. What we do can stay here."

"That's not a good idea." But his voice is strained.

"Neither is dancing in the rain." And then I get up and let the blanket fall away from my legs.

Savage's fingers bite into the arms of his chair. "Princess."

"You said that you're not going to let me play with you any more." I walk over to him, I stand between his legs, and he tilts his head, running his hot gaze over my thighs, to the hem of his sweater brushing against them, over my stomach, breasts, my throat, until it rests on my face.

"You said you were going to ruin me." I brace my legs on either side of his and straddle him, just like I did last night, except this time, there is nothing separating me from the front of his sweats.

"Princess."

"So do it, Savage," I say. "Ruin me. I want you to." I planned on making him beg, but this is way better.

I settle down on top of him, and his hands move to my hips, over the sweater. He's holding me there, just inches from sitting down. He lowers me slowly, inch by inch, until my pussy rests against his length, the only thing separating us is a bit of fabric.

"Fuck." Savage's jaw is clenched. "Fuck."

I'm so wet, and I rock back and forth a bit, watching as he sinks a little lower to get more contact with me. His dick is huge. I felt it last night, but I underestimated just how big it was. I ride back and forth, rubbing my wetness over him, relishing the thought that it's soaking through to make contact with his skin.

"Savage," I whisper.

"Yeah." His gaze is locked on my face, rather than the point of contact between us.

"You realize I'm not wearing any underwear."

He looks down right away. He witnesses the wetness seeping through his sweatpants. And his hands instantly slip underneath the sweater and grab hold of my naked hips.

And then there's a quiet. He holds me still for a moment, staring down at my pussy, exposed for him.

I can almost hear it. The moment his resolves snaps.

He grits his teeth, his chest rumbling with unspoken words, and finally, he meets my gaze again. "Fuck it."

Twenty-Two

SAVAGE

I'M TOO FAR GONE to care any more.

She's so wet for me, it's soaked through my sweat-pants, and the thought of her wetness on my dick is pure fucking destruction. The sight of her slick pussy, seated against my cock shatters every complaint before I can summon them up.

I grab the back of her neck, then tip us both out of the armchair and onto the floor in front of the fire. I grab the blanket and shove it under her head while she whimpers, then part her legs and stare at her.

She's glistening for me.

I kneel and grab the inside of her thighs, pushing them as wide as they will go so I can drink in the sight of her. If this is the only chance I'll get to make her come, I want to savor it. I want it to be a memory that lasts me for the rest of my fucking life.

My fingers bite into her thighs, and I drag her lower half into my lap, looping my arm underneath her ass and lifting her pussy as high as is comfortable for her.

Those shimmering blue eyes are locked onto me, and she's panting for me and whimpering.

"Savage," she moans.

"Just this once," I say. "Just one time."

She writhes in my lap, arching her pussy toward my face, and I exhale over her mound. Goosebumps spread up her legs, over her stomach, sweater falling back over her full tan breasts, those nipples puckered for me.

I let out another breath, hovering my mouth over her clit.

She jerks in my arms. "Savage, now." She balls up a fist and drops it onto the floor.

I touch the tip of my tongue to her clit, and she loses it, arching upward to meet me again, her eyes rolling back in her head.

"Oh my God," she whines.

"Scream as much as you want," I say, and then I take my tongue and draw it from her entrance up to her clit, spreading her wetness over her pussy.

Hannah screams my name, and the tension that she's held in her body for years breaks instantly. She's coming against my face and moaning, before I've even had the chance to taste her properly.

"That's it," I say. "That's it, Princess. You're my good girl. Such a good girl. Come for me again."

"Savage." She's just coming down from her high when I suck her clit into my mouth and circle it with my tongue. She screams again, rocking into me, and I hold there this time. I hold her dead still so I can punish her completely.

If I can't spend a night without thinking of her, she's going to spend the rest of her life coming to this memory.

I work her pussy with my tongue, focusing only on her

clit, and bringing her into an orgasm only moments after the first. She's losing her mind for me, completely swollen, dripping, even more perfect than she's always been.

"It's too good," she whispers. "Oh my God, it's so good."

I insert two fingers into her warmth, and I nearly come in my pants. It's soft and smooth. I pound my fingers inside her, opening her up, imagining that it's my cock inside her rather than my fingers. I close my mouth over her clit again and make her come a third time.

Hannah screams. I moan against her pussy, savoring her taste.

I need more of it.

I lift her and fold her so that she's all ass and legs in the air, open for me, and then I bring my mouth down on her entrance and pump my tongue inside her relentlessly. I use my thumb to slap and circle her clit, bringing her to another orgasm.

I like this method the best, so I do it again, playing her body and wringing out every last bit of pleasure.

She screams so loud during the fifth time she comes, that she starts losing her voice. My name on her breathless lips is enough for me.

Finally, I release her thighs. I lift her off the floor and lay her down on the sofa, then I cover her lower half with a blanket and walk out of the room, stumbling, almost tripping over the coffee table. I make it to the bedroom before I tug down the waistband of my sweats, grab my dick and start stroking it.

My hips thrust of their own accord, and I stumble again, grabbing at the bathroom door to keep myself upright.

"Savage." Hannah's standing in the bathroom doorway, a mess. Cheeks pink. Hair in disarray. Her voice is
hoarse just like I fucking promised. "Savage."

"Get on your knees, Princess."

She lowers herself onto them, writhing for me, even
though her pussy must be raw from how I've destroyed it.

I stand over her, working my cock. I pause, open my
hand in front of her mouth. "Spit."

She doesn't hesitate, and my dick throbs at her willing-
ness to comply.

I smooth my hand over my shaft, my head. "Mouth
open," I say.

Hannah sticks out her tongue, grabbing her breasts
through my sweater.

I take a handful of her hair, and tip her head back,
pulling tight, losing myself, and then I come all over that
pretty little tongue, moaning as she drinks me down.

Twenty-Three

HANNAH

I'M SHAKING, hoarse, and utterly ruined.

Savage picks me up off the ground and holds me upright. "Hannah," he croaks. "Hannah, I'm sorry."

"What for?" I ask, looking up at him.

"I shouldn't have done that," he says. "I shouldn't have disrespected you. I lost control, and I'm sorry."

"Disrespected me?" I pull back a step. "What is this, the fifties? You made me come like five times." My throat hurts. "You made me scream. That's not disrespectful, that was unreal."

But Savage is shaking his head, and it's already pissing me off.

"I made you get on your knees," he says. "That's not how I wanted something like this to go. I lost control."

"Yeah, well, so did I. And I wanted to get on my knees." I blush, because I can't believe I'm saying these words to Savage, or that we just did what we did. "I wanted all of what happened, and so did you, whether you want to admit it or not."

"That's not what I'm saying, Hannah."

"Oh, I see we're back to Hannah, are we? Princess is gone?"

Savage pinches the bridge of his nose. "Let's get you freshened up, and then we can talk about this."

"Sure." I strip the sweater off and drop it into the laundry basket in the corner.

Savage grunts. "I'll give you some privacy." He turns on the water in the shower, tests it until it's warm, and then he heads for the bathroom door.

"Seriously? You just came in my mouth."

"We'll talk after you're done." And I hate the expression he's wearing, the frown, the way he strokes his beard, shakes his head, like he can't believe what he's done. Savage regrets it. I don't.

I don't regret finally feeling what it would be like to have him, even just once. And I didn't get to have him all the way.

Savage shuts the door with a quiet click, and I get into the shower. I scrub myself down, muttering under my breath as I do, sluicing water over my skin. I'm super sensitive, so sensitive that I gasp when I clean myself, but I like it. I like what he's done to me.

Flashes of what happened come back as I wash myself.

The darkness of his eyes, the fixation on my pleasure, the way he moved me how he wanted to, to get at the parts of me he wanted to touch. There was no hesitation anymore, no regard for anything other than us. Me. He was hyper focused on me, and I've never experienced anything like that in my life.

And now, you never will again, because he's going to pull back.

"Ugh." I finish up in the shower quickly, dry off, and go out into the main bedroom. I hurriedly throw on my PJ shorts, and spot another sweater that Savage has laid out on the bed for me. I'm not sure if that's a good sign or not, but I'm actually so done looking for signs.

Now that I'm sure Savage wants me physically, I don't see why we have to hold back.

This can be just sex until I leave, right? It's not like we're going to fall in love and get married.

I exit into the hall and find him in the living room. Savage gets up and nods. He walks past me and out into the hall and the shower turns on a minute later.

I plop down on the sofa and stare at the spot on the floor where Savage just blew my mind.

He doesn't shower for long, and he returns a minute later, dressed in yet another pair of those cursed sweatpants and a long-sleeved shirt. Savage sits down in his armchair, frowning.

"Hannah," he says.

"Don't you dare," I reply. "I don't want to hear it. I don't want to hear how you regret what we just did. I'm still coming down from it, for God's sake. And it's not fair. I've spent years pining after you like a lovesick puppy dog, and the minute we touch, you're going to start acting like it's the worst thing since... I don't know, mayonnaise."

"You don't like mayonnaise?" Savage pulls a face.

"No, I don't like mayonnaise. It's essentially tangy cream. It's disgusting," I say. "But that doesn't matter."

"You know the French invented mayonnaise."

"That's aioli. It's different. And, oh my God, stop doing

that," I say. "This doesn't have to be a huge deal. It can be just physical. It can be between us—"

"I told you, Hannah, you deserve more than just physical."

"I don't care what you think I deserve," I say, shaking my head. "I'm telling you what I want. I want you until I leave, and it doesn't have to be complicated. It doesn't have to be about the pieces of your heart that you can't give me. It can be about just this. And we don't have to tell Cash, if that's what's on your mind."

He opens his mouth and shuts it again.

"I'm not going to beg you," I say. "That was amazing for me. I don't know how it was for you, but I'm not going to beg. I'm being straight with you, because I'm tired of being the person who keeps all her feelings and desires locked up inside." And a part of that is because of him.

"I don't want to do anything that's going to hurt you," he says. "Hannah, you don't know me. I am not the type of man you want in your life."

"Why? Because of the bad stuff you did in this motor-cycle club?" I ask.

"Partly. There are other things too. I'm not in control around you, and I don't fucking like it," he says.

"You think this is easy for me? To see you all the time. I choked on a mouthful of habanero peppers because of you."

"Because of me?"

"Yeah." *Why did you tell him that?*

He leans forward, bracing his forearms on those muscular thighs, his gaze fixed on me. I don't know what he's about to say, but if he wants to keep this distance between us, there's nothing I can do to stop it.

"I've never felt anything like what just happened," I say. "I guess you weren't kidding about ruining me. It would suck if we couldn't keep doing that."

Savage sits back again, his nostrils flare, his gaze tracks over me.

And his phone rings on the coffee table.

"Wait, your phone!" I point at it. "It's working."

Savage grabs the phone and checks the caller ID. "It's your brother."

"Right."

"I have to take this," he says, and gets up. He moves from the room briskly, and I hear a door open in the hall, the dull hum of him talking.

"Great," I mutter. "That's just perfect." I snatch my phone off the coffee table and open the group chat with the girls, because if there's a signal, I need to talk to them.

> Is anyone out there?

JUNE
Oh my gosh, Han! Are you okay? I've been worried sick about you.

> I'm fine. Actually, I'm not sure what I am. Let's just say, I've got a lot to talk to you about when this storm finally blows out of town.

BELLE
Ooooh, what's going on? Is it Savage? Did you bone Savage? Is it finally happening?

LILY
Fill us in!

Marci's probably asleep or cavorting with my brother, which is for the best, because she's got a special brand of humor that kind of makes me want to rip my eyes out when it's directed at me on a bad day.

> It's complicated. I'd rather talk to you guys in person about it.

LILY
That rules me out then.

JUNE
Lily, I wish you'd visit.

BELLE
Me too. Especially because I'm going to be in Heatstroke in about a week.

> What????!!!????

BELLE
I know, right? Yeah. But it's for a really weird reason. And I think it would be better if we talk about it when I get there.

> Color me intrigued.

JUNE
Can't wait to see you, Belle. <3

LILY
You guys have to set up a video call so I can talk to all of you.

I sit back and stare at the texts, and I feel strange. Beyond strange. Because one day ago, I was the obsessed pining girl who was hopelessly obsessed with her brother's best friend. And now, I'm… I don't know what I am any more, but I can't go back to who I was.

Twenty~Four

SAVAGE

I WALK OUT of the back door of the ranch house, along the flooded path that leads past the greenhouse. The rain has stopped, thankfully. The path is flooded, but my sweats are protected by the thick rubber boots I keep next to the back door.

"You hear me all right?" I press the phone against my ear, angry at myself and the situation, and the fact that I caved.

"Yeah, it's way clearer now. Cell signal not great out there?"

"It's been spotty since the storm started." I glance up at the sky, then out over the greenhouse and the distant fields, the trees rearing up on the border of the fence. I love it out here. It's quiet and hidden, fog drifting between the trees.

"Yeah, I've been worried fucking sick about June and Alex," Cash says. "Turns out, this wasn't a great time to take a trip out of Heatstroke."

"Have you heard from them?" I ask.

Usually, I wouldn't. I care about my friend, but I don't pry unless he asks for input. But it gives me a second to bring my thoughts to order.

Hannah's in there, irritated at my hesitation.

She thinks we can keep this quiet, emotion and complication-free, but I don't believe it for a fucking second. Maybe she can keep her heart in check, but I'm already falling into a state of obsession, and it's dangerous for her.

"—so they've been holed up at Ganny's. Apparently, the backyard is flooded. Alex is excited about it, of course."

"Sure," I say. "I've heard that about teens."

"She's the exception to the rule," Cash replies. "She gets excited about things like that. But she's always willing to tell me how cringe I am."

I hum a noncommittal answer.

"Anyway, how are you? How's Hannah?" There's a sharp edge to his tone.

"She's fine," I say. "She's indoors. Power is out at the ranch house. Not sure how long it will take to restore, but the rain has stopped."

"That's good. She's safe?" Another loaded question.

"Yeah, she's fine," I say. "But we did have a problem the other night." I tell him about the person we caught on camera.

"You're fucking kidding," Cash says. "That's weird."

"Why?"

"Because I came out here to find this Fucklin asshole, and he's here. He's at his place," Cash says.

My shoulders sag. Tension leaks out of them, and I release a breath away from the phone. Fuck. "Then it must have been someone else looking for shelter."

"Hmm. Maybe."

"So what happened?" I ask, and I pace further down the pathway, away from the house, to the glass greenhouse that is one of my favorite places to be.

"I came out here to find him, and I did. I told the little asshole that if he talks to my sister again, messages her, or even thinks of coming near her, I've got a bullet with his name on it."

"The picture of calm as always," I say.

Cash laughs. "Yeah, well, fuck that guy. He thinks he can threaten my family? I won't let anyone mess with Hannah."

"Hmm."

"What?"

"You realize you're going to have to let your sister spread her wings one of these days," I say.

"What the fuck are you talking about, Savage? Spread her wings? She's not a baby bird."

"That's exactly what I mean. She's grown. She can handle herself."

Cash falls silent. "Suddenly, you're the expert on Hannah?"

"We've been talking."

"Talking?" The word whips out.

"Of course. Unless you expected me to give your sister the silent treatment while she's here."

Cash exhales through his nose. "I'm tense. I expected this guy to put up a fight, but he caved. Which is a good thing, because I didn't particularly feel like going to prison, but if the cops aren't going to do shit, then fine."

"What happened, exactly?"

"I arrived here, knocked on his door, and he nearly wet himself looking at me," Cash says. "He recognized me."

"Did that help?"

"I think so. Given that I told him I'd out him as a stalker in front of the entire country if he didn't leave her alone. And then I said the bullet in the brain thing, so yeah," Cash says. "He pretty much fucking crumpled after that."

I grunt.

"I deleted her number off his phone, and stood over him while he deleted the many profiles he'd made on different social media sites to talk to her. And I told him that if she so much as hinted at the fact that he had contacted her in any way, I would be back."

"And he agreed?"

"Yeah," Cash says. "He has no choice."

The fact that Cash had to do that is fucked up. That little piece of shit didn't respect Hannah's "no", but because Cash is a man who's big and scary—

"It's over," Cash sighs.

"So you don't need me to be your sister's bodyguard any more, correct?"

"I doubt this guy will do anything after our little chat," Cash says. "But I don't want to take any chances. Keep watch over her for the next couple of weeks. Let's see what happens."

"You mean until she leaves?"

"I doubt she'll leave," Cash says. "Why would she need to now that this stalker is taken care of?"

"Because she wants to."

"Is there something going on here that I'm missing?" Cash asks. "Seems like you've got a lot of opinions about

Hannah all of a sudden, and I gotta tell you, buddy, I'm not that comfortable with it."

"You've trusted me for years, haven't you?"

Cash sniffs. "Yeah. Listen, make sure that she stays safe. Let's not let our guards down now."

"Are you heading back soon?" I ask.

"Yeah, once the weather clears, and I can get back into Heatstroke."

"Any news about that?" I ask. "We've been cut off for a while."

"Storm is passing, but there's an instruction to shelter in place. There are emergency teams working to provide for those who have been hurt or displaced by the storm. I don't know what the timeline is like, but I'm hoping this should clear up by the end of the week, at least in the sense that the flood water will have gone down, somewhat."

"Right."

"Savage?"

"Yeah."

"Keep her safe. Don't let anything or anyone hurt my sister." I can hear it in his voice—the trauma, the memories. It must have been real fucking tough to deal with Hannah's illness as a boy. Cash is already hyper-protective of the people he loves.

"I won't, brother."

"I believe you." And then he hangs up.

I stare at the phone, squeezing it, a cold wind plucking at the back of my neck. It's icy out here, but I don't care. I can't go back in there and see Hannah right now. How can I simultaneously regret what happened, but want to go back and do it over again anyway?

She drives me crazy. She's always driven me crazy, and I've been so fucking diligent about avoiding contact with her for fear I will lose control in exactly the way I did.

My dick is already twitching again at the memory of her on her knees, her greedy mouth open for me, desperate, and the taste of her still on my lips and tongue while I came.

I haven't had sex in years. The build up to having her was too much for me, and now I've done it. I've broken everything.

I have no choice. I have to tell Hannah that it can't happen again. I have to try to make her understand why, but that would mean telling her the truth about everything.

"Fuck." I stare down at the blackened screen of my phone, shaking my head, then turn to head back to the house.

Twenty-Five

HANNAH

SAVAGE HAS BEEN OUT THERE for a while.

Talking to Cash. Great. I'm sure that's going fantastically. Cash is such a friggin' psycho about keeping me safe, that he's probably putting extra pressure on Savage to protect me. And that's going to complicate things.

I press my hands to my face and groan.

This is ridiculous.

I want him, and he wants me. And I'm leaving. It's not like I'm any threat to his private idyllic life here. I need to talk to him.

I push up from the sofa and walk out into the hall. I don't care if he's on the phone with Cash, and I don't care if my brother hears what I have to say, either. I want us to hash this out, because I'm not keeping it bottled up inside.

"Savage?" I call out.

I don't hear him talking on the phone any more. I try the front door, but it's locked, the library is open and empty, and the bedroom is too.

The back door?

The one he told me not to go through at the start of my stay here. *He took that back, remember? He said you can go wherever you like.* Technically, he told me I could use the library as much as I liked.

"Stop equivocating," I mutter, and then I open the back door and step out onto the porch.

It's wet, the backyard flooded, but it's beautiful and crisp out there. Water stretching out toward the borderline, mist drifting between the distant trees, and a glass greenhouse rising ahead of me. It's slightly raised on a platform just above the water.

A greenhouse?

That makes sense, given the horticulture book Savage returned to the library.

And it's dry in there. Could he have gone in for a quiet moment to talk on the phone? *Out of earshot.* Ugh.

I grimace at the wetness then slosh across to the greenhouse, my skin prickling at the cool water. I shiver and then head up the stairs and open the glass door. I step inside and it's like entering another world.

"Oh my God," I whisper.

The scent of flowers fills my nostrils, and I walk down a long aisle, past tables and racks of soil and seeds, and then between the beds. A sea of roses stretches out in front of me. Roses of every color, red, white, peach, pink, and yellow. There's even a row of peach roses. I'm drawn to that row.

I move over to it and crouch in front of the beautiful flowers, shaking my head.

Savage grows flowers? Not just any flowers, but roses? My favorite flower.

I lean forward and sniff the closest rose, smiling. The

scent is light, not overpowering, but distinct. There's a white plastic plaque sticking from the bed that contains the peach roses. I brush my fingers across it, tracing the lines of Savage's handwritten text.

For Charlotte

"Charlotte?" I murmur. "Who's Charlotte?"

A door slams, and I jerk upright.

Savage stands between the tables near the front of the greenhouse, and his face is contorted. A mixture of pain and anger. "What are you doing in here?" he asks.

"Savage? I—"

"What the fuck are you doing in here?"

"I-I was trying to find you. I wanted to talk about what happened, and I—"

"So you thought you would come in here and snoop around?" he asks. "Is that it?"

"No. What are you talking about?" I ask. "I was trying to find you, and I thought because it's so cold out, that maybe you came in here to keep warm while you talked to my brother." I swallow.

Savage is breathing like a winded bull. "I told you not to leave through the back door, didn't I?"

"Yeah, but then you said that I could—"

"I fucking told you." He turns and shoves one of the tables over, releasing a frustrated shout.

I jolt back a step. "What are you doing?" My throat tightens. "What the hell is wrong with you?"

He glares at me, his gaze dark and unyielding. He takes several breaths like he's forcibly bringing himself under control. "Get out of here."

"What?"

"Get out of my greenhouse. Now." He points to the door.

Tears well in my eyes. I stare at him, shaking my head. "Whatever. Just, whatever." I walk past him, holding my head high, ignoring the waves of heat and anger that radiate from him.

I walk down the steps into the water and head toward the back of the house, my pulse racing. I don't know what I just found, but I'm guessing that whatever it is, Savage didn't want me to see it or know about it.

Fuck him. Fuck him and his broken heart, and his rage, and anger. Fuck him and his stupid beard.

I might've done the wrong thing, but I don't have to put up with a man yelling at me about it.

I head into his bedroom and slam the door behind me, and the tears spill over and stream down my cheeks. I slap them away and enter the bathroom. I blow my nose and release a breath, staring at my reflection in the mirror.

My hair's a mess, my cheeks are pink, my eyes red. "What is this?" I ask. "What the hell is going on?"

I am not about what I'm feeling right now.

I don't understand what's going on with Savage. He's been kind to me, caring, and protective, but I won't accept a man yelling at me like that. Not when he won't even tell me what the hell he's yelling about. Everyone has boundaries, and yes, I crossed his by going out of the back door, but he's crossed mine by raising his voice at me a second time.

I go back into the bedroom and lie down on the bed, hating that I like the smell of the sheets, that I'm so confused and hurt.

The back door shuts, and Savage's footsteps track past

the bedroom door. They hesitate in front of it then continue down the hallway.

"Asshole," I mutter.

I pull a pillow over my head and lie there, staring at the ceiling.

He wants me, but he doesn't. He's caring, but he won't let me in. He won't help me understand why his rules are the way they are, or what any of this is about.

And who's Charlotte?

Did Savage breed those roses specifically for her? For this Charlotte woman? That's why he's angry? Because he's holding a candle for another woman and he deeply regrets doing anything with me?

It makes the most sense.

I feel sick and stupid, and I roll over onto my stomach and bury my face in the pillow.

I'm such an idiot.

For a second there, for a few beats, I was sure that finally, I was getting what I wanted out of a relationship, even if it was sex. But of course, Savage doesn't want me, he wants this Charlotte woman, and not only has he lied to me about why we can't do anything, but he's also yelled at me for finding out the truth. If that's not toxic, I don't know what is.

I squeeze my eyes shut, the tears leaking out of them.

My fault for thinking something could happen. My fault for pushing too hard. Not my fault for being yelled at. It's not my job to manage Savage's emotions.

And screw him! He's into some other girl, and he's folding me like a fucking accordion in his living room and making me come like five times in a row? Screw that.

I sit upright and punch my hands down on the bed.

Footsteps creak on the wooden floor in the hall. The house is silent now the rain has stopped. A sliver of sunlight peaks through the clouds outside, and I glare out the window at it. Traitorous weather.

A knock comes at the bedroom door. "Hannah."

"Fuck off," I yell.

I'm not much for cursing, but this moment seems appropriate.

"Hannah, please, I'd like to apologize to you for the way I acted."

"Save it," I say. "That's the second time you've yelled at me, and that's not even the biggest issue we're having so just... Why am I even talking to you? Go away."

"Please, Hannah."

"Go away! Or in your words, get the fuck out."

He leaves again.

"Asshole." I flop back down on the bed and let the tears come.

Twenty-Six

SAVAGE

I CAN'T THINK, can't breathe after what I've done.

I sit on the floor across from the locked bedroom door, staring straight ahead. I've replayed what happened in the greenhouse in my head what feels like a million times. Her shocked expression, my anger, the betrayal in her eyes.

I walked in on her, muttering "Charlotte", and something snapped inside me.

And that's exactly why she deserves better than you.

My heart is pounding like a fucked clock. My palms are slick with sweat.

It's been hours, and apart from the sound of her using the bathroom once or twice, Hannah is silent.

She doesn't want to talk to me, and I deserve this. I'm a piece of shit. I'm not going to feel sorry for myself about it, but I have to make this right. I can't… I can't have her cry over this or blame herself. I'm the one with the rules and the problems, not her. I should never have put this on her. I should never have yelled.

I scrape my hands through my hair.

Fuck. Fuck, please, Hannah. I'm sorry. Fuck.

There has to be something I can do.

The lock on the bedroom door clicks, and I straighten.

Hannah cracks the door open and sees me sitting there. Her eyes are red. My stomach sinks, and I hate myself so thoroughly, I feel sick.

"Hannah," I murmur.

"Not your princess any more, huh?" she asks.

"Hannah, I'm sorry."

"I don't want apologies. You can save that for Charlotte," she says. "I assume she's your real princess, right? Or no, maybe she's your queen."

My stomach turns, and blood rushes to my ears. The sound of screaming. My own screaming. Pain. A memory that threatens to drag me back into the past. I start shaking. "Hannah," I manage. "Please." My throat tightens with emotion, my eyes are hot, prickling. I'm on the brink of an episode.

I focus on my breathing. I reach into the pocket of my jeans and find it. The soft chain links. I run my fingers over them. *Here. Present.* I fix my gaze on Hannah, breathing hard.

Her face has fallen into concern.

Even now, when she's furious with me, she's worried.

"Hannah," I manage.

"What's going on?" she asks. "Savage? Are you okay? Do you need help? What's wrong?"

"Hannah, I'm sorry," I say. "I... Just give me a second."

She stands there, watching me. I trace my fingers over the bracelet in my pocket, fixating on it. I breathe slowly, bringing myself back.

Inhaling and exhaling. Slowly.

"There are things," I say, finding the strength inside, "that you don't know about me."

Hannah sits down in the doorway, keeping her distance but watching me. She's wary, and I don't blame her. She must think I'm crazy. Maybe I am.

"Charlotte," I say, "is dead."

Hannah's eyes widen.

"She was my wife." The words are clipped. I'm hanging on.

Hannah's mouth drops open. She lifts her hand to cover it.

"She died sixteen years ago," I say, and the breathing helps. But I fixate on Hannah's face to help me even more. She's wide-eyed and listening, and right now, she is my anchor. "She died because of me."

Easy. Slow breaths.

"I was on active duty when it happened." I can do this. She needs to hear it. "Charlotte and I were married for three years. She was two months pregnant with my daughter when it happened."

"Savage, you don't have to—"

"I want to," I say, exhaling forcibly. "We lived in Coronado. Charlotte was an author, so she worked from home. She was intelligent and beautiful, but she liked to take risks. All kinds of risks. I let her do what she wanted, because I was a SEAL, and I couldn't tell her not to be careless when I put myself in danger on a daily basis. I— But—" Another exhale. "She wasn't adventure-seeking or doing anything crazy when it happened."

Hannah tucks her hands under either arm and watches me, her bottom lip trembling at my pain.

"She was shopping at the local grocery store. Our

grocery store. The one we went to every other week. It was normal. It was a normal day."

"It's okay," Hannah says. "I'm here."

I shake my head, holding out a hand so she doesn't come any closer. She looks like she might try to comfort me, when this is my burden to bear, and I've already upset her enough. "It was only a couple of weeks after we found out we were having a baby. I'd put in for leave so I could come home and see her. She... She went into the store," I say, and my voice shakes hard, "and some fucking piece of shit was in there, robbing the place."

Hannah sucks in a breath.

"He turned the gun on her and shot her. In court, he said that he panicked. That he didn't mean to pull the trigger, but she startled him. He got life in prison because of a plea deal. That motherfucker got life. He gets chocolate milk at Christmas, but my wife and child are dead, and I wasn't there to stop it. I wasn't there to protect her. I wasn't there to be a man. I wasn't there. I wasn't there." The words repeat.

"Savage. Oh my God." Hannah chokes up. Tears stream down her cheeks. "I am so sorry. I'm sorry I went into your greenhouse. I'm sorry that you lost her and your baby. I'm so sorry." She sobs and bursts into tears, covering her face. She's timid, she looks like she wants to come to me, but doesn't.

I'm grateful because I don't deserve her affection. "I wasn't there," I say, "and after it happened, I wanted to die, Hannah. I quit the SEALs, I joined a motorcycle club, and I started hurting people."

"Savage."

I shake my head. "Every man I hurt, I saw his face. He

took everything from me. He took my soul. He took my heart. He took my life." I'm breathing easier now. My cheeks are wet. "I am a broken man, Hannah. I have been broken for years."

I get on my knees and crawl toward her. I stop in front of her.

She's crying for me. Not for her. But for me.

She's such a caring, loving person, and I've known that since the start.

"When I first saw you, Hannah, I couldn't breathe. It was the first time I felt anything for a woman, for anyone, in the years since it happened," I say. "But you were just out of college, young, and Cash's sister. He saw how you affected me."

Her eyes widen.

I have to get it out. The truth about her, about Cash, about Charlotte.

"I swore that I would never get involved with a woman again, because I am not strong enough to protect the people around me."

"That's not true. You teach people how to look after themselves. You—"

I shake my head, on my knees for her. She gets onto hers as well, wringing her hands, tears streaking her cheeks.

"I was not strong enough to be the man I needed to be. And I've always been on the brink of this. Of another episode, of breaking down, of rage. I am not healthy," I say. "And your brother knows that."

"What has Cash got to do with this?"

"Because he saw the look on my face when I first met you, Hannah," I say. "He saw how I lit up for the first time. And he made me swear that I would never touch you."

"What?" Her tone is icy.

"He made me swear. And I promised him, not because your brother can tell you what to do, or me what to do, but because he saved my life. Because I owe him. Because he knows the type of broken I am. And because I have always known that I am not strong enough to be the type of man that you need."

She's stunned, staring at me like she's never seen me before.

I wait for her gaze to turn cold. For her to reject me. For anger.

"I am sorry," I say. "There is nothing I wouldn't do… *for* you. Hannah, there is nothing I wouldn't do. You make me weak."

"I don't want to make you weak," she whispers. "I want to make you strong. I want to make you realize that you are everything a man should be."

I ache all over, the tension rippling down my spine. "I can't be the man you need."

"Savage," she whispers. "You already are."

Twenty~Seven

HANNAH

HE'S on his knees in front of me, this huge, strong man, his shoulders heavy with the burdens he's been carrying on his own for years.

I can't imagine what it must be like to lose a child. To have lost the woman he loves, and the promise of a future together.

"Savage," I whisper, rising to my feet.

He remains kneeling in front of me, but he looks up, those dark eyes fixed on me.

I put out my hands. He takes them, holding them to his forehead. It's like all the pretense has been stripped away—the avoidance, the aloofness, the disconnection.

His hands are warm. "Forgive me."

"Please, Savage."

"Call me Carter," he says.

My heart nearly shatters. "Carter," I whisper.

He straightens. Slowly, he gets to his feet. He towers over me. "I'll do anything to make it up to you," he says. "Anything."

My heart pounds against the inside of my chest. "Can I have two things?"

"Anything you want. Anything."

"I want you to consider this," I say, carefully. "I don't want you to do it because I say you must. It's got to be something you want to do, but I really, really, hope you will consider getting therapy. Because the pain you are going through isn't something you should have to bear on your own."

He swallows. "I will."

I let out a breath.

"What else do you want?" His gaze fixes on mine. He's not shaking any more, but he's never been more open.

"Kiss me."

His burly chest rises and falls rapidly.

I wait.

Carter's hands move up my arms, fingers brushing over the sweater, raising goosebumps even though he's not touching my skin. He brushes them over the sides of my neck, my cheeks, and rests his palms against my cheeks.

This is happening.

I'm sure that he'll pull away and say no at the last second.

Carter brings his face to mine, slowly, and hovers his lips an inch from mine, so close that his breath brushes over my face. "I've wanted to do this for years."

And then he presses his lips against mine.

A tremor moves up my body.

His kiss is warm, soft at first. His fingers brush over my skin, his right hand moving into my hair, the left resting against my throat and collarbone. He parts my lips and tastes me, and a low rumble in his chest is all the warning I have.

He lifts me off the floor and walks me back into the room, kissing me hard, his hands moving over my body like a man unleashed.

I gasp against his lips, tugging at his shirt, ripping at it like I can tear it free.

His lips and tongue are relentless, his hands on my ass now, gripping, biting through the cotton of my shorts.

"Please," I whisper. "Oh my God, yes."

He presses me against the wall beside the bed, kissing me hard, his hand wandering up to cup my breast. Savage groans and pulls back to stare at me. "Hannah, are you—"

"I have never wanted anything more in my life," I say. "I need you."

He captures my lips with a moan, grinding into me, his cock pressing against the fabric of my shorts. There are too many layers between us.

"I want it," I say. "Please. I want it now."

"I don't have a condom."

"You don't need one," I whisper. "I'm clean. Are you—?"

"I haven't had sex in sixteen years, Hannah."

"Oh my God." I moan and grind against him, desperate. "I can't wait any longer. I can't."

Savage rips his pants down, and I glance between us, my eyes widening. His cock is long and hard, thick with arousal, veiny, the tip wet for me.

"Hold onto me," he says.

I do as I'm told.

Savage grips the side of my PJ shorts and rips them free. My body rocks forward from the motion, but I don't care. It's the hottest thing I've ever experienced, including earlier. He tosses the ruined shorts off to one side.

Finally, there's nothing separating us. He presses me into the wall.

My pussy is bare, and he stares at it, groaning as he takes his cock and runs it over my mound and between my lips. "Fuck, you are wet." He presses the tip toward my entrance then stops.

I slap my hands down on his shoulders. "What are you waiting for?" If he backs out now, I'm going to scream.

"I haven't made you come," he says, frowning. "I can't fuck you without—"

"You made me come five times this afternoon. Please, just—"

The permission is all he needs. Savage notches his head inside me, and I cry out, rising high on his body. He's huge, and it's been a long time since I've done anything physical with a man.

"You can take it, Princess," he growls, grabbing a fistful of my hair and making me look at him. "You want it all, don't you?"

I whimper and nod.

"You're going to come on my cock," he says, pressing another inch into me. "Say it, Princess."

"I'm going to come on your cock. I'm going to come on your cock as many times as you want me to."

He grunts and slides in another inch, parting me, and my eyes roll in my head. I'm breathless, a mess, and I grab hold of his shoulders, trying to cling to what's left of myself before I lose it completely. I've never had an orgasm without my clit being stimulated, but it feels like I'm seconds away from it.

"You're mine," he says. "Tell me you are all mine."

"I'm yours, Carter."

"Fuck." He slides in more of himself, and I glance down. Halfway in. "You're taking it like such a good girl. Like such a good fucking girl."

"I can take it all."

"Yes, you fucking can." And then he drives himself into me all the way, and my pussy clenches around him so tight and hard, I scream his name. "That's right," he says, and draws himself out of me. He slams home again, and the window beside us rattles.

"Carter." I scream it, like a curse or a blessing or both. "Carter. Oh my God. Carter."

He drives into me, again and again, and he manipulates my legs as he wants, unfazed by my weight in his arms, pressing me against the wall. We both watch his cock sliding in and out of me, glistening and hard.

"Look at that pretty pussy," he says. "Who does it belong to?"

"You."

"Nobody else touches this pussy again. Nobody. It's mine," he says, and spits on it. "Got it?"

"All yours," I pant. "It belongs to you."

He pounds into me again, adjusts us, and then rubs his thumb over my clit. That one tiny flick of motion is all it takes to send me over the edge. I slap my hands down on his shoulders and yell his name, my fingers digging into his flesh.

"Yes, come for me. Come for me." He presses into me again and again, taking every beat of my orgasm to the next level, and I can't believe it.

This is finally happening. We're finally happening.

Carter pounds into me, one hand on my throat, squeezing gently, the other helping him work my body on his length, gripping my ass tight. He fucks me like he can't get enough, like I'm the reason he's waited, like I'm the only woman in the world.

I let out strangled moans, halfway between his name and wordless pleasure, and my second orgasm rocks through my body just as his dick grows thick inside me. Savage pulls out and aims himself at my clit. Thick ropes of cum hit my flesh, and I cry out.

He drives inside me again, still coming, and holds himself there, grunting, panting, eyes on me.

SAVAGE

I CARRY Hannah to the bed, still deep inside her. She's warm and velvet-soft, and I don't want to pull out of her. Whatever spell we're under, I don't want it to break.

I'm expecting her to pull away, to tell me how broken I am.

She's a princess, but I've just treated her like a whore, and it's not how I wanted our first time to go. Not that I believed there would be a first time.

I lower her down on the sheets and lie on top of her, bracing my arms on either side of her body.

Hannah smiles at me, and it's that smile that convinces me of how thoroughly fucked I am. Because I will do anything for that smile. I will burn down the world for her. I will break every promise.

"That was amazing," she whispers, and presses a kiss to the tip of my nose.

I capture her lips with mine again, tasting the sweetness of her mouth.

She moans against me, her pussy tightening.

If she keeps this up, I'm going to be ready to go another time and fast. "You're amazing," I say, and then I pull back and frown at her, taking in her lips that are bruised red from our kisses, the rash of red across her chin from my beard. "Are you okay? Was I too rough?"

"You were perfect," she says. "You were— I mean, let's be real, I came seven times today."

"Not enough."

"The day's not over yet." She gives me another impish smile. I kiss her again.

Now that I'm allowing myself to do this, I can't get enough. Enough of her kisses, the way she tastes, how she smells, her movements, her voice, her name on my lips. I'm already growing hard inside her again.

"I lost control," I say, against her mouth. "I should've been more gentle for our first time."

"F-First?" Her eyelashes flutter.

"Yes," I say, and move inside her. I'm ready to go, and even though I've just come, I have to measure my breathing to not blow inside her right away. "You are a dream come true, Princess. I'm going to treat you the way you deserve to be treated."

"Carter," she whimpers, as I move inside her again. Gentle, slow thrusts.

I'm making love to her rather than fucking her out of control like a beast.

"I'm going to show you what you deserve." I kiss her, stroking her hair back from her forehead. I sweep her into my arms as I move inside her. I trail a line of wet kisses down her neck, frustrated at the sweater that's separating us.

"Take it off me," Hannah whispers. "I want to feel all of you."

I sit her up and place her in my lap so that I stay inside her. Carefully, I remove the sweater and toss it aside. "You are unbelievable." The tan flesh, the smooth planes of her stomach, her full breasts, the nipples' soft peaks. I brush my fingers over her back, and she shivers and tightens on my cock.

"That feels amazing."

I strip off my shirt and toss it aside, and her gaze lands on my tattoos, then sweeps over my chest and down my abdomen. "Oh my God, this is actually happening."

I lift her on my dick and settle her back down again. "It's happening."

Her breaths hitch, and she shudders against me. I wrap my arms around her, pulling her close. "Ride me, Princess. Show me how you like it."

"I like everything you do to me," she whispers.

Hannah places her hands on my shoulders and moves up and down my cock. She circles her hips, moaning, tossing her head so that soft dark hair slides over her skin. She is immaculate, perfect, and I pulse inside her.

"You're so fucking good at that, Princess," I say.

"Carter." She presses on my chest, and I lay down on the bed for her, watching as she grinds her pussy against me, working herself toward an orgasm. Her body fits mine, and she is fucking magic.

Her lips part, and her eyes are hazy and hooded. I bring my hands up her thighs, squeezing them, and urging her with my touch.

"I'm going to come. I'm going to—"

"Come for me, Princess."

She tightens around me, and arches her back, holding herself in place, head dropped back and her throat working around silent screams.

"That's it," I whisper. "That's my girl." I sit up and take hold of her, roll her over so I'm on top, then start working myself inside her.

The animal in me wants to fuck her raw, until she's nothing but a keening, wet mess. But there will be plenty of time for that over the next few days. Right now, I want to show her what she deserves, and that means taking my time with her.

Making her come, making her feel as special as she is.

I kiss her neck and suck on her throat. I kiss a path up toward her jawline, down it, and to her gasping lips, all while I move my hips and work my dick inside her.

Hannah whines and clings to me. "It's so good. It's so good."

"Look at me, Princess."

Those bright blue eyes lock onto me, and she shivers.

"I've dreamed of this too," I say.

She clenches tight.

"Fuck, you like that, don't you?" I whisper, stroking her hair back from her head. "You like hearing how much I've always wanted you. How hard I get for you."

"You've always—"

"Always, Hannah," I say.

She moans against my lips.

"I've always wanted this pussy," I say. "Your mouth." I take a handful of her hair and tug lightly. "I've always wanted to make you come while you sit on my face."

"Oh my—"

"And I've spent fucking years thinking about you

naked. Resisting you. All while you walk around looking like my girl."

She's speechless, her gaze on me, her body soft and mellow, moving with mine as I work inside her, nice and slow.

"I'm going to make you come once for every time you've tortured me," I say.

"How many times?"

"I've lost count, Princess." And then I pull back and move my hand between her legs. I toy with her clit, circling it until she's rising toward me, on the brink of her climax, then stopping again. By the third time I've brought her to the edge, she slaps her hands down on the comforter.

"Carter!" she shouts. "I can't any more. I need to come."

"You want to come?"

"Yes, please."

"Tell me how many times you've come for me when you were alone."

"I've… lost count." She circles her hips, seeking release as I kneel between her legs. "Make me come. Make me come!" Hannah slaps her hands down again and grasps fistfuls of the comforter, twisting it like she wants to rip it apart.

"And how many times have you pictured it was me fucking you when you were with one of your exes?"

Her eyes widen.

I'm circling her clit again, and she's panting, working her pussy on my shaft, losing her mind for me.

"How many times, Princess?"

"Every time." The words escape her on a whine.

"Good girl," I say, and, this time, when she reaches the edge, I don't stop, I drive her over it.

Hannah screams my name repeatedly.

I wait until she's come down before I move on top of her. "Arms around me. This is going to be fucking rough."

And then I grab hold of the headboard behind her and start fucking. I pound into Hannah, and her skin flushes, as her eyes roll back in her head, as she comes for me again, speechless, breathless, screaming nothing.

I want to fucking ruin her for all other men on this planet. I want her to remember me when she's gone. I want her to think of me every night for the rest of her life.

I take us both to the edge, and then I spill inside her, grinding it out. I tug on the headboard hard, and the sound of wood snapping fills the bedroom.

After, I lower myself on top of her again, still inside, and roll onto my back with her on my chest.

Hannah moans a couple more times, but the sounds wane as she drops off to sleep. I grab the comforter and pull it over both of us.

We'll deal with the broken bed tomorrow.

Twenty~Nine

HANNAH

I WAKE up on top of Savage. It's toasty warm underneath the blanket, and I'm resting on his chest, my hair plastered against my cheek, and my legs curled up on either side of his body. He's not inside me any more, but I'm considering remedying that.

It happened. It actually happened.

Savage and I finally happened in a way that we both wanted.

But I can't help thinking about yesterday afternoon. The things he told me. The way he broke apart.

His ex. The baby he lost.

My heart breaks for him. I can't imagine how difficult that had to have been, or how much he must hurt just thinking about it. He clearly blames himself.

I have an overwhelming urge to wrap my arms around him and squeeze. To protect him from his own feelings, but I can't do that. Savage and I aren't together. And I can't fix him. He has to put in the work to get through the trauma.

If I was staying, I would be there with him through it, but I'm not.

And I *have* to remember that.

The alternative is letting myself feel things for a man who is clearly not ready for love. Sex or not, nothing has changed. Savage still wants to live out here on his ranch. He still wants to be alone. I'm not naive enough to think that incredible sex will change that.

Even if he hasn't been with a woman in sixteen years.

I peer down at his chest, the tattoos that arc down his neck, over one pec. He has a flaming skull tattoo along his ribs, and I press my hand to it.

Savage shifts underneath me, and his hands move up my naked thighs to my bare ass. He strokes his fingers down and between them, gently. He pauses before touching me.

"Princess," he murmurs, his voice rumbling and warm.

"Carter."

"Hmm." It's low and warm, the noise he makes as he sweeps his fingers over my pussy.

I suck in a breath and hold it.

"You're wet." He inserts one finger inside me, and I tense against him.

He's exquisite. The way he moves and touches me, the way he wants to give me pleasure.

Savage's dick presses against me, and he removes his fingers and sweeps the tip of his cock against my pussy. "Fuck, Princess, you are so ready for me. You're swollen."

"Yes," I murmur. "I want it."

He grabs both of my ass cheeks and lifts me. Savage

slides me onto his dick, and we're already panting for each other, me moaning his name, him grinding his teeth.

"Fuck, I want to live like this," he says.

"Like what?" I ask.

"Inside you." And then he pounds into me again.

The sex is hot and fast, and he's focused on making sure I come, even as he moves my body how he wants it. It just so happens to be how I want it too. I'm screaming his name and cross-eyed from pleasure when he pulses inside me again.

Afterward, Savage slips out of me and presses a kiss to my temple.

"Fuck," he says, "you are just too good to leave alone."

I gnaw on my bottom lip. "Am I?"

"Yes." He kisses my forehead.

And then the light on the bedside table clicks on.

"The power," I say, grinning at him, and I sit up in bed, holding the comforter to my chest. He pulls it down and sucks one of my nipples into his mouth. "Oh my God, okay. Screw the power."

"Once we're done, we can take a shower."

"Once we're done?"

"Yes." He growls it against my skin. "Once I'm done with you, Princess."

My eyes roll back in my head as he circles my nipple with his tongue and slips his hand between my legs.

———

IT'S two hours later when Savage carries me out of the bedroom and into the bathroom. He stands me up, then turns on the shower and makes sure the water is the perfect temperature before he guides me into it.

"Oh my God, that feels good," I say, as the water washes over my skin.

"How good?" Savage asks, his dark brows tipping downward.

"You're kidding, right? You're jealous of the water?"

"I'm jealous of anything that gets to touch you naked."

I stick out my tongue at him, and he takes the soap and lathers it over my skin. He's gentle with me. He washes my hair and my body, worshiping every inch of me, even kneeling at my feet and lifting them one by one.

"You really don't have to do this."

"I do," he says. "If I'm going to come on your face and disrespect you in the bedroom, I've got to show you how much I care in other ways."

"I— You know what, I don't have a problem with that," I say. "Come on my face anytime you want."

He finishes washing me, then starts lathering up himself. I run my hands over his broad, muscular back, then press my fingers into the muscle along his spine. He groans and places both hands on the white tiles of the shower wall.

"Holy crap, you're tense," I say, kneading him.

He turns and takes my hands. "I'm good," he says. "Thank you, Princess. But I don't want you to exert yourself."

"Why? Because I'll break into pieces?" I roll my eyes.

"No," he says, grasping my throat. "Because I'm going to fuck you until you have nothing left later."

"Oh," I squeak.

He gives me a devilish smile, and my stomach flips. He

has a beautiful smile. It's genuine and warm, and full of his personality. When he smiles at me like that, I feel like I'm going to lose my mind or part of my heart to him.

I look down at my feet.

Savage brushes his hands over my breasts and between my legs. "I can't keep my hands off you," he says. "But we'd better get something to eat."

I nod.

We dry off and dress, and Savage leaves me to check my phone while he goes to the kitchen.

The first thing I want to do is send a text to the group chat and tell them what happened, but I don't. That would ruin the moment, and for now, this feels like it's just us. Also, I don't want to go bragging to them when I have no idea what Savage wants. Carter. *God.*

And then there's the fact that we slept through the afternoon, and it's just past midnight.

The smells of cooking are too good to resist, so I join him in the kitchen.

A single pink rose sits in a vase on the kitchen counter, and I lean in and sniff it, smiling. "Thanks for cooking," I say. "I would love to help."

"Next time, you can," he says. "I wanted you to relax while you are here. Feel cared for."

"Oh, trust me," I say, "I feel cared for. I don't think I've ever felt this taken care of in my life."

"Good." The word comes out rough, but his gaze is soft as he flips a pancake on the stove. "You know what? If you want to help, there's some cream in the fridge. You can whip it for the pancakes."

"It's a good thing that the power came on," I say. "I guess that means things are going to clear up soon."

He nods, but there's tension in his shoulders.

Savage's kitchen is neat, and I squeeze past him where he stands in front of the gas burners, spooning pancake mix onto his skillet. I grab the whipped cream out of the silver slab that is his fridge and he directs me to the bowls in the dark wood cupboards.

I whip up the cream, standing next to him at the counter. The corners of his lips are tilted upward, and he occasionally strokes his beard and gives me a sideways glance. Savage slides his arm around my waist and pulls me to his side, and I let out a squeak.

"Hungry?" he asks.

"Yeah," I reply. "I'm starving."

Savage dishes up the pancakes onto plates while I get out the butter and syrup. He places the whipped cream on the table, and it's giving me all kinds of ideas.

He pours us two glasses of water and we start eating.

"You're not going to check your phone?" I ask.

"Later," he says.

My heart thumps in my chest. I have to get this situation under control, because I'm already so into him, I can barely think straight. "So," I say, with a grin. "We should talk."

He arches an eyebrow. "What about, Princess?"

My skin prickles at the nickname. "About that," I say. "You calling me that. The insanely good sex we've been having. The fact that I can get out full sentences in front of you for once."

He chuckles, and I'm stunned. I don't think I've ever heard Savage laugh. Not properly. It's an uninhibited sound, and an easy smile slips onto my face.

Trouble. You are in trouble.

"You don't want a relationship," I say. "You said you don't have a heart to give, and I understand that you've got a lot of stuff going on."

He doesn't answer, but that smile has faded, and his hand goes to the pocket of his sweats. "I'm not worth your time emotionally, Hannah. I come with too much baggage."

"And I appreciate that and your honesty," I say. "But I don't want to stop… this." I point at him with my fork and then back at me. "Not until I leave town."

"You're still leaving," he says.

"Yes. Of course."

A frown wrinkles his brow. "All right. I— Fine."

"Is there a problem with that?"

The wrinkles deepen. "No. You're your own woman and person. You should do what makes you happy. Just, uh, I want you to be safe."

"Well, while I'm here, you can continue being my bodyguard," I say.

He grunts but doesn't answer.

"You don't have to tell Cash about us." I lift my chin. "In fact, I'd prefer it if you didn't. Because we're not serious, right? So, we'll fool around, have some fun, and once I'm gone, you can pretend it never happened."

His chair scrapes back and he circles the counter toward me. Savage catches my wrist, removes the fork from my hand and sets it aside. He lifts me out of my seat and into his arms. "I will never pretend this didn't happen."

"Carter," I say.

"I will never forget it happened, Princess," he says.

"You will be with me for the rest of my fucking life thanks to last night. Thanks to now."

"Yeah, but you made a promise to Cash, and you wouldn't want to break it. I just want to give you an easy out. And honestly, I don't want Cash getting weird about this. I want it to be something special. Between us."

"My promise is not your problem," he says.

"O-Okay, but you're happy to keep doing this, even after I leave your ranch?"

Savage's gaze darkens. He releases me then sweeps his arm across the table, clearing it of dishes, sending them smashing to the ground. He lifts me onto the table and rips down my yoga pants, then brings me to the edge of the counter and sucks my clit into his mouth.

I cry out, shocked, aroused, everything in between.

"You're mine until you leave this town," he says, around a mouthful of me.

I forget my fears as he presses me back onto the counter.

Thirty

SAVAGE

I CAN'T GET ENOUGH of her. I can't get enough of the way she tastes or smells, the way she moans my name or comes on my dick. I don't want it to end, but the power is back, the cell signal is fine, and it's only a matter of time until the water dries and she leaves.

Hannah's curled up on the sofa, a book in hand, her head resting on my lap while she reads. I stroke my fingers through her hair, watching her. I have a book in hand too, but I can't stop thinking about this beautiful woman in my lap, and it is fucking me up.

I don't want feelings. I don't want to care.

The last time I cared, my heart was shredded to shit. I have dealt with the trauma in the best way I can, but it's not enough.

There's a reason Cash wanted to keep me away from his sister. I can't function in a relationship. I'm barely hanging on most days, and it's not fair to Hannah to put that on her.

Stop considering it.

Be happy with this.

She shifts in my lap and sits up. "You know, our sleep schedule is going to be all fucked up." She's adorable in my sweater, and she pushes her glasses up her nose as she smiles at me. "It's like three in the morning. We should probably try to get some sleep."

"I struggle to sleep with you around," I say.

Hannah rewards me with a smile that rips right through the center of my chest. "Beautiful," I say, and brush her hair back behind her ear. I lean in and press a kiss to her lips, and she responds with a greedy hunger that makes me hard.

"Princess," I say, warning in my tone. "We're going to injure ourselves if we keep fucking at this rate."

She blushes and presses another kiss to my lips. "I can't help it," she whispers. "I've wanted this for a really long time."

"I have too."

She crawls onto my lap, straddling me, but she doesn't grind into me, thank God. Sore or not, if she did that, I'd lose it all over again. "I'm glad we're doing this," she says. "As lame as that sounds. I've wanted you for so long, I can scarcely believe this is true."

I nod. "Me neither."

"Carter, about what you told me yesterday," she starts. "With the flowers and the—"

"Charlotte?" I ask.

"Yes. And the… your…"

"The baby was a girl. My daughter," I say, and my vision blurs around the edges. I reach into my pocket and feel the soft, cold links of the bracelet. I breathe through it.

"I shouldn't have brought it up," Hannah says. "I

wanted you to know that even after I leave, I'll be there for you. You can call me any time if you need to talk to somebody, or if you're feeling any type of way."

I nod, grinding my teeth. "It's just—" The words come out choked and slow. "I wasn't there. I should have been. That is what is fucking me up. I should have been there for her when she needed me."

Hannah rests her head on my chest, and I inhale her scent. It's beautiful and perfect. I have lost so much, and now that she's with me, I can't imagine her not being there. Or watching her leave.

How the fuck am I going to stay calm when she goes? What if this stalker ass fuck doesn't listen to Cash and comes to find her?

"I'm here," she says, and presses a kiss to the side of my neck.

She's dangerous for me to be around, but I want to stay with her anyway. I want to make sure she's safe. The thought of losing her after everything I've been through is too much to take. My vision blurs, and I shut my eyes, holding the bracelet.

"Carter?"

"Mmm."

"What are you doing?" she asks.

"It's just something I hold on to to keep me calm," I say. "When I start talking about this stuff, I need an object to focus on." *You shouldn't have done this.*

"What is it?"

Shit. I remove the bracelet from my pocket and hold it out in the palm of my hand.

Hannah gasps. "Oh my God," she whispers. "My bracelet."

It's a silver charm bracelet with thick links. There's only one charm on it—a small key, the end of which is shaped into the number 21.

She touches her fingers to it, frowning. "I lost this on the night you, uh, rejected me."

"You were drunk," I say. "I wasn't about to take advantage of you, Hannah."

"But you took my bracelet?"

I keep my palm open so she can take it from me. "I'm sorry," I say. "I found it on your living room floor, and I was going to give it back to you. It was broken." I turn it over in my fingers and show her the clasp, the metal that's misshapen from where it bent and I fixed it. "The chain snapped there, but I fixed it."

"Thank you."

"But then, I kept it, because it felt good to hold."

"And it helps keep you calm," Hannah breathes. "My bracelet helps keep you calm."

"Take it, Princess," I say. "It's yours. I should've given it back to you the minute I fixed it."

She runs her fingers over my palm, holds the sides of my hand and closes my fingers over her bracelet. "You keep it," she says, with a small smile. "It was a gift from my mother, and she gave it to me so that I would always have luck and happiness."

"I'm an asshole," I say, and hold it out to her.

Hannah puts up her hands. "I'm not taking it back, Carter. Keep it. I want you to have it. Maybe it will bring you luck."

"I've already got you sitting in my lap," I say. "How much luckier can I get?"

"I think you're about to find out." She runs her hands

through my hair and brings herself closer. Her lips press against mine, and it's further confirmation that she's what I want. I'm not right for her, and I can't allow myself to have her, but god damn if I don't want those two things to be true.

"Oh, Carter," she murmurs.

I deepen the kiss and place the bracelet in my pocket. I get up, and she wraps her arms around my neck, her legs around my waist. I carry her through the house to the bedroom, then lower her onto the bed, still kissing her.

The headboard clacks, and Hannah pulls back, a smile twisting her lips, her glasses askew. "I can't believe we broke the headboard."

"Mmm. Let's break the rest of it." I undress her slowly, place her glasses on the bedside table, and then I ravish her with attention, taking my time as I trail kisses over her skin, and take her to new heights.

If she'd asked me for the bracelet back, I would have given it to her.

And I'm coming to realize that there isn't much I wouldn't give Hannah, if she asked for it.

Thirty-One

HANNAH

IT'S BEEN three straight days of sex and heaven and eating good food. Drinking wine. Spending time with a man I thought hated me at best or was indifferent to me at worse, and I have come out the other side, a changed woman.

I don't know how that's possible, but it is. The Hannah Taylor who arrived on the ranch was without hope. The one leaving it is seriously sore from another night of intense sex and also, completely satisfied.

"Yeah, that's it. Remember what I said, let your momentum take you. Don't punch from your shoulder, and you've got it."

I take aim at Savage and do as I'm told. He's wearing pads to catch my fists, and he gives me a grin of fierce pride as I land the punch.

"Fuck, Princess, you are really good at that. Well done."

"Thanks," I say with a grin.

We're outside the ranch house together, with the blue

sky above, the water finally having soaked into the ground or dried up, and the trees are swaying in a gentle summer breeze. I'm going to have to drive back into Heatstroke in a car that smells like a rotten vegetable patch.

"I should hit the road," I say, biting the corner of my lip.

We discussed it last night over wine. I'm heading back into town today. The road is passable, and I still have work at the library for the next couple of weeks to get back to—and my plan to get the local schools involved in the reading program. I am *not* giving up on that before I leave.

Savage walks me back into the house. He grabs my bag for me and carries it through the hall, bare-chested, slightly sweaty from our training session.

I would stay and shower, but I'm afraid I'll never leave if I do. Because I'll want him to join me in the shower, and then we'll end up having sex against the tiles, and I'll stay another night.

I know, because I was meant to leave yesterday and that's exactly what happened.

Savage stops at the front door, his hand on the knob. "Any time you want to come back," he says. "You come back."

"Oh really?" I bat my eyelashes at him dramatically. "You mean, the notorious loner Carter Savage doesn't want to be left all alone on his ranch?"

Savage hooks a muscular arm around my waist and drags me to him. He kisses me so hard, my toes curl in my tennis shoes, and by the time he sets me down, I'm gasping for air.

"Not when it comes to you, Princess," he says. "The rest of them can get out of my swamp."

I laugh, but he silences me with another kiss, and my mirth turns into a moan. "Carter," I whisper. "I'm never going to leave if we keep doing this."

"That's part of my evil plan," he says, that deep voice sending a thrill through me. "Keep you here forever, like a princess trapped in a castle."

"Except I want to be trapped with you."

He kisses me again, pressing me against the wall, and we knock over a vase on a table in the entry hall.

I laugh against his mouth. "You had me this morning."

He grunts. "Not enough of you."

"You can stop by to bodyguard me tonight," I whisper. "Or this afternoon. You know, whenever you're free."

"I'm free right now. Why don't we go unpack your bag?" He sucks on my bottom lip, and my heart flutters. "You can stay here for a month."

"I'm leaving, remember."

A throaty noise of displeasure. "Fine. Come on. I've got to call Cash and tell him you're on your way home anyway."

"I'm surprised he isn't freaking out at me over the phone." I follow Savage down the creaking wooden steps of his ranch house.

"Hmm, that's because he's pretty sure that your stalker isn't a stalker any more."

I stop dead in my tracks. "Oh God. What did he do?"

"He went out to meet ol' Fucklin and warn him not to come near you."

"You're kidding." I can't be mad at my brother for that. He's a dick for not telling me, but I'm grateful. The cops won't help me because Franklin hasn't "done anything" yet.

"Nope."

"That sounds like Cash," I say. "So, wait, does that mean you're not my bodyguard any more?"

"You're disappointed." He smiles, and I can't get enough of it, the way his eyes wrinkle at the corners and his face lifts from that usual surly expression.

"Maybe. Okay, definitely."

"Cash wants me to watch you until you leave."

"Good."

Savage waits for me to open the trunk of my car and then places the bag inside. The scent of waterlogged and ruined upholstery floods my nostrils, and I recoil. "That's wonderful."

"Mmm. I know a guy who can help. I'll give you his number. Engine should be fine. The flood water didn't get high enough to choke it."

"Thanks," I say.

He shuts the trunk and leans against it. "You're not freaking out about Cash overstepping his bounds."

"I would," I say, "but there's this whole... I had an amazing time at my bodyguard's ranch thing to take into account. If Cash hadn't been such an overprotective brother, I never would have wound up here. So, it's his fault, really. Kind of."

He grabs me by the hips and pulls me close, and I swear I'm never going to get used to that, or the way he sends butterflies tumbling through my stomach with a glance. It doesn't matter that we've been together. I'm lusting after him like we've hardly touched, so each time we do, I squirm and gasp.

I'd be embarrassed, but I deserve this feeling. Even if it's only for the next six weeks.

He captures my lips in another soul-destroying kiss, and we're grinding against each other like two horny teenagers within the span of a couple of minutes. Savage's feet slip in the wet grass, and we break apart, me touching my lips, and him readjusting himself in those cursed gray sweatpants.

"Okay," I say. "I'd better go."

"Don't touch yourself," he says.

"What?"

Savage comes over and brushes my hair from my neck. He kisses my throat then nips it, overpowering me with that smoky cedar scent and his presence. "Do not touch yourself until I'm there. I want you to wait. Understood?"

"Yes, Carter."

He fists a handful of my hair and gives me one last kiss before backing up to my door and opening it for me.

I wince at the disgusting smell and the way the carpeting in my car squelches as I sit down. I turn the key in the ignition then roll down the windows with a press of a button. Savage shuts my door for me and leans down, leveling me with another of those butterfly-inducing gazes.

"Be careful," he says.

"I'm just driving home," I reply.

"I should take you."

"I'll be fine. I insist."

He hesitates, and after what he's told me about his past, it has to be hard for him not to be overprotective. I squeeze his arm. "Carter," I murmur, "I promise you, I'll be fine."

"Call me when you get home."

"The minute I'm there," I say.

He pats the top of my car then backs up.

I reverse out of my parking spot, making the turn and I head off down the dirt road. It's too damp to kick up dust, but I keep glancing in my rearview mirror.

Savage stands in front of the ranch house, arms folded, watching me until I turn the corner.

———

THIRTY MINUTES LATER, I park outside a worse for wear Bagel's Bakery, my heartbeat wild against the inside of my chest.

When we were trapped out on Carter's ranch, the sex was like a hazy fantasy, but now that I'm back in Heatstroke, what happened is too real. We had sex. A lot. And he wants me. He actually wants me.

I squeeze my steering wheel out of sheer excitement and let out a giggle. I feel like a schoolgirl again, and even though it's childish, I love it.

I grab my phone out of the center console and shoot him a quick text.

> Here safe. Parked outside Bagel's Bakery.

> **SAVAGE**
> Text me once you're inside. I'll be by tonight.

> Can't wait.

> Remember the rule. No touching yourself.

You'd better come stop me.

How about I just make you come.

"Oh God," I mutter.

I'm still sore from the storm, but I don't care. I want more of him. I want as much as I can have until I leave.

Already, the thought of leaving makes me nervous, and not in the good way it did before.

Don't be weird, Hannah. You want to go. And he doesn't want you to stay.

I get out of my car and glance up and down the street. There's debris from the storm. The striped awning over Bagel's Bakery is torn on one side, a few of the benches are damaged, and one of the lampposts has been knocked over. It's bad, but it's not catastrophic. Across the street, Mrs. Wilson is already opening the doors to the antique store.

"Hannah!" The sound of my best friend's voice sends a shock through me. "Han!"

I turn toward the glass front door of Bagel's Bakery and let out a happy squeal. "Belle?"

My bestie, dressed in a black pencil skirt that fits her like a glove, matched with a cream silk blouse and a pair of slingback pumps, marches across the sidewalk. "There you are! I was worried sick about you."

"About me? Belle, what are you doing here?" I circle the car and run toward her.

We collide and I hug her tight, squeezing so hard she lets out a wheeze. "I missed you," I whisper.

"I missed you too, Han," she says, and she pulls back,

her brown eyes sparkling with unshed tears. "No offense, but you smell kind of funky."

"What?"

"Like mushrooms or something."

"Oh," I say, with a laugh. "It's my car." Another laugh, and I can't stop smiling. "It got damaged in the storm."

"Now," Belle says, taking me by the arm and leading me back toward my car, "don't take this the wrong way, but that's kind of a strange thing to get excited about."

"I'm not excited," I say, grabbing my keys and phone. I pop open my trunk and grab my bag, slinging it over my shoulder, still smiling.

"You're not excited." Belle tucks dark curls behind one ear. She's pale, with crimson lips, and I've always thought of her as Sleeping Beauty. With a little bit more sass. And less weird guys trying to kiss her while she's asleep.

"No."

"But you're smiling from…" Belle's eyes go wide. "You little—" She grabs me by the arm and tugs me close, peering into my eyes.

"What are you—?"

"You had sex."

"I… What?"

"You. Had. Sex. I can see it in your eyes."

"That is a seriously strange talent to have," I say.

"So, you admit you had sex." Belle smiles at me. "Man, I'm good." And then her eyes go wide as dinner plates. "Are you kidding me? Did you… You and Savage?"

I press a finger to my lips and shush her like there are people trying to eavesdrop on my conversation.

"No. Way." Belle does a little happy dance on the spot. "I can't believe it. It finally happened?"

"Let's talk about this upstairs," I say.

Belle and I walk up the stairs together, and she shoots questions at me. Once we're inside, I send Carter a quick message, then put my phone on the coffee table and plop down on my floral-print sofa.

Belle sits down next to me, grinning. She looks so well put together, the big city girl in her professional attire, sitting on the edge of my sofa. She's out of place in Heatstroke, but I don't care, because she is the kindest, sweetest person I know. And she throws a mean left hook.

When we were at college, a guy grabbed my ass on a night out and Belle clocked him on the nose so hard, he had to go to the ER.

"Okay, so, are you going to tell me what the hell is going on?" Belle asks, clapping her hands excitedly. "Do I need to break out the wine and the tissues?"

"It's meant to be a secret," I say.

"Ninety percent of my job is keeping secrets," she says, fluttering long lashes at me. "Come onnnn. I won't tell anybody."

"Why are we even talking about me? How about the fact that you're in town. And here. In my living room. I haven't seen you in, like, six months. And Facetiming most days doesn't count."

Belle pulls a face. "It's work-related."

"Wait, you're in Heatstroke for work?"

"Enough about my chaotic life," she says, trying to brush it aside. "What about you? And your new older hunky mountain man?"

"He doesn't live near a mountain."

"It still counts."

"You are hiding something," I say, narrowing my eyes at her. "Do you want to tell me over coffee?"

Belle lets out a breath. "I'm afraid it might make things worse if we're both hopped up on caffeine."

"Tell you what," I say, "you tell me why you're here, other than to soak in my presence, and I'll tell you how things went with Savage." Now that I'm used to calling him Carter, it's strange to say Savage out loud.

"You're not going to like it," Belle says.

"Try me."

"Well," she says, "you know that jackass rugby player I have to babysit and keep out of trouble?"

"Sure?"

"It's your brother, Leo."

Thirty-Two

SAVAGE

THE HOUSE IS TOO quiet with Hannah gone.

And it still smells like her floral perfume. It's driving me crazy, because all I can fucking think about is her, what we discussed, how badly I want to go over there and talk to her.

It took everything in me not to follow her into Heatstroke. She's not technically in danger any more, but I can't shake the feeling that something might be wrong. Either I'm paranoid because of my past, or there's an active threat.

You need to get your shit together.

I stand on the front porch of my house, staring into space. It's quiet out here, idyllic, and I've always needed this separation from the town, even though it's not exactly a bustling hub of activity. During tourist season, the ranch is a haven. Shit, it's a haven all year round.

But now?

Empty.

Empty.

Hannah is gone.

I walk back into the house and shut my front door. I grab my laptop and sit down on the sofa where Hannah crawled into my lap. She's everywhere now, and there's no going back to the way things were. Fuck, I'm going to see her later, and I still feel like I've lost something.

I'm going to have to come to terms with this real fucking quick, because she's gone in six weeks. I'm not going to stop her.

She sent me a text a little while ago, but I can't help opening my laptop and checking the feed from the camera I placed outside her front door. When Cash asked me to be her bodyguard, I took it seriously.

Cars pass by in the street, and it *seems* peaceful, but my shoulders are tense regardless.

I rewind the video feed from earlier and watch as she comes up the grated stairs with her friend, Belle. They're chatting excitedly. Or rather, her friend is chatting, and Hannah is wearing an adorable smile.

I grab my phone to text her, but hesitate.

She's with her friend, and I don't want to come on too strong.

What the fuck are you talking about? This is just sex. Sex that might bring an end to one of the only friendships I have left, but I won't be able to quit Hannah.

Instead of texting her, I bring up a new browser tab on my laptop and do a quick search for therapists in and around the area. There's one in Heatstroke, but I hesitate to click the link.

I haven't gone to therapy since I arrived in Heatstroke. I prefer to ignore my problems until they go away, or attack them with rage. Neither of those options are healthy, but filling in the contact form will mean coming face-to-face with a stranger and talking about things I'd rather leave locked away.

The bracelet is in my palm again, and I run my finger over the cool silver links. What am I doing this for? Who am I doing it for?

Hannah isn't my woman. I can't be what she wants.

Unless you got therapy.

The thought is so out of pocket, I almost shut the laptop, get up and walk away.

I type my details into the contact form and hit enter. Fuck.

My phone rings on the coffee table, and I grab it, frowning at the lack of Caller ID.

"Who is this?" I answer.

"Who is this?" The person on the other end asks. It's a male voice, gritty, but altered to be impossibly deep.

I set the laptop aside and rise, gripping the phone to my ear. "Who the fuck is this?" I repeat.

"I think you know who it is, Carter." A pause. "Or should I call you Savage?" The tone is mocking.

It's *him*. Davis. "What do you want?"

"You didn't think you could run for long, did you? Or hide like a rat?"

"I'm not hiding," I say. "Come pay me a visit. We can talk man-to-man."

"Pay *you* a visit," the voice says. "I'm not going to pay you anything, given that you're the one in my debt." And then the line goes dead.

I hit the button to call the number back, but it clicks and doesn't go through. There isn't even a voicemail message. A burner phone.

I'm already on my way to the door. I burst out onto the porch and glare around, scanning my surroundings for any threat. The field to my left is empty, the trees could potentially hide an attacker, but that's the least of my worries.

I dial Hannah's number.

"Hey," she answers, her voice a squeak.

"Are you okay?" I ask, charging back into the house. I open the feed that shows me the view of the front of her apartment.

"I mean, apart from being sore from the past three days? I'm great, actually." Her voice softens. "I miss you. I can't wait to see you tonight."

"I'll be there in half an hour. Lock your door. Don't leave the house."

"I—"

"See you soon." And then I hang up, grab my shit, and head for my SUV.

Thirty-Three

HANNAH

THE PAST THREE weeks have been a blur of good memories, excitement, and anxiety. Savage spends every night at my apartment now. We fall asleep together, him cuddling me, and I wake up to morning sex and coffee right after. It's honestly a dream come true.

The only thing that taints it is the fact that my plane ticket is booked, my bags are half-packed, and I can't stop hoping that Savage will ask me to stay.

It's ridiculous, given that he doesn't want that and I'm not meant to either, but the time I've spent with him is the happiest I've been in my life.

I sit behind the counter in the library, the phone in my hand, smiling at the rubbery buttons like a goof.

"You're in an awfully good mood lately," Irma says, patting her curls. "You got me worried that you're going to stay in Heatstroke."

"Delightful as always, Irma."

"Well, whatever do you mean?"

I laugh and tap my fingers on the side of the phone.

I've spent the last couple of weeks calling the local schools and asking them to participate in a fundraising initiative for my Middle-Grade Readers Group. The local middle school agreed to help, but there are a couple others in the county, and they've been tougher to crack.

If only I could—

"You know, you're usually so mopey when you're at work," Irma says. "I'm really surprised you've stayed on this long. What's got you all excited?"

"I'm excited for the reading program," I say, but that's only a quarter of it. I'm excited to see Savage later, and I'm nervous because Ganny's hosting a potluck this weekend, and Savage is going to be there, along with the rest of my family. It's going to be difficult to avoid him.

"Mmm." Irma sniffs. "I've seen that look before."

"Huh?"

"That goofy 'in love' look. Who's the lucky guy?" Irma asks, because she wants to pry. Irma's never particularly interested in me unless she can tease me about it later.

"I'm not in love," I say. "I'm just excited for the future."

"Ah. So there's a guy at this place you're flying to?"

"I'm going to New York," I say.

"Right, right."

I've told her my destination a couple of times, but Irma spends most of her time in her own world or gossiping, and my travel itinerary doesn't rank high on the list of juicy gossip in Heatstroke.

I punch in the number for a local school on the phone, and I'm about to hit dial when Savage walks through the open library doors.

He's flawless in a tight-fitting white T-shirt that

stretches across his pecs. "Savage Self-Defense" is printed across the front of the shirt, but it's not like I can focus on the damn logo. His gaze is locked onto me, a twinkle in his eye, his hair curls at the ears, and he runs a strong hand over his beard as he approaches the front counter.

That same hand has been around my throat, and my skin tingles at the memory. I smile at him, trying to measure my reaction, since we're technically keeping this a secret from Cash and everyone in this town.

"Hi," I say, as he bypasses Irma's portion of the polished counter and stops in front of me.

Savage smiles at me.

Irma perks up in her seat. "You're happy today, Mr. Savage," she says.

He sends a blank look in her direction, but that only makes her eyebrows lift. *Shoot. She's onto us.*

"Returning," Savage says, tapping his finger onto the front cover of the book he's placed on the counter in front of me.

Irma keeps watching, her lips pursed.

"You aren't checking out another book?" I ask, as I slide the romance novel across the counter toward me.

Savage shakes his head. The corners of his lips twitch, but he keeps a straight face.

It's so good to see him smile. It's even better knowing that I'm the one putting that smile there.

I focus on the task at hand so I don't give him a dreamy-eyed stare that will rouse Irma's suspicions. I open the library book to check the date on the card inside.

A folded note is tucked inside the cover.

I cast a sidelong glance at Irma, but she's returned to tapping away on the computer, her tortoiseshell reading glasses perched on the end of her nose. It's a pity that Shana isn't working today. I vastly prefer her company, and she wouldn't pry into my business.

Carefully, I unfold the note and read what's written inside.

Princess, I can't stop thinking about you.
Also, I'm going to donate all the kid's books
in my library to your reading program.
Thank me later.
Carter.

Blood rushes to my cheeks, and I look up at him. He gives me one last smile before turning and walking off toward the exit, and my, those jeans he's in are snug.

"Don't stare, Hannah," Irma says. "It's not becoming of a lady."

"Bless your heart, Irma," I reply.

Her head snaps up.

"When did I ever say I was a lady?" And then I stare back down at the note. Is he serious? All the books? We talked about the initiative once when I was out on the ranch, but it didn't come up after that. And his wife was a children's book author, wasn't she?

My insides twist with grief for him. How can he do this? Is he serious?

"Excuse me." I get up and take the note with me to the bathroom. I slip my phone out of my pocket and shoot him a text.

> Are you sure about this? I don't want to take those books from you if you don't truly want to donate them, because it's a big deal, Carter.

SAVAGE
I want you to have them.

> I don't know what to say. Thank you, but I'm not sure I can accept. They have so much sentimental value.

It's a good step for me to take. My therapist thinks so too. I want to respect Charlotte's memory, but I also have to find a way to move on from the grief. She would have wanted me to donate these books. Her whole life was about giving to others and to kids in particular.

> Wow. I'm so happy for you, that you feel like you can take this step.

You're the reason, Princess. You are the reason I'm ready.

Tears well up in my eyes and my throat closes. He's been through so much, and I can't ever replace what he has lost, even if he wanted me to, but what he's saying is just…

> I don't have the words.

Then I'll have them for you. You are a life-changing, giving, amazing person, Hannah Taylor. You are the most special woman I have ever met.

I stare at the screen, shaking from head-to-toe, because he feels that way about me.

Get it together!

But I'm fast running out of reasons not to fall for him.

You can't stay here. You won't stay here.

It doesn't matter that Franklin doesn't text me anymore or send me flowers, or even that Cash has given me space. I wanted to leave Heatstroke for a reason—to experience life. To find myself and my independence.

I can't do that here. Can I?

I'VE BEEN THINKING about her all fucking day.

I park my SUV in a spot outside Bagel's Bakery, enter it, and stand in line, my arms crossed over my chest. Nobody talks to me—people have learned to avoid conversation with the angry guy who lives out on his ranch—and I don't mind it. The only person I want to talk to today is Hannah.

The inside of the bakery is cute. The type of place Hannah would enjoy spending time in, with squeaky polished wooden floors, and dark wood tables, wrought iron chairs, and a special board done in chalk with a crude drawing of a cupcake. The servers wear black aprons, the pockets on the front bearing slogans like "Bagel Today, Bagel Tomorrow" or "This is Knot Your Average Bagel!"

I don't care for any of it, but god damn, Hannah loves donuts, so I'm buying her a box before I head upstairs to see her.

I shift my weight from one foot to the other, scanning the interior of the bakery out of habit, marking anyone who might be a threat. But it's clear of weirdos, and the faces are mostly familiar.

The line shifts, and a girl at the front counter smiles at me. I swear, I recognize her from somewhere.

She sweeps curly blonde hair behind her ear and gives me a wide smile that shows off a small gap between her front teeth. "Hi, Mr. Savage."

"I know you?"

"Riley," she says, tapping her name badge, then she does a double take when she realizes it's missing. "I usually work at the Heartstopper in the afternoons. I picked up some extra work here in the mornings."

"Right."

"What can I get for you?" She's young, probably in her twenties. I would expect her to be off at college, not working double shifts at two different places in town to make ends meet.

"Strawberry stuffed donuts. Half dozen. Please."

"Sure. I'll get that wrapped up for you." She rings up my order on an old-timey bronze register, and I pay her with a hundred dollars. "Oh, shoot, I'll get your change. Just give me a—"

"Keep it," I say.

She blinks. "Oh. Thank you. That's very kind of you. Thank you." She wells up, but turns away quickly.

Poor kid. I walk over to a table and sit down to wait for my order.

I grab it when my name is called then head out, taking the stairs that lead up to Hannah's apartment two at a time. I can barely fucking wait to get there.

I want her to stay.

The realization hits me as I knock on her door.

I want this woman to stay. My ranch house is empty without her in it, and my life is slowly changing because of her. I feel lighter than I have before, more focused. I want to help her. Fuck, I want to keep her. I can't put her in danger but I can't let her go.

That phone call fucked me up, even though nothing came of it.

Hannah opens the door, and her face lights up. "Carter," she says, those pretty lips parting.

I take her by the back of the neck and bring my mouth down on hers. She opens up to me immediately, moaning against my lips, kissing me back with as much need as I have for her. I kick the door shut with my heel, walk her backward, and drop the box of donuts on the coffee table. I lift her into my arms.

Hannah's legs wrap around my waist, and I hate that she's wearing jeans.

I grip her thighs and kiss her hard, walking her backward until she hits the opposite wall.

"I'm going to cut these off," I say, tugging on the fabric. "I want that pussy now."

Hannah trembles. "It's yours," she whispers.

I slip my hand over the front of her jeans and rub her, frustrated that I can't reach her.

She moans and rides against my hand, arching her back, her head bumping against the wall.

"You okay?" I ask.

"I don't care about my head," she whispers. "Just take me, please."

"How do you want it, Princess?"

"In my mouth."

I suck on her collarbone and drag the front of her shirt

down so I can reach the slope of her breast. "That right?" I ask. "You want a mouthful of me?"

"Yes," she hisses, trying desperately to rub herself against the front of my jeans. She wants release, and I want to give it to her.

"You can only have it if you behave yourself."

"But—"

"Stop moving, Hannah. You're going to hurt your head."

"Carter! I want it," she says. "Now."

"You're in no position to make demands." I carry her to the sofa and sit her down on it. She scrambles onto her knees, and I wrap my hand around her throat. The excitement in her eyes, the way she lifts her chin to stare at me, daring me to make a move, drives me fucking wild.

Hannah squirms on the sofa. "Please," she whimpers.

I unzip my jeans and pull out my cock. It lolls in front of her, and her eyes widen.

"You think you can take this?"

"I want to try."

I slide my hands up to her head and bring her forward. She opens her mouth and trails her tongue over the head. My cock throbs at the contact. "You… are going to drive me fucking crazy, Princess."

We've never done this before. Her sucking my dick. Even though I've pictured it countless times. She takes me in her mouth and sucks, and my eyes roll back. I grip her head a little harder so she feels the pressure. And guide that smooth warmth up and down my shaft.

The pleasure is exquisite, and so are the noises she's making. Gagging, sucking, moaning and whimpering. Her head bobs in front of me, and she stares up at me, those blue eyes wide and almost pleading. She wants me to come.

"Why are you looking at me like that?" I ask, pulling her back.

Her mouth pops free, and she frowns at me. "Why did you stop? I wanted to finish you off."

"You want me to come in your mouth?"

"On my face," she whispers.

"Fuck, Hannah. You are—"

Footsteps thud up the stairs outside, and we both freeze, staring at each other, wide-eyed.

"Crap," Hannah whispers, and scrambles off the sofa. "I have no idea who—"

A knock rattles the front door. "Han? You home?" Cash's voice.

Her jaw drops, and she covers her mouth.

I tuck my dick back into my jeans and make sure my arousal is hidden. Hurriedly, I look around the room. The donut box is on its side, so I right it.

Hannah hurriedly checks her hair and fixes her shirt.

"Han?"

"Yeah, just a minute." She gestures for me to sit on the sofa.

I do, my phone in hand, and I fix a frown on my face, like I'm intensely focused on something.

Hannah unlocks the front door and lets Cash inside. He steps into the tiny living room. "Took you— Savage?"

I glance up and raise a hand. "Hey," I say, and the look on his face is fucking dangerous. Suspicious, his brows drawn inward. He strokes his jaw, clean-shaven for once, and flicks his gaze from Hannah to me, then back again.

"What are you doing here?" Cash asks.

I open my mouth to reply, but Hannah saves me the trouble.

"What do you mean, what is he doing here? You were the one who set him on me." She shakes her head, her hair brushing back and forth. Fuck, she is so gorgeous. "You told him he has to be my bodyguard, remember? And to teach me self-defense? Or have we moved past that? Finally, might I add."

Hannah's snark dissipates some of the tension, and Cash sighs. "You're learning self-defense."

"Yeah," I say. "I'm teaching her." Fuck, it wasn't the only thing I was teaching her. I feel a tinge of guilt, but just a tinge. It's nothing compared to how I felt about this before. Cash is important to me, one of the most important people in my life, but Hannah is...

Fuck, she is Hannah.

And I'm starting to think I can't let her go now that I've had her. And that if Cash doesn't like it, well, he's going to have to fucking deal. I might owe him, but he can't tell his sister what to do.

"Right," Cash says. "I was actually coming by to ask if you wanted me to come with you." He says to his sister. "June is in the mood for a vacation, so we could come with you to New York, help you get settled into your hotel. Alex would like to stay with Ganny for a while and—"

"I don't know how long I'm going to stay for," Hannah says. "And no offense, but this is something I need to do on my own."

"Hannah, when are you going to let this go?" Cash asks. "You're obsessed with proving that you're independent and that you can do stuff, but why do you want to do any of that when you have people to look after you?"

"Because she's a grown woman who makes her own choices," I say.

The words are out before I think about them. I want to keep Hannah, especially because the last time I left the woman I loved alone, she died.

The woman you… what?

"What do you know about it, Savage?" Cash asks, pulling a face. "This is family business."

"Savage is family," Hannah says.

My chest aches at the words.

"And I don't need you to come with me." Hannah places a delicate hand on her brother's arm. "I appreciate the sentiment, but I'm good. I can manage on my own."

He grits his teeth and grumbles. He's always been a grumpy bastard, and that's part of the reason we get on so well. We're both assholes, but he needs to take his asshole down a couple notches when he's speaking to Hannah.

I don't want her to go alone either. It's driving me fucking insane, the thought of her in trouble or without help, but I've got to be a man about it. Sometimes, that means letting go, which turns out to be the hardest thing in the world.

"You good?" Cash asks me, over Hannah's head.

"Just waiting to get started on our self-defense training," I say.

But Cash isn't going to let this one go. "I'll see you at the potluck this weekend."

"You will."

Hannah watches the tense exchange, then sighs and walks to the sofa. She flops down, grabs the box of donuts, and opens it. "Anybody want something to eat?"

Thirty-Five

HANNAH

IT'S ONLY two weeks until I leave for my trip, and I should be excited, but there's a sick feeling in the pit of my stomach this morning that I can't shake.

I sit upright in bed, staring at the cutesy bluebells that decorate the pale cotton duvet. I pick at a hole in it, wriggling my nose left to right.

It's the potluck today, and everyone's going to be there. Which is great, except Savage is going to be there too, and my doubts about leaving are growing by the day. I want him to ask me to stay. Even scarier, I want to stay, and if he does ask, I don't know if I'll be able to leave.

And I don't want that either.

Because I've never experienced a damn thing.

But at the same time, I've experienced more in the past few weeks than I have in years in Heatstroke.

"Ugh." I get out of bed, draw back my curtains so that sunlight streams into my tiny, cozy room, then head out of the door and across the hall for a shower.

The morning passes in a haze of indecision and

thoughts about Carter. About how he makes me feel, about how he touches me, about how we spent last night together, curled up on my sofa, reading together, my legs in his lap.

I prepare a lasagna, cover the dish with foil, then drive over to Ganny's house. A lot of the storm damage has been repaired, but there are a couple of stores and homes in Heatstroke that are either under construction or need work. I roll down my windows, grateful that my car doesn't smell like a mushroom patch anymore. It's a perfect summer's day, the sky blue, the grass green and lush, and Ganny's house, all shiplap, with its porch swing drifting in the breeze, is the picture of home.

Home. I park my car and gnaw on the inside of my cheek.

Savage's motorcycle is parked out front, and my heart skips and flutters. He's already here. He's inside. With my family. Waiting for me.

Run before you lose your heart.

But that battle's already been lost. He has my heart, and he won't return my feelings. It will be too much, too soon for him.

The screen door bangs open before I can get out of the car, and Belle comes down the stairs, taking them expertly in high heels. "Ugh!" She lets out a frustrated cry, balling up her fists.

"What's the matter, Sweetheart?" Leo saunters down the stairs behind her. My brother is built like a house. He's even taller than Cash, closing in on Savage, and he's got a rugby player's build. He's also a playboy and an asshole, and he's wearing a shit-eating grin as he walks up behind Belle. "You can't take a joke, can you?"

"You," Belle says, spinning toward him. "You better watch your tongue, because I am not going to take this. We're meant to be keeping this professional, and you are making that very difficult."

Leo towers over her, he strokes his jaw, his eyes glinting with excitement. He's got our mother's green eyes, and they've always made him look like a bird of prey. "Maybe you should stop talking about my tongue, then."

Belle pokes him in the chest. "You're going out of your way to make my life hell, and you know it."

"I would never try to make your life hell," Leo says, still grinning. "That's just a happy side-effect of being me."

I can almost see the steam coming out of Belle's ears. She hates fighting. She hates any kind of friction, and my brother is a professional at getting under people's skin.

It's why he's always getting in trouble. He loves to compete. He loves to win. And he doesn't understand what it means to back down.

"Can't you be serious for just a second?" Belle asks, still with her finger pressed into his right pec. "Just for a god damn second?"

"Language, Sweetheart." He catches her wrist and encircles it. "You got to watch that dirty mouth of yours in public. I'm meant to be keeping my image clean, remember?"

Oh, boy. This is about to go south fast.

"I'm not the problem," Belle says.

Leo releases her and steps back, brushing his hand through his dark hair. It's shorter on the sides and he's added yet another tattoo to the collection on his arms.

"Yeah," he says. "I'm the problem." He's still smiling, but it doesn't reach his eyes. "I won't kid around with you again, all right, Miss Simms? We'll keep it as professional as you need." And then he turns and heads off back inside, still with that swagger.

Belle's breathing like she's run a marathon.

I grab the lasagna and get out of the car. "Are you okay?"

"Christ on a cracker," she says, jumping on the spot. "You scared me."

"I've never seen you lose your temper like that."

Belle presses her hair back from her forehead. "It's so bad. I don't usually act like this. Your brother is driving me crazy. Like… I want to quit crazy."

"You know what they say." I join her and give her a sideways hug. "There's a thin line between love and—"

"Pure, unadulterated hatred and irritation?"

"That's how they etched it onto the side of a Pharaoh's tomb somewhere."

"You're kidding," Belle says, "that saying is from that far back?"

"Oh, no. I have no idea where it comes from," I say. "I was just being a weirdo. It's kind of my thing. Just like being an insufferable, wounded asshole is Leo's thing."

"I'm not sure you should ever say the words "wounded" and "asshole" in the same sentence together," Belle replies, quirking her eyebrows. "You know, unless you're a proctologist."

"I love you," I say, hugging her again and laughing. "God, I missed you. It's super selfish, but I'm so glad you're here."

"My torture is your joy."

"So dramatic," I say.

"I'm serious, Han. I can't stand being in the same room as him. We're just such different people," Belle says.

"Leo's a good guy," I reply. "He likes to mess with people, but when my mom got sick, he flew back and spent every day at her side. He helped keep my father from total collapse and Cash too, in his own way."

Belle licks her lips. "Great. Humanize him. That will make my job easier."

I punch her elbow, and she grins at me.

"I missed you too, Han."

We head inside Ganny's house, and it's already full of noise and the smells of good cooking. My grandmother totters into the hallway, spots me, and grins from ear-to-ear. "Hannah!" She opens her frail arms, and Belle takes the lasagna from me so I can give Ganny a hug. She smells like her special rose cream and her cheeks are smeared pink with rouge.

"It's good to see you, Ganny."

"Oh my, sweet child. I missed you." Ganny pulls back and smiles at me. She looks older than the last time I saw her. "You know the drill. Dishes in the kitchen as per usual."

Belle and I walk the lasagna through to the kitchen. June and Cash are in there, him with his arms around her, whispering sweet nothings in her ear and pressing her into the counter. She giggles and runs a hand down his chest.

"Hey," I say. "This is a house full of rooms. Maybe you guys should find one of them."

June separates from Cash and gives me a hug. "Hey, Han. How are you? I owe you an apology for missing out on the training—"

"It's not needed," I say.

I should be thanking you.

"How's Alex?" I ask.

"Oh, the flu? Yeah, it passed pretty quickly. She's out back playing with Fireball." The furious yipping of Ganny's Chihuahua punctuates her words, and Alex's yell of excitement from the backyard is adorable.

Belle places the lasagna on the counter. Her phone rings, and she takes it out of her pocket then winces. "I've got to take this. It's Mr. Peters." She steps out of the kitchen with a regretful glance. "Mr. Peters. Yes, sir. Yes, sir, I saw the article in the…" Her voice fades as she heads down the hall.

"Fucking Leo," Cash says.

"Don't gripe." June strokes his arm, smiling up at him. "Your brother's going through it."

"My brother has been going through it since we were kids. How many excuses are there for being a fucking asshole?"

"And I love you too, Cash." Leo sticks his head around the doorway to the kitchen, eyes sparkling. My brother oscillates between annoying and charming. "We don't say it to each other often, but I really missed you."

Cash's frown deepens. "What do you want?"

"I don't want anything," Leo says, still half hidden. "How about you come outside and we'll talk about your repressed rage. I bet I can get Ganny to set up the kiddie pool for some wrestling. I heard you let Jesse win the last fight."

"You—" Cash steps toward Leo, raising a finger.

Leo gives his best shit-eating grin and points a blue plastic water gun at him. He shoots off a stream of something brown, and it hits Cash square on the nose. Cash splutters and runs a hand over his face. "What in the fuck? Is that piss? Did you just squirt piss at my head?"

"I was aiming for your mouth," Leo says, then aims the gun at his mouth and sprays some liquid into it. He swallows. "And it's whiskey, dumbass. Why would I squirt piss at you? I know you're getting old, but that's out of pocket, even for you."

"Leo." Cash growls it out and storms across the kitchen.

Leo lets out a demonic cackle and disappears from sight.

I laugh.

Jesse and Leo have a similar sense of humor, but Leo always takes things to the next level. Jesse would tease and mess around, but Leo would do that and more. He once put an open can of tuna fish underneath Cash's bed and left it there for weeks. Nobody knew what the hell the smell was until Mom made Leo confess.

She was good at that. She was kind and gentle with him, where Dad was all about tough love with the boys.

June and I head out of the kitchen together, chatting about her week, and how she's adapting to Cash going on tour.

We enter the living room and find Dad and Ganny chatting on the sofa. Savage is seated across from them, a can of Coke in hand. His gaze drifts up to meet mine, and heat floods my entire body.

I have the strongest urge to go over to him and kiss him, but I don't. He taps his fingers on the soda can and maintains eye contact with me.

"There you are June, honey pie," Ganny says. "Now,

darlin', I've been meaning to ask you when I'm going to get another great-grandchild?"

June chokes beside me and nearly does a spit take, wine glass clutched in hand.

Dad turns to Ganny and pats her leg. "Come on, now, Mama, she's not a prize cow. She can't just pop out babies because you want her to."

"Just saying, I want more great-grandkids," Ganny continues, her eyes glimmering blue and focused on June. "And given that—"

I don't hear the rest of what my grandmother is saying because I excuse myself and move out into the hall, past the family pictures that peer down from the walls. I run upstairs to the guestroom and shut myself inside, taking deep breaths to calm myself down.

Relax. She didn't mean anything by it.

But it's difficult to feel that way when I'm one of the grandchildren who will never give her what she wants. Sweat breaks out on the back of my neck and I sit down on the edge of the queen-sized bed, picking at the snowy white comforter. Outside the window, our favorite tree, complete with the treehouse Grandpa built us, stands like a solid reminder of my childhood and my life.

It feels like the pretty cream walls are closing in around me, like I'm trapped and—

A knock taps against the bedroom door, and it opens. Savage enters and shuts the door.

He doesn't say a word. He doesn't have to. I get up and take two steps into his open arms.

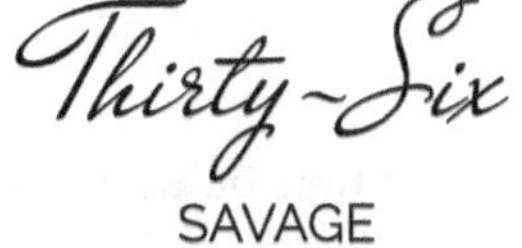

Thirty-Six

SAVAGE

SHE HAS to know how amazing she how much of a woman she is.

Hannah doesn't need to have babies to be the perfect woman. Her value isn't intrinsically tied to that, no matter how much she feels it is, but there is no good way for me to say that without sounding like an ass. I have no idea how she's feeling. It's an emotion I'll never be able to comprehend. I lost a baby, but I can't imagine what it must be like to want kids and not be able to have them. To feel like you are less because of it.

"It's not your fault," I say, and cup her cheeks in my hands, stroking my thumbs across that smooth skin. "Hannah, Princess, look at me."

Her eyes flicker down and then up. Her lips part on a breath, and the tears are a continuous stream.

"It is not your fault," I say.

She presses her lips together and nods. "T-Thank you. I shouldn't cry. It's ridiculous."

"It's *not* ridiculous. You have every right to feel how you fucking feel."

"Man, that therapist is really doing a number on you," she whispers.

I chuckle and tuck her hair behind her ears. "Don't give her all the credit," I say. "I'm taking small steps to get there, and I could not have done any of this without you. You are all woman, Hannah. Strong, intelligent, proud, capable, independent."

More tears come, and she grabs the front of my shirt, twisting it in her fingers. "Thank you," she whispers. "It's hard to feel that way sometimes. I feel weak right now."

"Well, you're the strongest person I know."

She slides her hands over my chest and down my biceps. "Sure, I am," she says. "Have you seen you?"

"You know what I mean," I say. "And bonus, you can pack a mean punch now."

A smile transforms her face, and it feels like I'm being torn apart looking at her. Fuck, she is everything. She is everything.

I am in love with her.

I am so in love with her that I can't think of anyone else, but if I tell her, she will want to stay. I'm not sure how I'm going to handle having a woman in my life again, because I'm terrified that I'll go feral and overprotective, and act like an idiot.

And I am not sure that Hannah wants me to love her.

She rises up onto her tiptoes and kisses me on the lips. "Thank you, Carter. Thank you for coming."

"June was caught up in that conversation with your grandmother and father. I'm sure she'll come to find you soon enough."

"Then we'd better make this quick." Her hands move to my jeans.

"Princess," I say, stopping her hands. "You're vulnerable."

"I don't feel that way when I'm with you."

I clench my jaw because her hands sweeping over my shirt, down to my belt, to the zipper of my jeans, has me instantly hard.

"We could get caught," she murmurs.

"Mmm." I catch her wrists in mine and hold them tight. I catch her lips with mine and kiss her softly. I want this to be gentle and sweet, but Hannah returns the kiss with such desperation, such roughness, that I push her back onto the bed.

"Quick," she whispers. "I want it quick and hard and—"

"Anything you want, Princess." I unzip my jeans and pull them down just enough, then slip my cock out.

Hannah's wearing a pair of jeans herself, and I strip them down, along with a pair of lacy pink underwear that's been a permanent feature in my dreams for months. Her pussy glistens wet for me, and I hurriedly press into her.

She cries out, and I cover her mouth. "Quiet."

Hannah's eyes light up. She nips the side of my hand, and I remove it. "What if I don't want to be quiet?"

"Then I'll have to punish you." I pound into her pussy, and she moans, her lips tip upward at the corners in a mischievous smile.

I wrap my hand around her throat, and she gasps. I bring my mouth to hers and catch every moan with my tongue while I work her pussy with hard thrusts that take me closer and closer to my fucking breaking point.

"You want my cum?" I ask.

"In my mouth," she whispers. "I want it in my mouth and on my face."

"Here?"

"Yes. Here. I want you to."

"Jesus, Princess. You're fucking—"

"Do it, Carter. I want it."

"Whatever. You. Want." I drive each word home with a thrust, removing my hand from her throat and sliding it down her body to reach her clit. I bring her to the edge, and she bites her bottom lip hard as she orgasms.

She rocks against me, hissing and breathing, clenching and bringing me to the brink.

Once she's come, once I am sure that she's taken care of and she's come down from the edge, I pull out of her and stroke my shaft.

Hannah squirms off the edge of the bed and onto the throw rug. She kneels, tucking her hands between her thighs, and opens her mouth, tipping her head back to accept what I've got for her.

"Fuck, Princess. You are so fucking—" I'm transported, in fucking ecstasy as I let loose on her lips, her greedy little tongue, her face.

She closes her eyes and lets out a tiny moan, squirming on the spot.

After, I rush to the guest bathroom and come back with a wet towel. I clean her face, carefully, and then help her up.

"That was amazing," she whispers. "It's kind of weird, but I've always wanted to do that."

We get dressed, and I can't keep my eyes off her. She drives me to heights I've never experienced before, not just when I'm inside her, but in conversation. When she smiles or moves.

"I'm going to wash up," she says, and heads for the bathroom, taking that ruined towel with her. I wait until she's done then take my turn cleaning up.

She's waiting for me on the bed when I exit the bathroom, and I head over to her, lift her into my arms, and kiss her.

I love you, Hannah.

I want to say it, but I don't. I can't.

I can't hold her back, but I also can't deal with the thought of her in harm's way or out of sight. And the idea that any man might put their hands on her, or feel anything like the way I do about her, makes my palms sweat, fists clench.

"Are you okay?" Hannah asks, rising onto tiptoe so she can kiss me.

I nod, but keep my silence.

As long as you're with me, I'm happy.

Thirty-Seven

HANNAH

"ARE YOU EVER COMING BACK?" I ask, pressing my phone to my ear as I start up the stairs to my apartment. "It's been over a month. Just how much money does my brother have that he's not telling me about?"

"Listen, when it's right, it's right," Marci says. "But we should be home within a couple of days." She lowers her voice. "Jesse's feeling very threatened."

"Threatened?" I frown.

"Mr. Skitters appears to be in love with June," Marci whispers. "It's confirmed. Every time we have a video chat with him, he's always purring in June's lap or staring up at her in adoration."

"Bullshit," Jesse shouts in the background. "He's my cat."

"Our cat, Taylor," Marci says.

"Fine. Our cat. But mostly my cat. He loves me. Marci, you think he loves me, right?"

"I've never heard him this insecure," I say. "And that includes the whole running for sheriff debacle."

"Don't let him hear you say that," Marci replies, with a giggle.

"What did she say?" Jesse calls.

"Nothing, nothing. Just girl talk. Speaking of girl talk, Han, what is going on with you and Savage?" she asks. "When last we texted, there was something, uh, brewing in the coffee pot, if you know what I mean."

"Is that a diner metaphor for sex?" I ask.

"Don't say diner," Marci whispers. "I'm having a panic attack about the Heartstopper, even with Greer in charge."

"It's doing great," I say.

"You're avoiding the question."

"I'll text you about it," I say, as I come up the stairs and stop on the grating. My stomach drops.

There's a dusty pink rose resting against my door. "I'll talk to you later. I can't wait until you guys are back."

"Love you," Marci says.

I hang up without replying and crouch down in front of the rose. My heart sputters in my chest as I lift it from where it was placed. There's no card, but this is… It's got to be *him*. It's not Savage, right? No way.

It's Franklin.

Why would he do this, even after Cash warned him off?

I don't understand it. I stare at the rose, and the soft click and whine of something mechanical catches my attention. It came from above my head, and I search the eaves of the building for what it was. My gaze lands on a distant and tiny red blinking light.

What on—?

The red light is attached to a black box that's seated against the side of the building. And it has a tiny lens. A lens that is focused on me. It's so small that had I not heard the noise, I wouldn't have realized it was there.

My breaths come in gasps, and I drop the rose and insert the keys into my front door. I burst through into my apartment and shut the door behind me, then lock it.

Relax. Breathe.

But I can't.

This isn't the first inexplicable flower from my stalker. And the camera? That is brand new, and incredibly disturbing. I pull my phone out of my jeans, shaking.

> I need you to come over here, please. I'm really afraid.

> **SAVAGE**
> On my way.

That's all, and it brings me so much comfort, my shoulders ease. I pace back and forth between the coffee table and my sofa, trying to work this out in my mind.

Franklin has sent me how many flowers now?

There was that bouquet, the white one, and then this pink rose, and the worst part is, that rose was sent after Cash talked to Franklin about leaving me alone. And I haven't received any texts from him either. What the hell is going on? And the camera? He set up a camera?

I pace back and forth for half an hour. Waiting for him.

Savage's knock on my door sends me scattering toward it. "Carter?" I whisper.

"It's me." His reply is in that rich, comforting rumble.

I unlock the door to admit him, but freeze as he steps through it, holding the discarded pink flower. He holds it out to me.

"What are you—?"

"It's for you," he says.

"Yeah, that's kind of the problem, wouldn't you say? I thought Cash got rid of him?"

"Wait, what?"

"What?"

"Hannah, I put this flower in front of your door," he says.

"Oh. Oh," I say, and exhale. But the relief is momentary. I take it from him and inhale the sweet scent. Of course. Savage has an entire greenhouse full of roses. Even ones named after Charlotte. So, there's that.

"Why did you think it was from your stalker?"

"Because he used to send me roses. Bouquets of roses with a card. And then there was that time he sent me a white rose without a card, and a few times before that. It's always a bouquet with a card or a single rose, and—"

Savage pulls a face. "Shit."

"What?"

"I had no fucking idea he was sending you flowers."

"That's okay," I say. "I shouldn't have freaked out, but—"

"Hannah, every rose you've received that came without a card was from me."

"But—" I do the math. "But then you've been leaving flowers on my doorstep for months."

Savage remains still.

I suck in a breath. "Ever since… Ever since the night you rejected me. When I was drunk."

He nods once.

"Are you kidding?"

A shake of the head, his dark eyes focused on me, like nothing else exists.

"Why?"

"Isn't it obvious?"

"Carter, what do you—?"

He crosses the space between us and takes my hands. The rose drops from my fingers onto the floor between us. "I've been obsessed with you for fucking years, Hannah."

I swallow.

"For years. And when that night happened, when you wanted me, I had to get out before it was too fucking late, and I broke my promise. But the way you were hurting was criminal. I wanted to put a smile on your face, so I left you the roses. If I'd known that they frightened you, I would never have done it."

I'm shaking, but I have to keep myself under control because no matter how romantic and perfect this is, there's still a camera outside.

"There's a camera on the roof," I say.

Savage brushes his fingers up my arms. "I know."

"You put it there?" I step out of the protective circle of his arms. "You put a camera up outside my apartment."

"The morning after your brother asked me to be your bodyguard."

"So, you've just been watching me without my consent."

"Not you, Princess. The front of your building. I've been making sure that you aren't being targeted by anyone."

I squeeze my eyes shut and try to get my bearings in this moment.

Savage cares enough to look out for me, but I don't like

the fact that he never *told* me about the cameras. "Did you put cameras up inside my apartment?" I ask.

"Absolutely not. I wouldn't do that."

"No, you would just put them up outside and not tell me about them," I say, backing up another step.

"Hannah," he says. "I should have told you I put it up, but you can't tell me you don't feel safer without me around."

"I do feel safer with you around," I say, breathing through my anger. He has helped me. He's been every-thing to me over the past couple of weeks, but this is a struggle for me. "You know I want to be independent."

"You can be independent and still be safe."

"Not with the man I— I'm seeing watching me without my consent. That's weird. That's weird and kind of creepy."

Savage grits his teeth. "I was your bodyguard. I tech-nically still am. It's not like I put a camera up in your bedroom without your consent. I have some boundaries."

"But you're not going to respect mine."

"What?"

"You're not going to take it down, are you?" I ask.

"Fuck, do you really want me to do that?" He cracks his knuckles. "Because I'm trying to protect you here."

"Protect me from what? The stalker thing is not a thing any more."

"I have a past too, Hannah. Someone might try to use you to get to me." Savage scratches the back of his neck. "I got a weird fucking call a couple of weeks ago."

"From who?"

"Davis. He was using a voice changer."

"Well, that's just amazing news," I say. "That sounds like something you should have told me about."

"It didn't involve you."

"But it involved me enough for you to keep watching over me with your cameras."

Savage takes a breath. "Look," he says, "I crossed a boundary here. That was wrong of me. I shouldn't have put up the camera without asking you first. I'm sorry."

I wait for him to try to gaslight me like one of my exes. To tell me that it was for my own good, and I'm over-reacting.

"I hope you can forgive me, Hannah."

"I need a little air," I say. "I'm… look, Carter, I'm stuck on you, and I'm not going to stop seeing you because of this, but I need a minute to think, okay?"

Thirty-Eight

SAVAGE

I CAN'T FUCKING STAND this.

I stare at the open doorway and listen to the sound of Hannah's retreating steps on the stairs, grinding my teeth.

Yeah, I put up the camera. Sure, I should have told her, but I acted on impulse. I wanted her safe, and fuck it, I would do it again. With the caveat that I'd tell her about it first. And now she wants space. Space I have to give her, even though I'm fucking aching inside to take her in my arms and hold her close.

The fact is, I don't want to give Hannah space.

I've spent the last sixteen years wanting only space. Space from the world and all the people in it, but now that she wants it, all I want is her.

In my house. In my life.

"Fuck this." I exit onto the steps. Hannah has just reached the bottom. "Hannah," I say, and then jog up to her. "Princess."

Hannah looks up at me, those blue eyes shimmering with tears.

I jog down the stairs to her. I don't take her in my arms, but I itch to do it. I'm never going to come back from touching her.

"Princess," I say, moving toward her again, then stopping myself. *Space.*

"Why do you call me that?" she asks. "What's the reason? Is it because you think I'm spoiled? Because I'm some cloistered, cared for little princess who needs everyone to look out for her? Is that why?"

"No."

"Then why?"

I scratch the back of my neck.

"Carter."

I take in a breath. "A couple of years ago, the Heat-stroke Public Library hosted a reading of the Princess and the Pea," I say. "You remember that?"

She nods, sucking the corner of her bottom lip between her teeth.

"I attended."

"You attended a reading of a children's book?" she asks. "I don't remember seeing you there."

"That's because I hung back between the bookcases in the sci-fi fantasy section. I caught glimpses of you, reading to the kids about the princess, the pea, her fucked up family who sold her off to some random lonely prince," I say.

"And what, you thought I was like this princess who has to sleep on a million mattresses to be comfortable?"

"No," I say. "You were wearing a crown, Hannah. And you looked so goddamn beautiful. So fucking perfect. It looked like you were born to wear a crown, and it stuck in my head. You as a princess. Not a spoiled princess, not someone who has to be cared for or pandered to, but a regal, beautiful woman who deserves to be worshiped."

Hannah stares at me, wide-eyed.

"And anyway, none of this makes up for the fact that I went behind your back and installed that camera, but fuck it, Hannah, I've been obsessed with you for years, and the thought of you in danger...." I clench my fists.

"What?"

"It makes me want to burn the world down for you. It makes me want to find whoever upsets you and make them pay for it with fucking blood."

She trembles. "You can't be serious."

"And I would expect nothing less from you. I expect you to punch anyone who fucks with you in the nose, then tell me about it so I can finish what you started," I say.

Hannah takes a step toward me.

In the street, cars pass by, but we're further back from the mouth of the alleyway. They can't see us, and even though this is the least romantic place ever, I want to tell Hannah how I feel. I hold back, because when I do that, it's going to be perfect. I'm going to show her exactly what she means to me, so there's no doubt left.

And then you are going to let her go.

My throat tightens at the thought, and I shove my hand into my pocket, touching my fingers to the bracelet.

"Carter, I—"

"You want space, and it's going to take time for you to get over this."

"I'd like a heads up next time."

I nod.

She steps even closer.

"Is the space thing over now?" I ask, the urge to hold her nearly unbearable. What the fuck is wrong with me? I can't go a minute without her. It's insane.

"You'll really do it?" she whispers, tracing a hand down my arm.

I catch her wrist in mine and lift it to my lips. I press a kiss to the warmth of her palm, trailing my lips down the inside of her forearm.

"Do what?" I ask, between kisses.

"Burn the world down for me?"

"Hannah," I say. "There isn't a god damn *thing* I wouldn't do for you. You ask for it, and it's yours."

She steps into my arms, and I bring my lips down on hers, my hand resting against her throat, moving up to her cheek. The kiss is gentle at first, but I can't help myself with her. I lift her into my arms, and she kisses me back, stroking her fingers through my hair, tugging, gasping.

I need to get her upstairs before I fuck her up against the side of the bakery.

"Oh my goodness." The words come from the entrance to the alleyway.

Hannah freezes in my grasp.

We turn, and find Irma, her colleague from the library, standing inside the mouth of the alleyway, holding a gift box, her one hand literally clutching the string of pearls at her neck. She's wide-eyed, and I'm surprised her gray curls aren't standing on end.

I clear my throat and let Hannah down slowly.

"Hi, Irma," Hannah says.

"I suppose that explains why he's been visiting the library so much lately."

"Why, because big guys like him can't read books?" Hannah snaps it out.

I hide my smile, stroking my beard.

"You always were a bit loose, weren't you, dear?" Irma mutters.

I step past Hannah and glare down at the woman. "What did you just say?"

She lifts her pointed chin.

"I suggest you keep your opinions about my woman to yourself," I say. "Or I will make sure your inappropriate behavior is reported to your superiors. Understand?"

"Are you threatening me?"

"I'm making a promise," I say, trading her stare for mine.

Irma pats her hair. "Yes, well. I didn't mean anything by it. Just kidding around, isn't that right, Hannah, dear? We like to have our little jokes."

"It's fine," Hannah says, and squeezes my arm.

Irma sucks in a breath through her teeth. "I wanted to give you a parting gift, dear." And she hands the box to Hannah. "I'm sure you will put it to good use." And then she waddles off, casting glances at me over her shoulder as she goes.

"Nice lady," I say.

"She's harmless." Hannah opens the gift box and snorts. She takes out a pack of condoms. "Condoms and an info-pamphlet about the dangers of teenage pregnancy. Oh, and a coupon for Bagel's! That part is nice."

"Harmless, huh?"

"Eh." Hannah waves a hand. "If you give a crap about everyone's opinion of you, you'll never figure out who you really are."

I take her by the hand and lead her back up the stairs to the apartment, thinking of all the ways I'm going to show her just how perfect she is for me.

Thirty-Nine

HANNAH

I **OPEN** my apartment door and let out a squeal.

Marci barrels into the room and throws her arms around me. "I missed you so much! Oh my god, girl, you have got to tell me everything. There is something fishy going on here, and I want to know what it is."

I'm so nervous, my stomach turns, and I swallow bile.

Marci frowns at me. She's tan from her honeymoon and practically glowing, but I've been feeling down and under the weather all morning. I don't care, though, because she's here! She's finally back. And just in time.

"What's going on?" she asks. "You said you need to tell me something?"

I shut my door and guide her to my comfy sofa. I've already put out the coffee pot, filled to the brim with steaming hot coffee, and two mugs.

"Where's Belle?" Marci asks.

"Busy babysitting Leo. Those two are fighting like cats and dogs." I pour Marci a cup of coffee then make one for myself. But the scent is seriously making my nerves and nausea worse, so I set it aside and watch Marci drink hers instead.

"I have to get all the details about that later," Marci says. "What's going on with you?"

My palms are clammy. "Don't worry about me," I say. "Let's talk about your honeymoon. Was it everything you dreamed?"

"If you mean did I eat a whole bunch of pasta, make love, drink wine, and see Rome, then have to look after my sick as a dog husband on the way home," Marci says. "Then yeah."

I grimace.

"Oh, don't worry." Marci raises a hand. "It's not contagious. I think he just overate."

"That sounds like Jesse. Let me guess, concessions stand at the airport?"

"Pretty much," Marci says, with a laugh, and then she sweeps her gaze over me. "What's with you? You look different."

And then I break, because I can't not tell one of my best friends that I'm leaving Heatstroke in literally a couple of days. Or that I'm having a sordid, amazing affair with the man of my dreams. I tell her everything while she listens with wide eyes, coffee mug forgotten in her grasp.

Afterward, she puts down her mug and takes my hands. "Holy crap, that's sweaty." She lets go of them again.

"Sorry," I say. "I was super nervous to tell you."

"What did you think I would say?" Marci asks. "No, don't leave. I want you to stay and watch me be happy while you slowly waste away?"

"Gee, thanks."

"You know what I mean. Han, I will always want what's best for you. And I know you. You're always prepared to take on the world. You've been ready for this for ages, and you deserve happiness. Which brings us to the next part... Savage? Are you serious?" She pinches my arm.

"Ow!" I rub the sore spot.

"How could you not tell me? We've been waiting for this to happen forever." Marci's older than me, but she's got a young soul, and I'm half-convinced she's also my soul mate. Just like Belle's my soul mate. And June.

And... *Don't even think about it.*

"I didn't want to overshadow your trip. Can you really say you would've been entirely focused on your honeymoon if I'd dropped that little nugget of information? I know you. You would've blabbed to Jesse instantly."

"Guilty as charged," she says. "But still. I resent that." She sticks her tongue out of the corner of her mouth. "So? How was it?"

Nausea nearly overwhelms me at her words.

I suck in a breath and try to calm myself down. Why am I so stressed about this? I swipe my hand over my forehead.

"Han?" Marci tilts her head.

"I'm fine," I say, waving a hand. "Maybe I'm coming down with something."

"Not it." Marci unties her auburn locks then scoops them back into a bouncy high ponytail again. She smells lightly of coconut and sunscreen and it's making my nausea worse. "So, you were telling me how Savage was in—?"

I can't keep it in any more. I get up and sprint to the

bathroom. I burst into it and make it to the toilet just in time.

What feels like five meals later, I look up and find Marci leaning against the door jamb, gnawing on her lip. "That bad, huh? I'll be sure not to tell him."

"Marce."

"Han, do you need me to take you to a doctor? I've never seen you like this before."

Another wave of nausea hits me, and I cling to the toilet.

"Han?"

I fight it down, my eyes watering, and look up at her.

"When last did you get your period?" Marci asks.

"My periods are irregular," I say. "So, I don't really keep track of them. Why do you...?" And then it hits me.

———

"THIS IS NOT HAPPENING," I whisper. "It's not happening."

We sit on the edge of my tiny bath-shower combo, the shower curtain mocking me in the mirror over the sink with its happy, vibrant yellow ducks.

"Not happening," I repeat.

"It's possible, isn't it?" Marci asks.

"I have POI," I say. "There's a remote possibility, but it's tiny, and it's wrong."

"Wrong?"

"This doesn't happen for women like me."

"What do you mean, Han?"

I take a breath of cool air—I brushed my teeth and tongue while Marci ran to the drug store and brought back like twenty different pregnancy tests. "I mean, infertility is a serious issue. I get that people can sometimes get pregnant by accident, but usually, it's a struggle. It takes years worth of hormone treatments, IVF failures, it's rough. I looked into it when I was hoping that maybe I might be able to have a baby, but even then, the OB GYN said there's like no chance for me. My best option would be adoption, which is really something I would consider if I met the right guy or I wasn't about to leave forever but this is just… it's just not happening. It's not possible. It's not fair to other women. It's not—"

"Hannah."

"Yes?"

"You're doing that thing where you panic ramble," Marci says, stroking my back. "Do you need me to get you some water? Is there anyone you want me to call? The girls? Do you want Belle and June?"

"Maybe? I don't know. I feel weird. It's got to be the flu, right?"

"We'll know in about thirty seconds." She points to the first test lying on the basin. "And then in a minute. And then we can do like five more after that."

What will I do if those tests are positive?

My heart swoops at the idea.

Of having a baby. Of it being my baby. And Carter's baby. Of a home.

But I'm going to leave. Or I was going to leave, and I can't possibly go running off to New York without telling Carter, or while I'm pregnant. *He lost his child.*

My insides clench. I am so confused about how to feel.

Guilty. Happy. Afraid.

I have to tell Carter, sooner rather than later.

"Han, no matter what happens, it's going to be okay."

Marci draws me close, and I rest my head on her shoulder. "I promise you, it will all be good. You have an entire family who loves you, and all your friends and…"

"And Carter? I don't know if I have him. He says he's obsessed with me, and he's been doing these amazing things for me, but that doesn't mean he's instantly going to be over the moon about having a baby."

Marci is my tough love friend. She never sugar coats things, and she's not like June with her optimistic streak. She takes me by the shoulders and gives me one of those sharp stares that are her trademark. "Yeah? Well, if he doesn't want it, he's a fucking dick. And you'll have all my support. Also, I have a baseball bat in my closet, and we can totally beat the crap out of that stupid motorcycle of his."

"Marce."

"I'm just saying." She shrugs then checks her watch. "Are you ready?"

"Yeah. I— Yeah, I guess so." I squeeze my eyes shut.

The part of me that was sure I would never be able to have kids is overjoyed. The woman who's in love with Savage doesn't know what to think.

Marci lifts it off the counter and looks at it. She keeps her expression blank then hands the stick to me.

I take it and slowly lift it into view.

Two pink lines stare at me.

"But that's just one," Marci says. "We can check the other one in a minute."

I swallow, my mouth dry.

I never thought this was a real possibility. My doctor said pretty much no. Absolutely not. No chance.

Another wave of guilt besets me, followed by that fear,

the joy. I'm all over the place and it makes my stomach swim and my head hurt. I clutch my forehead, massaging my temples with my thumb and middle finger.

"Okay, let's check the next one." Again, Marci looks at the test, then hands it to me with a blank expression.

I lift it into view. "4 Weeks Pregnant." In bold black letters on the little screen.

"Four weeks? Four weeks. Oh my God."

"Yeah, it's one of those early detection things," she says. "But you must be pretty darn pregnant if the other test is showing it too."

"Thanks, Marce," I say, and pull a face.

"How do you feel?"

I take a breath and stare at the two tests.

"I mean, apart from grossed out 'cos you're holding those and you literally peed on them."

I hand her the tests. "Can you call June and Belle? I—I don't want to tell them this over the phone."

Marci whips out her phone and calls them. She paces back and forth in the bathroom. "Ugh, neither of those bitches is picking up."

"Oh." My stomach sinks.

Marci drops down in front of me, and she looks so pretty in her strappy top with her new Italy tan. "You know what? I'll run out and get them. You stay right here. I'll be back in no time."

"Okay," I say, nodding. "Yeah. Thanks, Marce."

"Of course." She presses a kiss to the top of my head then dashes out of the bathroom. The front door clicks closed a few minutes later.

Forty

SAVAGE

STOP THINKING ABOUT IT.

Stop thinking about it.

Stop thinking about her leaving town. She won't be gone for that long. She'll check in with you. She'll call.

But I cannot fucking stop thinking about her, no matter how god damn hard I try. So much so, that I want to go over to my laptop and check the video feed from that camera above her doorway. I haven't taken it down—I managed to convince Hannah to let me keep it there for the last little while she's in town.

I'm feeling extra fucking protective over her. Maybe because of that call I got a couple of weeks back, maybe because I'm madly in love with her, and I can't stand the thought of her leaving.

You should tell her.

But I can't tell her.

If I tell her, it will stop her from leaving, and she wants to go. I have to let her fucking go, and I hate it.

I square up to the punching bag in my garage. I'm

covered in sweat, and I've already discarded my shirt. I dart close and punch the bag, watching it swing and rattle with every punch. The door to my garage is open, letting in the summer air, and I have a view of the spot where Hannah clung to me in the rain, laughing and staring up at the sky.

It's fine. She's fine. I punch after the thoughts.

I'll get through this. So will she.

And the call I got a couple of weeks ago appeared to be a fluke. I made a couple of calls to my contacts and it looks like Davis is still in prison.

But it's still under my skin. I've told Hannah, she doesn't seem concerned about it. Why would she be? It's not like we're married.

We should get married.

I'm torturing myself.

The crunch of tires on gravel brings me back to the present. Cash's pick-up rolls up to my log ranch house and parks out front. He hops out, the engine ticking under the hood, and walks over to me.

"What the fuck, Savage," Cash says.

"And hello to you too, brother."

"Don't you dare fucking call me that." Cash charges toward me, his fists clenched. He's always let his anger get the better of him, and he squares up with me now, even though he's a good couple inches shorter.

He pushes me back a step, and I stand my ground. "You good?"

"You broke your promise."

Fuck.

"You touched Hannah. You messed with my family, Savage. You—"

"I thought I was your family."

"You know what the fuck I mean." He raises a finger and points it at me. I consider it and him.

I'm not going to fight my best friend. It won't achieve anything, and Cash might be strong, but I'll fuck him up and he has to know that.

"Cash," I say, and take a deep breath. "I should never have made that promise."

"I don't give a fuck whether you should have made it or not. You did. You swore you would stay away from her. You are damaged fucking goods, and she doesn't need a man like you drifting in and out of her life. You can't give her what she needs."

"And you know what Hannah needs."

His hands contact my chest again and he pushes. This time, I don't budge. "She's my sister," he roars, pushing his forehead against mine.

I push him back a step. "I'm in love with her."

Cash's rage seeps away. "What?"

"I am in love with Hannah," I say. "And it's taking every fucking ounce of self-control I have not to go over there and tell her that I want her to stay in Heatstroke. That I need her in my life. I have spent weeks in fucking therapy trying to fix myself for her. I have listened to everything she needs and tried to accommodate her, so forgive me, Cash, but I do not give a fuck whether you like it or not. I don't give a fuck about our promise. I would crawl across burning coals to get to your sister. I would take a bullet to the head for her. I would literally beat your ass if you stood in my way. I love her, and I do not give a fuck what you think about it."

Cash opens and shuts his mouth.

"And quite frankly, brother, she's her own woman. You don't get to tell her what she can and can't fucking do. I shouldn't have to tell you that," I say.

Cash stands there with a mouth full of teeth and says sweet fuck all.

I turn back to the punching bag and set to work.

Cash folds his arms and watches me in silence. "You've been going to therapy?"

I catch the bag in both hands as it swings back to me. "Yeah."

"For weeks?"

"Yeah, it hasn't been long, but I'm going to keep at it. Even after Hannah leaves. Fuck, especially after she leaves, because fuck me, that's going to hurt," I say, and it feels good to get it out.

"It's going to hurt?"

I stretch out my arms. "Yeah. What?"

His mouth has dropped open. He snaps it shut and scratches under his dark, close-cut beard. "Just never heard you talk about your feelings before."

"Is that a problem?"

"No, it's just... yeah, it's different."

"What should I do, not talk about them because I'm a guy?" I ask.

"That's not what I'm saying," Cash replies. "You're different, that's all. You never used to talk about shit, and all of a sudden you're talking about feelings. Just how good is this therapist of yours?"

"She's great," I say. "But it's not just her. It's Hannah too." I go over to my workout bench and sit down on it, resting my forearms on my thighs. "Don't know how to describe it, but this has been like a dam wall breaking under strain. It's been sixteen fucking years of trying to cope with what happened to Charlotte and my baby girl. And then trying to deal with who I became afterward when I joined that club. I don't want to do it on my own any more, and Hannah helped me realize that I don't have to."

Cash pulls his lips into a line and nods. "Well, damn, okay. Good for you. I'm proud of you."

"Thanks." I grab a towel and wipe my hands on it.

"And you're just going to let her leave?"

"I'm not going to let her do anything," I say.

"You know what I mean, Savage. You're in love with her, and you're going to watch her walk away? Without telling her?"

"Yeah. I don't want her to stay on account of me," I say. "I want her to live a life that makes her happy, and I can't make her happy out here." I gesture to the ranch. "She won't want to live out here, all alone. She wants to travel and see the world."

"You could travel with her."

"For a guy who wanted to head butt me for breaking my promise, you sure seem happy about me being in love with your sister," I say.

"You know I was trying to protect her. That was the only reason I made you swear you wouldn't get involved with her." Cash folds his arms. "Come on, now, you're clearly working through your shit, and everyone with eyes knows that Hannah's been crazy about you for years."

"Doesn't give me the right to tell her how I feel."

"Is that it?" Cash asks.

"What?"

"That you don't want to stop her from leaving? Or is it that you're afraid."

"I've already got a therapist, Taylor."

"I'm serious. You're afraid that she won't love you back, aren't you? Or that she won't want to stay if you do tell her," Cash says. "Well, fuck it, you were the one who told me to stop being an idiot about June. And look at me now."

I bow my head. "It's not that simple."

"Oh, but it is," Cash says. "Hannah might not need me meddling in her life or being overprotective, but she does need to know that you love her before she leaves town. She deserves to know."

I don't say anything back, but I glare at him like he's an asshole.

Cash comes over and pats me on the shoulder. "Think about it." And then he heads for his truck and gets in. He honks goodbye and drives off, while I stare into space. Finally, I get up and head inside to the laptop. I open it and check out the feed that shows me the front of Hannah's house.

Ice travels through my veins.

A figure in a dark hoodie walks up the stairs toward Hannah's apartment and opens the front door.

Forty-One

HANNAH

THE FRONT DOOR clicks in the living room, and I let out a breath. "Marce? Did you find them? That was super quick."

Footsteps move down the hallway and toward the bathroom.

I stare at the pregnancy test in my hands, thinking hard. There's got to be a way to break this to Savage that won't make him freak out. But he's going to freak out either way, and if he takes it badly, it's going to rip my heart to shreds. I just know it.

Marci enters the bathroom and stops dead.

"What's wr—?" I look up, and thoughts about the baby, about my love for Savage, about how I feel about being pregnant, vanish.

A man in a hoodie stands inside the bathroom.

"Who are you?" The pregnancy test drops from my fingers. "What are you doing here?"

"Hannah Taylor?" His voice rasps.

I don't recognize it. "What are you doing in my apartment? I'm calling the cops." But my phone is in the living room.

The hoodie guy laughs softly. He reaches up and removes his hood, and I recoil. A scar runs down the left side of his face, twisting his lips into an awful grin. His eyes are a silvery gray, and his hair is too. There are tattoos down his throat, and one of them, a flaming skull, is familiar. Savage had that same tattoo along his rib cage.

"You are a pretty little thing," he says. "I'm going to enjoy this." And then he makes a grab for me.

I scream and jump up and away from him. But there's nowhere to go. He's blocking my path to the door, and I can't climb out of the window—I'm two stories up.

Savage's voice rings in my ears. *Easy breathing. That's it. Calm. Remember, move from the hip. Let that power flow through your body into your arm, and through his head.*

My fists come up, and the intruder smirks. "Come on, now. You don't really think you're going to—"

I center my weight, exhale, and then I give him my best right hook.

It happens in slow-motion. Maybe it's my brain in panic mode, or maybe it's adrenaline, but my fist lands on his nose. I feel a sickening crunch, and blood fountains from his nostrils. He keels backward and grips his nose.

And my path to the door is free. I run out into the living room, screaming like a woman possessed, and head for the door.

But arms grab me around the waist and pull me back a second later.

"You fucking bitch." His breath is hot against me neck. "I'm going to fucking kill you for that."

I ram my head backward and it makes contact with

him. His arms release me, and I start for the door again. *Carter!* It's a mental plea he will never hear.

He trips me, I flail and fall down, blocking my fall with my hands. Pain flares through my right palm, and I notice, in a half-dazed state, that one of my fingers has a cut across the front and is bleeding.

Fingers twist through my hair and pull my head back. "Bad move," he growls.

"Let go of me," I scream. "Help! Somebody help!"

"Nobody's going to hear you," the man growls, and drags me to my knees. "Nobody's coming to save you." He shuffles me backward until my back hits the coffee table.

The baby.

Terror lodges in my throat. I won't let this happen.

I kick and scream as hard as I can, wrenching free from the man's grasp, and get up again, backing away through my living room, my fists up, my stomach churning with fear.

The guy laughs, blood trailing from his nostrils, over his lips, down his chin. He doesn't care. In fact, his eyes are wild, his grin wide.

Nightmare. This is a nightmare.

All you have to do is stall. Marci will be back soon.

But the last thing I want is my friends in danger along with me.

I put my armchair between us, but the guy doesn't move, he simply watches me like a bird of prey who knows that the little mouse can't possibly escape.

"You," he says, pointing at me, "are interesting. I never thought Savage would take another wife after what happened to the last one."

I'm too afraid to answer him. I swallow, but my dry throat won't work.

"What do you say we give your man a call?" he asks, taking a phone out of his pocket, casually. "I'm sure he'll be excited to hear your voice. Your screams."

"Who are you?"

"Does it matter?" he asks. "You're going to die anyway."

"Are you from that motorcycle club?"

His grin widens, his teeth stained with blood. "That's right. He told you about that? But did he tell you all the evil things he's done in the name of our club? Torturing men, beating people into submission, running drugs?"

My stomach turns.

"Ah, so he didn't tell you." The guy taps away on his phone completely unconcerned by me.

I glance around desperately. There's got to be something I can do. A way out.

"You know, out of all the shit he did when he was a part of our club," the guy continues, "there was one mistake he can never go back on. One thing that I will never forgive."

I try to wet my lips and swallow.

"Want to know what it is?"

I inch toward the door.

My attacker steps calmly in front of me. "He betrayed us to the cops," he says. "So that he could forget his fucking sins, and run off to this bumfuck nowhere town to start a new life. He thought he hid himself good." He snorts, nostrils flaring. "And that's where he was wrong. Savage took everything from me. And now, I'm going to take everything from him."

I raise my fists and pull back for another punch, but he's too fast for me.

He catches my fist in his palm, then twists my arm. "You and I," he says, "are going to sit down, and have a nice little chat with Savage."

Forty-Two

SAVAGE

MY PHONE BUZZES in my pocket. Caller ID hidden. It's Davis. It has to be.

I don't answer, because it's not going to achieve anything. I called the cops on my way over. Fuck safe driving, fuck everything. I'm half-naked, driving like a maniac, because if anything happens to Hannah, I will lose my mind.

I will lose it all.

He's got her.

Adrenaline courses through my veins as I tear down the street and pull to a stop outside Bagel's Bakery. I leap out of my SUV and dart up the stairs.

I reach the door and listen for any sounds of movement, or of Hannah inside, but there's nothing.

I'm coming.

I kick the door open with such force that it rebounds off her apartment wall and march into the room. Davis is seated beside Hannah on the sofa. He's got his arm around her shoulder, and a knife in his hand pressed to her throat.

Hannah's blue eyes are wide and filled with fear that makes me sick. I want to reach into my pocket for the bracelet, but I won't.

My vision tunnels on Davis, and the smile he's wearing.

"Savage," he says. "You didn't really think I wouldn't find you, did you? I know you called your buddies in the cops. Guess you're not the only one with friends high up. I've been out for months." He laughs.

I didn't go into a protection program, even though I should have. I didn't plan on living through the night when I arrived in Heatstroke. I was going to throw myself off that fucking cliff and never look back, because there was nothing left to live for.

Now, I have everything to live for, and she's sitting next to a murderer.

Rage like no other rises inside me, and I take a step toward him.

"Nuh-huh," Davis says, tapping the blade against Hannah's throat. "One step closer and you're going to end her life."

"Let her go." I am helpless in this situation.

As helpless as I was when Charlotte was attacked, and I was out of the country.

My senses are tuned to a fine point. Every micro-expression on Davis' face, the beads of sweat near his hairline, the skull tattoo on his neck that dances and moves when he talks or swallows.

"Let. Her. Go," I say.

"Or what? What are you going to do, Savage?" he asks. "Hannah and I have been having a nice little chat. Isn't that right, Hannah? Or should I call you, Princess?"

I grind my teeth.

"You're not as sly as you think, Savage. Christ, even during a storm, it was easy to spy on you two."

"This is your plan?" I ask. "To monologue like a cheesy villain from a cartoon."

"My plan is to torture Hannah," he says. A single droplet of blood trickles down her throat, and she freezes, her eyes wide. "And thus, torture you. Because that is what you deserve. I lost everyone because of you. Everyone. And I'll tell you, it might have taken me a long time to get out of prison, but I spent each and every night in there thinking of the day I would find you, and make you pay for what you did."

I glare at him.

The police will be here soon. There's no telling what he will do once he hears the sirens.

There has got to be a way.

Hannah's trembling, and I have to be calm for her.

I take a breath and shove everything aside, the adrenaline, the need to break his face and squeeze his throat until his eyes pop out of his fucking skull.

"I don't care," I say, and turn to go.

Davis doesn't say anything.

I walk toward the exit.

"Where the fuck are you going?" he asks. "I'll kill her if you leave."

"She's nothing to me," I say, drawing on a well of calm. "She was just a quick fuck."

Hannah makes a noise that's so painful, I almost turn back. I step out onto the grated steps.

"You really expect me to buy that?" Davis shouts. "You

came rushing over here and kicked the fuckign door in. Now, you're not interested in her?"

"Not worth my time." He doesn't buy it, but he doesn't have to. I have to disarm him enough for him to get up.

This is a huge fucking gamble, but I have no choice. The alternative is him toying with me while Hannah bleeds out on the sofa beside him.

I walk onto the landing and don't glance back as I start down the stairs.

"The fuck?" Davis mutters, and then I hear him getting up.

And it's my fucking chance.

I turn back and race through the room.

I catch him halfway to standing. Hannah's still on the sofa, wide-eyed, tears streaming down her cheeks. He spots me coming and lunges toward her with the knife, but I'm on him in a heartbeat. I take hold of his fist, the one holding the knife and pull it away from her.

And then I crush his fingers.

Davis screams and tries to punch me, but I catch his left fist in my other hand, so I have him trapped. I pull him close to me, listening to the satisfying crunch of his bones breaking.

Davis' face is inches from mine.

"You'd better hope the police get here in time to stop me from breaking every fucking bone in your body," I hiss, and then I pull my head back and bring my forehead down on his already broken nose.

He screams, raw and terrified.

I release his crushed hand and the knife drops from his grasp. I pick it up from the floor, test its weight, then flick it free. It lodges in his right shoulder.

He yells again, stumbling back.

And then I tackle him to the ground, my vision hazing red. I punch. Again, and again, and again, the sounds lost on me, until hands pull me away from him. I'm fighting to be free, to end his fucking life for what he's done, but more arms hold me back. More people stop me.

Police stream into the room, and I search for Hannah, the haze dropping away. She's gone.

Forty-Three

HANNAH

"I'M FINE," I say. "Seriously, I'm fine. They're just keeping me here until the doctor comes in to discharge me."

Marci, June, and Belle are crowded around my hospital bed. Belle's mascara is ruined, leaving dark streaks down her pale cheeks. Marci keeps walking back and forth in the room, lifting her hands and shaking them in front of her like she's got her hands around someone's neck. June sits on the edge of the bed, occasionally smoothing the pale green bedspread with her free hand, the other is holding mine.

"I can't believe this happened," June whispers. "I'm so sorry, Han."

"I should never have fucking left you alone in that apartment." Marci's raging. She stops, throttles the air again, and glares around the room. "I should have locked the door behind me. I should have—"

"This is not your fault," I say.

"No," Belle says, and hiccups around a sob. "This is

Savage's fault. It's his fault. He brought this down on you."

"That's not fair," I say. "He—"

"He nearly killed that guy," June says.

I gnaw on the inside of my cheek. Nothing can wipe away what happened yesterday. Every time I close my eyes, the events repeat in my mind. I've already talked to a therapist at the hospital, and I'm going to make a booking with a woman at a private practice in Heatstroke after I'm out of the hospital.

"He should be arrested for it," Belle says. "For everything. I can't believe—"

"Guys, stop," I say. "Savage had no idea that this dude would get out of prison and come after me. It's not his fault. He saved me." Even if he did act like he didn't give a crap about me to do it. The least of my worries right now.

I'm in hospital because the doctor was worried about the baby. I fractured my hand on that dude's face, so it's in a cast, and though most women with POI who do fall pregnant aren't high-risk, the OB GYN wants to be sure everything is fine before they let me go.

I'll be walking out with a prescription for prenatal vitamins. And a conversation I need to have with Savage.

I can't get the memory of what he did to that man out of my mind.

It was violent. Visceral.

His pupils were so large and so focused on my attacker, it was like his eyes had gone completely black. And then he... He did those things to him.

What's even weirder is that I'm not sickened or afraid of him. Savage protected me. He did what he could to make sure that I survived that encounter.

"I don't like it," Belle whispers, and grabs a chair from next to the bed. She pulls it closer and sits down, fiddling with her hands in her lap. "I don't like any of this Hannah. It should *not* have happened."

"This is so fucked up," Marci says. "And now you're pregnant with his baby too. Like what the fuck."

June and Belle already know. I told them when they first arrived at the hospital.

"Guys, relax. I love you all, but you have to trust that I have this under control."

June strokes the back of my hand, reaches up and brushes my hair back from my face. "We know, honey. We're all a little stressed out."

"Han, I can't imagine my life without you," Belle warbles.

I smile at her. "Yeah, who will talk to you about how awful Leo is?"

She gives me a watery grin in return. "He's not so bad."

"That," Marci says, pointing at her, "is something we'll be discussing in length. But first, Hannah, what are you going to do about Savage? You can't be with him, right? I mean, he's clearly unhinged."

"He saved me," I say. "And you don't know what he's been through."

A knock rattles the door, and a police officer, a female with her hair tied back in a glossy bun and kind eyes, smiles at me. "Miss Taylor?"

"Yeah?"

"My name is Detective Cortez with the Heatstroke Police Department. I'd like to talk to you about what happened at your apartment. Do you have a minute?"

I glance around at the girls. "Talk to me?"

"About Carter Savage. He's currently in our custody. I'd like to go over what happened with you and get a couple facts straightened out."

I sit up and nod to my friends. "Yeah. I can do that"

———

IT'S BEEN three days since the attack, and I can't go home. It makes me uncomfortable, being in my apartment and remembering what happened. It doesn't feel safe anymore, so I've been staying with my grandmother and my Dad.

I sit on the sofa in the living room, book in hand, my phone on the cushion next to me. Ganny's making chocolate chip cookies. She's been baking nonstop since I arrived, like she can keep me safe with sugar and carbs.

The girls are the only ones who know about the baby.

And Savage is going to be released from jail, all charges dropped, because he saved my life. The scumbag who attacked me isn't so lucky. He's severely wounded, and he's going back to prison, but even still, I don't feel particularly safe.

I let out a breath and try to focus on my book, but the words blur together on the page.

Carter saying he doesn't care for me.

The pregnancy tests.

A knife against my throat.

Stop.

It's difficult. I struggle to fall asleep at night, and when I do, I end up having nightmares about what happened.

A knock at the front door sends a shot of hot fear streaking through my veins.

"I'll get it," I call out.

"Are you sure, honey pie?" Ganny calls from the kitchen, sounding frail. "I can get that for you, honey, you don't got to—"

"I've got it, Ganny. Don't worry about me."

I head through to the hall and look through the peephole.

Carter is on the front porch.

Relief and fear thread through me, and I open the door right away.

"Princess." His voice is as deep and comforting as ever. And his dark eyes are fixed on me, searching, like he thinks I'll disappear.

There are dark circles under his eyes, and his beard is rougher than it was before. He's wearing another of those shirts with the logo "Savage Self Defense" on the front, and his hair is damp, curling at the ears in that way I like.

Instead of fear, I'm filled with joy at the sight of him. But I have to measure my reaction. Savage told me he had nothing to offer from the start, and I'm not going to pressure him. He saved my life. He saved our child's life without even knowing it.

"Hannah," he says.

It takes everything in me not to step out onto the porch and into his arms. To kiss him.

"Carter," I whisper. "Thank you."

His gaze snaps from my lips to my eyes. "What?"

"Thank you for saving my life," I say. "A second time."

"You should never have been in that position in the first place," he says. "That was my fault."

"No, it's not your fault," I say. "You didn't purposefully expose me to anything. You thought that guy was in prison, right? And it wasn't my place to force you to tell me anything."

"I endangered your life."

"Stop." I put up a hand. "I don't want to hear this from you. You or anyone else. What happened, happened. We can't go back now."

"What I said was a lie." Carter stares at me like I'm the only person in the world. "I said that so I could take him by surprise."

"I don't care," I say. "I have—other things I'm concerned about right now." I want to hug him so bad. I'm aching for him. But he doesn't step in closer, and it scares me. How is he going to react about the pregnancy?

I have to tell him. Right now. I can't wait a second longer.

I open my mouth to say the words.

"Princess," he says, "I care so much about you it hurts. You're going to leave town, and there's nothing I can do to stop it, but I have to— Shit. I came here to tell you that I didn't want you to go, but the truth is, I can't imagine my life without you in it. Hannah, I want you to stay, but I'm going to let you go. I won't be the man who stands in your way."

"You want me to stay?" I ask.

"Yeah," he says.

"Why?"

Savage's throat works.

"Wait," I say. "Don't tell me." I let out a breath. "There's something I need to tell you first." And then I take a step back to admit him into the house.

Forty-Four

SAVAGE

I FOLLOW Hannah into the house then up the stairs to the guest room. Memories of us together here twine through my mind.

Hannah takes my hand, and I have the distinct urge to put my arms around her, to kiss her and claim her as mine. She doesn't flinch away from me after what she saw me do. She seems completely comfortable, and I am so relieved, I can't fucking speak.

"Sit." She guides me to the edge of the bed and sits me down on the white comforter.

Hannah stands in front of me, wearing a cute flowery dress that hugs her curves, cups her breasts, and exposes her tan cleavage. Pink roses on white cotton. Her hair falls around her shoulders, and she's wearing no makeup, her eyes fixed on mine.

"Carter," she says. "I am going to stay in Heatstroke for a while."

I want to punch the fucking air and scream for joy.

"Not only do I have stuff to do at the library," she says,

and swallows, "but there's... uh, there's other stuff I have to deal with." She bites the corner of her lip.

"What's wrong?"

"Carter, there's something you need to know," she says. "And before I say anything, I want you to hear me clearly. I don't need you to be involved, if you don't want to be. I don't expect you to be my boyfriend or husband or whatever else. So just... Just bear that in mind."

"Princess."

She puts up that palm again. "Please. Let me just—" She puffs out her cheeks and exhales. "I'm pregnant."

My jaw drops, and my vision tunnels on her then returns to normal.

Pregnant?

Pregnant.

Pregnant?

"What?"

"I'm pregnant and you're the father," she says, and then she brushes her hand over the back of her head. "And it's super unexpected, I get that. I only found out on the day that... That the guy came over and he—"

I rise from the edge of the bed. "You were pregnant when he— You." My breaths come in gusts. My gaze flickers from her to the door. I want to find him and fucking kill him. My Hannah, my baby. My baby?

"Carter, please." Hannah's hands press against my forearms, and my vision snaps to the present, to her. She tries to force me to sit down. "I need to finish what I was saying."

But I can't think straight. She was pregnant when he attacked her. And I wasn't there.

Except this time I was. I saved her. I saved them both, and I—

"I don't expect you to want to be with me," she says, rambling fucking nonsense, because there is no way I'm letting her go now. "I want you to know that I'm not leaving yet, due to, you know, I have to figure out what I'm going to do next. I can't go cavorting around the friggin' country when I'm pregnant. This baby is going to need a home, and I've always wanted to be a mom, and I'm not going to let this opportunity go, so I'm keeping this baby, and if you think that I'm not going to do that then you're out of your mind, Carter, because I want to—"

"Princess, be quiet."

"What? Why?"

"Because I love you."

Her eyes go round, and she sucks in breath. "What did you—?"

"I love you, Hannah." I take her hands in mine, bring one to my lips and kiss the back of it, then move to the other. "I know that everything I've said up until this moment has told you the opposite."

"You said you weren't ready to love anyone. You don't have a heart."

"Yes."

She peers up at me, so painfully beautiful. "I don't want you to say this because of the baby, Carter. I don't want us to pretend everything is okay and this is normal when it's not. It's not normal that it happened this way."

"How is it not normal?" I ask. "What do you think normal is, Princess? Normal is what we make it and fuck what anyone else thinks."

Tears spring to her eyes. "Thank you," she whispers.

"Thank you, and Carter, I love you too, but we have to be realistic about this." She glances down and off to one side.

"You don't believe me."

She doesn't answer me.

"You don't believe that I love you or that I'm ready, do you?" I ask.

"I want to be with you," she says. "I want us to try, but I need us to take it slow. With you it's been... It's like a whirlwind. It's everything I've ever wanted, and it's all right there in front of me, and it is terrifying, Carter, because you can break me apart so easily."

"I would never break you," I say. "I'll break anyone who touches you."

"Yeah, I know." She manages a laugh.

And I live for it. I love the way she smiles. "But if you need to take it slow, then we'll take it slow, Princess. I want you to understand that I will do anything for you. And I will prove to you how much I want you, and this baby, and our future together."

I hug her to me and kiss her softly, cupping a hand to her cheek. "I will do whatever it takes, Hannah."

HANNAH

HE LOVES ME. He loves me and he wants to be with me and I'm pregnant with his baby.

And I'm never leaving Heatstroke.

The things I wanted don't matter any more.

I shake my head at the string of thoughts. They've been tormenting me for the past few days, and I can't help the way I feel. In disbelief, confused.

I want to keep this baby. I'm never going to find my independence because everyone is going to want to look after me.

I'm ridiculous for being unhappy about that. I should be grateful.

I'm afraid that Carter is only saying he loves me because of the baby, not because of us. But our chemistry is untouchable. It's everything. So how can I doubt it? Maybe because I've spent years pining for him and it's only been a month and a couple weeks since we started seeing each other.

And I love him. I love him. Oh my God, do I love him

and this baby too, and I can't stand the thought of being heartbroken.

But he wouldn't do that to me. I can trust him.

I sit on my bed in the guestroom with my laptop in front of me and consider apartment listings in Heatstroke. I have my job at the library, which is amazing, especially since I've got a reading with local kids from the middle school coming up, but I can't afford a lot. I also don't think I can live in my old apartment any more.

When I think about that place, I feel unsafe.

A knock taps on the door.

"Come in," I call out.

Ganny mentioned breakfast, and she loves to treat me when I stay over. She's giving with every single person who graces her home. I want to be like her when I grow up.

What is she going to say when she finds out?

The door opens and Leo enters the guestroom, followed by Jesse and Cash.

I straighten and press my palms onto my knees, pulling a face at my brothers. "What on earth are you guys doing in here?"

"What's the matter? We can't pay you a visit?" Leo asks. "I haven't seen you in ages."

"Try years," Cash grouses.

"Oh, relax, Grumpy Dwarf," Leo says. "You'll get over it."

"Dwarf?" Cash arches an eyebrow.

"You guys want to take this outside?" Jesse asks. "I thought we came here to talk to Hannah, not to argue."

"Yeah," Cash says.

Leo narrows his eyes at Cash, but turns to me. "Han, what's going on?"

My brother is so usually full of himself, that when he gets sincere like this, it always takes me by surprise. It's a reminder that he hides his feelings behind that bravado.

"What do you mean?" I ask, switching my gaze from Cash to Leo to Jesse and back again.

My brothers have always been my saviors. Cash is an overprotective asshole, but when the chips were down, Leo and Jesse were there for me too. They were always ready to kick ass if I needed them. And Lily would join in too.

"We know," Cash says.

"You're going to have to be more specific than that."

"About you doing the no pants dance with Savage," Jesse says.

Blood rushes to my cheeks. I open my mouth but no sound comes out.

"Making whoopee," Leo says, when I don't reply.

"Boinking?" Jesse next.

"Fornicating." Leo wears a serious frown and strokes his chin, his stubble rasping. "Coitus. Copulation."

"Stop it," Cash snaps.

Both Leo and Jesse chortle and nudge each other.

"What's wrong with you two? This is your sister you're talking about," he says.

"And so?" Leo asks. "She's not a nun, Cash. And this weird pseudo-protective big brother shit is weird as hell."

"At least I give a shit, Leo."

"Don't start," Jesse says. "I might not be in law enforcement any more, but I swear to God, I'll kick both your asses and report you."

"Do any of you actually want to hear what I have to say?" I ask.

The three of them settle into silence.

"You know that Savage and I are a thing?" I'm not going to call him Carter in front of them. I feel like that's a special thing just for us.

Cash grumbles under his breath but nods. "Yeah, I know. I talked to him about it."

"You did."

"Yeah. I wasn't happy at first, but we talked and he really cares about you, Hannah. He wants to do right by you," Cash says. "Are you still going to leave after what happened at your apartment?" The question is gentle, but the implication is clear. Cash is in his "overprotective" era.

"I don't know." But I do know, because I'm not about to go traveling while I'm pregnant and can't afford to. All the money I've saved is going toward the baby. And I'm happy about it, because I never thought that it would be possible for me. Those complicated emotions—guilt and fear mixed with joy, nearly overwhelm me.

"Han," Leo says, and takes my hand in his. He squeezes it. "We know that you've been through a lot. Not just over the past couple of months, but in your whole fucking life. You deserve to be happy, so if there's any part of you that's holding back because of what we'll think, especially this asshole's opinion—" He points at Cash. "Yeah, just know that you don't got to worry about us."

"So, you're here to tell me that I'm an independent woman who doesn't need her older brothers' opinions?" I ask.

"Yeah," Leo says.

"You realize that's a little tone deaf given that your

opinion is that I should be an independent woman who shouldn't care about her older brothers' opinions?"

"Hannah, please," Jesse says, grasping his temples, "I'm still recovering from a three week hangover in Rome."

"I told you not to drink red wine, you doofus. They make that shit different over there," Cash says.

"We'll support you no matter what," Leo says. "That's what we're saying."

"Thank you," I say.

They sit there, these seriously oversized brothers of mine, all watching me with concern or care or, in Cash's case, an unreadable frown.

"Are you going to tell us what's going on?" Jesse asks, brushing his fingers through his dark hair.

"Not today," I say.

"Hmm." The lines on Cash's forehead deepen.

"All right," Leo says, and smiles at me. "Let us know when you wanna talk." He leans in and kisses me on the cheek, then heads out the door.

Cash ruffles my hair like I'm a kid, and I glare at him. Jesse hugs me. "You're the best Hannah Banana."

And then they're gone, and I'm left with a smile and nerves bubbling in my belly. Cash and Savage talked about me. Cash knows that Savage cares. Then it's real. This is real.

Forty-Six

SAVAGE

I'M GOING to spend the rest of my life showing her what she means to me.

I cannot let this woman go, and I don't mean that physically. If Hannah wants to explore the world, if she wants to fucking go hiking in South America, or travel the world, I will help her do it. I want her to be happy.

I get out of my SUV into the warm afternoon and jog up the stairs of the Heatstroke Public Library. The familiar smell of books mingles with the scent of cut grass from outside. Irma, the librarian who saw us and likely ratted us out to the whole town and Cash, is at the front.

She makes eye contact with me and jolts on the spot. "H-Hello, Mr.—"

"Where's Hannah?"

"She's doing a reading, currently." Irma points a gnarled finger toward the reading area on the other side of the library.

I move between the bookcases and stop at the sight of her. Fuck, she is so perfect.

She's sitting in an armchair between the bookcases, her ankles crossed, wearing jeans and a silky blouse that ties at her throat, a book open in her lap. There are kids gathered in front of her, and every one of them is hanging on her every word as she reads from the book.

Her bright blue eyes flicker left to right as she reads, and fuck, I'm so in love with her, because even the way she forms words is sexy to me.

I stand there listening to her until the book is done, and she looks up and meets my gaze. A smile parts her lips, but there's uncertainty there, in the way her eyebrows drop one second and lift the next. I have to dismiss that fear.

The kids surround her and ask questions, while their teachers clap hands and call out to them to get organized.

They file out, and my eyes are locked onto her.

She shuts the book and smiles at me. "Hey," she says.

"That was amazing."

"Amazing? Yeah this is a pretty great book," she replies. "Thank you for donating it." She lifts the book and shows me the cover, and I spot the name on the front. "I hope you don't mind me reading it to them. I was interested, and I've got to say Charlotte was a fantastic writer."

Warmth spreads through my chest, and I close the distance between us in large strides. I sweep her into my arms and hug her to my chest. "You're amazing, Hannah. You are fucking amazing."

"Carter," she breathes.

My name on her lips is an addiction. I kiss her, and she moans against my mouth, going supple in my arms. I want to take her home and show her what she means to me, but that's only part of my plan for the day.

I pull back from the kiss, brushing her hair back from her face. "I wanted to check in on you," I say. "How are you feeling?"

She sets the book down on a table that's been pushed back from the central area where the kids were sitting. "I've had some nausea."

"You didn't drink the ginger ale I got you?" I ask.

"I did, but it didn't help that much," she says. "Thank you, though."

"Grated apple," I say.

"Huh?"

"Try grating some apple and letting it turn brown." I smile at her. "I've been looking up this shit online. I want to make you comfortable, Hannah."

She moves through the space and stops in front of me, tucking her hands behind her back. "I'd be super comfortable if I could just find a new apartment. The old one kind of... It's got weird memories now."

I nod.

I haven't asked her to move in with me yet because I don't want to spook her. I want Hannah to be fully ready for what I have to offer her. I want her to believe it, because she's struggling with that.

"Yeah, otherwise I guess I'm okay? Things changed really quickly." She rubs her arms. "But I've been meaning to tell you, I'm supposed to go to a doctor's appointment, like a check up for the baby? And I wanted to ask if you maybe wanted to come with me?"

"There's nothing I want more," I say. "Seriously. Call me any time of the day or night. No matter what you need, even if it's just a hug or to have your fucking pillows fluffed. Call me, Princess. I will come running."

"Thank you."

I reach into my pocket and draw out the black box I've been carrying with me all day. "This is for you," I say.

Her eyes widen. "Carter?"

"Open it."

She takes it from me and opens it, then gasps. Inside the box, nestled on a black velvet cushion is her mother's silver charm bracelet. It's still got the key charm, but I've added another one to it. A rose.

"But I thought you needed it," she whispers, and stares at the bracelet. She traces it with her fingertip. "The rose is so beautiful."

"I'm going to buy you a charm for every event in our lives," I say.

Hannah's bottom lip trembles. "Are you serious?"

"Yeah."

"But Carter, you said you—"

"I need you, Hannah. You are the only luck I need. The only calm I need. The only excitement. You and our baby." The truth is, I need the bracelet, but it's been bugging me that it was precious to her and I kept it. I want her to have it, I want her to know that I will suffer through anything to make her happy.

I remove the bracelet from the box, and she holds out her wrist. I place it on her, and she sighs, smiling at it, her eyes glimmering with unshed tears. And then she hugs me. I kiss the top of her head, my hands wandering down her back, stroking every bit of skin I can get at.

"When do you get off work?" I ask.

"In a couple of minutes," she says. "I'm just going to clean up here, move the tables back and then—"

I start moving the tables back from the corners before she can say anything.

"Carter, I've got it, don't worry."

"You're pregnant," I murmur. "You are not moving shit."

She purses her lips, but she's wearing a small smile. "Thank you."

I don't think she gets it yet, and I don't blame her. She is mine. She is so fucking mine, and I am going to care for her every need from now on. I finish up under her direction, and then I slip my hand into the small of her back and walk her back to the counter at the front. She collects her purse and says goodbye to Irma, who is reading one of the *Game of Thrones* books.

Before we leave, I lean in and make eye contact with Irma.

She stiffens.

"I hope your favorite character dies," I say.

And then I guide a shocked Hannah out of the library. She's laughing by the time I feed her into my SUV and start the engine.

Forty-Seven

HANNAH

THE RIDE to the ranch is comfortable and quiet. Savage switches on the radio and listens to me croon to the music, smiling as we take the dirt road. It helps me not think too much about how strange things have gone.

I didn't expect to *ever* get pregnant, let alone get pregnant with Carter's baby, or when I was on the brink of taking a big step and leaving town.

The more I'm in Savage's presence, the less stressed I feel. Before, I felt this weird tension with him, but now it's good nerves and warmth.

And he loves me.

But I'm still afraid that this is too good to be true. Or more than I deserve.

Savage parks his SUV outside the ranch house, and I smile at the gorgeous log cabin. Pleasant memories from our time together fill my mind and heat floods my body.

"Stay right there," he says, and gets out of the car.

"Why?" I call out.

Savage circles the vehicle, opens my door, and offers

me his hand. "Because you shouldn't have to open your own door."

I laugh, but it dies in my throat as he lifts me out of the car and carries me toward the front door. "What are you—?"

"I love you," he says, and puts me down on the front porch. "I want you to know how important you are to me, Princess."

I lose my breath.

The way he's looking at me, how tender he's being, it's everything.

"I have something to show you," he says. "Two things." He unlocks the front door and stands back to let me inside. The hallway is covered in roses. Beautiful red roses, the edges of their petals so dark, they're almost black, are arranged in crystal vases all the way down either side of the hall.

I'm speechless.

Savage places his hand in the small of my back and guides me inside.

The hall isn't the only room filled with roses.

The living room is occupied by them too. We walk down the hall together, between the beautiful flowers, and Savage stops beside the closed door that leads into the library.

"So," he says, "the first thing I wanted to show you was these flowers, Princess."

"They're beautiful," I say, choking the words out.

"They're for you." He kisses my cheek. "I bred them for you, and named them after you."

My jaw drops. "Are you serious?"

"Yes. I feel like you need to know how much I care,

Hannah. I'm not going to hide how I feel any more," he says. "And the way you've been with me has given me an idea." He takes my hands and kisses them. "There are a lot of women in this country, this state, who need support. Women who are alone or who have been abused or hurt. Single mothers. I want to start an initiative to deliver flowers to new mothers in hospitals. In honor of you, of Charlotte, of strong women everywhere."

I burst into tears and throw my arms around him. "That is *amazing*, Carter. That is so amazing."

"I love you," he says.

And every time he says it, it's like a balm for my soul. "I love you too," I whisper into his chest, grasping his shirt. He's so solid, and my love for him is implacable. I don't know how much longer I can survive this. I am so scared of getting hurt, but I am so into him it makes me dizzy.

"And there's more," he says.

"More?"

"Yeah." Carter pulls away and holds my upper arms, smiling down at me. "I want you to know how serious I am about you, Hannah." He clears his throat. "You love books, you're a librarian, so I don't want you to take this the wrong way."

"Uh oh, what?"

"Well, remember how I donated those books to the library?" he asks.

"Yeah?"

"There was a second reason I did that, Princess." He opens the door to the library, and my heart turns over in my chest.

Inside is a crib. The bookcases are gone. Light streams

through the gorgeous French windows and skates across the wooden floors. The room smells clean, of wood polish and the scent of flowers that surround us.

"Carter," I say, unable to get my emotions out.

"You're not ready to move in with me yet," he says, "and that's fine. I want you to be comfortable and take as much time as you need, but I need you to know that I am in this, Hannah. One hundred percent. The only reason I didn't buy anything else for this room, and trust me, it's killing me not to, is because I want us to decorate it together. I want you to have whatever you want for our baby. I want us to go all in."

My heart feels like it's going to burst. I can't believe this.

"And don't worry about the other books and bookcases, I put them in the master bedroom for now. When we're ready, we'll build on another room."

"Carter, I can't even process this," I whisper. "This is amazing. You're amazing."

"I will do anything to make you happy, Hannah. What else can I do to show you how much I care?"

I wrap my arms around his middle and squeeze, resting my head against his muscular chest. "There's nothing else you can do. You've done everything. You— You saved my life twice, you've given me hope again, and you just— you—"

He takes my chin in his hand and tilts my head upward, looking me directly in the eyes. "You saved me, Hannah. Without even meaning to. Without even trying. Every laugh, every look, just the way you move through this world saved my life. When I was in my darkest times, your smiling face saved me, when you didn't even know I cared. I tried so hard to avoid this moment because I was scared. But if I've learned anything about you and me, it's that we're inevitable," he says. "We're meant to happen. And I'm not going to fucking fight it any more, because I don't want to. The only thing I'm going to fight for is you. And our child."

He swipes the tears away from my face and kisses my cheeks, then my lips.

"When you're ready, Hannah, please move in with me."

"Yes," I whisper. "Yes."

"Yes, you'll move in with me?"

"I will."

His face lights up, and I love it. I love how beautiful his smile is, and that he saves it specifically for me. He kisses me, and I melt in his arms. This is it, this is what I've always wanted. I don't know what the future will bring, but I know that I want it to be with him.

Forty-Eight

SAVAGE

SHE'S MINE.

Hannah is mine, and there isn't a damn thing anyone can do to take her away from me. I will have her for the rest of my life, protect her and keep her, and fucking worship the grounds she walks on. But while I feel like I've been gifted a perfect future, I can't help thinking that Hannah had at least a portion of hers taken away.

I meet Hannah at her old apartment on a sunny morning—she's fully moved out as of today—and sweep her into my arms the minute she's handed the key back to her landlord.

Hannah laughs and grasps my shoulders, throwing her head back, and she's the most beautiful woman in the world. I put her down, grab her packed bag, and lift it onto the back seat of my car. I open the passenger side door for Hannah.

I get in beside her, but I don't start the car yet.

It's a Sunday morning, and we have a couple of hours to kill before her grandmother's pot luck.

I turn to Hannah and study her. I'm not sure when I realized I was in love with this woman, or if it's just something that's always been there, waiting below the surface for me to get my shit together.

When I look at her, she has this indescribable quality. A beauty that radiates from the inside out. It's like I can see all the different shades of who she is—the red of her passion for kids, for us, for life or the pink of her cheeks when she's looking at me. The past and the present mesh together and make her into this complete, loveable woman.

"Carter?" she asks.

"Hmm."

"You're staring."

"I know," I say, and laugh. "Open the glovebox and grab the envelope inside, will you?"

"Sure." She takes the envelope out then frowns at her name, which I've written across the front in slashing letters. "What's this?"

"Open it."

She opens the envelope and removes two plane tickets from within, along with a note. She opens the note and reads it. I smile at her eyes widening as they shift from side-to-side.

I remember every word I wrote.

Princess,

You've given me everything I've ever dreamed of.

You might think that your life will always be in Heatstroke. That you will never get the adventure you dreamed of. Let's fix that.

Love,
Carter

And those two plane tickets are to France, specifically to Paris. From there, we'll catch a regional flight to Bordeaux. The South of France, just like she wanted.

The note trembles in Hannah's hand. "Are you serious? These are tickets to—"

"Yeah," I say. "I thought we'd go next week."

"Are you kidding?"

"You can't go in your third trimester, so let's go now. We'll go away together, enjoy ourselves, and then come back and get properly settled in at the house. Figured it's a good way to start our life together."

"Our life." Her cheeks turn that beautiful shade of pink again. She scrambles across the seats and throws her arms around my neck. She kisses my cheeks, my nose, my lips.

I kiss her back hard, my hands wondering over her back, moving down her spine, tracing her curves. She isn't showing yet, but I can't wait until she is. I can't wait to treat her the way she's always deserved to be treated.

"Hannah," I say, against her mouth. "I love you."

"I love you," she whispers.

"Let's get you back to the ranch." And then I suck her bottom lip into my mouth and nip it.

She moans against me. "I don't know if I can wait that long. I'm so desperate for you, Carter."

I love hearing that. Even more because I know she would've been too embarrassed to say it in the past. Too shy. Now, there's nothing between us except too many clothes. "Come on, Princess. Let's go. We're giving the folks in front of the bakery a free show."

She lifts her head and glances out at them. "Who cares?" And she's shining with pride. Unabashed.

I'm so fucking proud of her. "I do," I say. "Nobody gets to see you moaning and coming except for me."

Hannah shifts back into her seat and clips her seatbelt into place. And then we're on our way back to the house together. Our house.

———

"We should go," Hannah sighs, as she takes a casserole out of the oven and places it on the counter. "It's ready."

We're due at Ganny's pot luck in a half hour. It's just enough time to drive out there. But Hannah and I have spent most of the morning in each other's arms. I've made her come three times, but it's still not enough.

When I said I was going to worship her body, I meant it.

Hannah's wearing a cute cotton dress studded with blue flowers.

I take hold of her waist and turn her around in my arms, brushing the backs of my fingertips over her cheek. "How are you feeling?"

"Good," she says.

"Just good? That's not right."

"What do you—?"

I tug down the front of her dress and expose her full breasts in the kitchen. Her nipples pucker in the cool air, instantly. "Oh my God," she whimpers.

"You're not wearing a bra," I say.

"Yes."

"Are you trying to drive me crazy?" I ask.

"Maybe."

I palm one of her breasts and pinch her nipple. She gasps and arches her back. My other hand slides over her torso, down to the hem of her skirt.

"Naughty girl," I growl, and nip her throat, scratching it with my beard. "You'd better be wearing underwear."

My hand slips between her legs, and I find her wet and quivering for me. So slick, I could slip inside her in the kitchen.

And that's exactly what I intend to do.

I move her away from the oven, to the other side of the kitchen counter, and bend her over it, so that her tits press against the cold countertop.

I rip her dress up and over her hips, and she quivers and cries out.

"How bad do you want it, Princess?"

She swallows.

I trace the curves of her hips with my hands. "How bad?"

"So bad, Carter. I want you inside me. I need you to fill me up again."

I slip my finger over her warm pussy, spreading her warm wetness toward her clit. "Whose pussy is this?"

"Yours," she cries out.

I torture myself by fingering her slowly, by refusing to let myself taste her. It's like I'm edging myself by giving her slow pleasure. I rub her clit and finger her pussy at the same time, standing behind her and watching the way she reacts. How she starts swirling her hips, getting so desperate for her release that she's begging for it. Pleading. Both with her body and her mouth.

"You want to come, Princess?"

She smacks her hand down on the countertop. "Now. Give it to me now."

I love that she's demanding it.

I bend and suck her clit between my lips, and almost blow my load when she instantly comes on my face. Quickly, I pull back, remove my dripping cock from my pants and slide inside her. I enjoy the last pulses of her orgasm, and she arches into me as I slide in inch by inch.

"Carter, please. Please."

"This is going to be fast, Princess," I growl, and slap her ass, grab and squeeze it. "You'd better hold the fuck on."

I pound into her, and she clings to the counter top. Shaking, her eyes rolling in her head, and unearthly fucking noises escaping her throat. I'm making her lose all sense of herself, but it's nothing compared to the way she makes me feel.

Out of control, protective, happy.

I show her how I feel with every thrust, bringing us both closer to the edge. I press my hand into her hair, and tug on it.

She cries out. "Harder. Pull it harder."

And I do, finding her clit with my free hand and working her at a slower pace until she comes again. This time, when she breaks, I go with her. We're a breathless mess of arms and limbs. We're late for the potluck. We're totally fucking out of control when it comes to each other.

But for the first time in sixteen years, I'm happy. And it's all because of her.

Forty-Nine

HANNAH

MY STOMACH TWISTS as we pull up to Ganny's house in Savage's SUV.

Ganny has no idea that we're together, and neither does my dad. Technically, the boys don't know that we've decided to move in together. Of course, my girls know and are sworn to secrecy like they are about the pregnancy.

"You sure you want to do this?" Savage asks, a deep crease appearing between his brows. "We don't have to tell anybody shit today, if you don't want to. It's our choice."

"Thank you," I whisper. "But I think it's important that they know the truth. They're my family."

"They're going to be thrilled you're staying in Heatstroke," Savage says. "At least they will be after we get back from the South of France."

My stomach twirls at the thought. It's a dream come true to have the opportunity to go there and see another country. It's not like we can drink wine, but we can have food, and we can tour the area. And if Savage wants to, we can go up to Normandy in the North and see where the troops landed on D-Day. Military history is important to him.

"I'm ready," I say.

Savage hops out of the car and helps me out of it. He does that every time, even though I'm capable of doing it myself, but I like it. I like that he cares that much, and that if I asked him to stop, he would.

I take the casserole dish up to the front of Ganny's house.

We hesitate on the porch. Savage pulls me into another embrace and kisses me gently. "I love you," he says. "I'm right here with you."

I kiss him back, and then we enter the house. As per usual, Ganny's home is filled with noise and laughter, and Fireball's annoying barking as he and Alex play together. I place the casserole in the kitchen and then head into the living room to find my family.

Ganna and Dad are on the sofa together, chatting amiably. Dad is holding a can of soda, the wrinkles around his mouth and eyes pronounced. He's smiling more these days, and I'm grateful for that. I thought he would never smile again after Mom died.

I clear my throat.

"Hannah, honey pie, I'm so glad you're here," Ganny says, trying to get up.

"Don't get up," I say. "I want to talk to everyone."

"Everyone?" Dad frowns, brushing his fingers through his silver-gray hair. He's a mirror image of Cash, or what Cash will be when he's much older, except he's got Jesse's height.

"Yeah," I say, brushing my hands over my dress. "Yeah."

"I'll get them," Savage says.

People filter into the living room. June and Cash, Alex shortly after. Marci and Jesse, hand-in-hand, scarcely able to take their eyes off each other. Belle. Then Leo, who's wearing a deep frown and keeps glancing over at her non stop.

Finally, all my family is here.

I take a breath.

"I'm pregnant," I say.

A stunned silence follows.

Ganny's about to say something, but I cut her off. "Savage is the father," I say, pointing toward Carter.

He keeps a serious expression, but he slips an arm around my waist.

"We're moving in together," I say. "And I'm not going to leave Heatstroke permanently, like I originally planned."

More shocked stares.

I wait for them to say anything, but before they can, Savage turns me toward him. He holds my hands in his, giving me that genuine, warm smile he reserves only for me.

And then he drops to one knee.

Gasps travel through the room.

Tears spring to my eyes. Is this real?

"Hannah," Carter says, reaching into his pocket and withdrawing a black velvet box, "Princess. We haven't been together long, but I have been in love with you for what feels like a lifetime."

My heart is pounding so hard, I feel like I'm going to pass out.

"I'm not proposing to you because you're pregnant.

I'm proposing to you because I can't see a future without you by my side, and I don't want to. I want you to be my woman. I want to protect you. I want to be there by your side as you grow as a person, as I grow, as we become stronger as a couple. Every day I have spent with you has made me realize that life is still worth living." He opens the ring box. A beautiful diamond ring set in a golden band sits on the cushion inside. The diamond is shaped like a star, and is accented with beautiful red stones. "Will you do me the honor of being my wife, my woman, for the rest of my days?"

Nearby, Belle sniffs and hiccups.

"Yes. Yes, of course, I'll marry you."

Savage lifts me into his arms and buries, his head in my neck, squeezing me to him.

We're not just together. We're engaged. We're going to be married.

Excited hoots and hollers come from my family members. We're surrounded by arms and pats on the back, and happy laughter moments later. The last person to congratulate us is Cash.

He stands in front of us with his hands tucked into his pockets, scuffing his shoe on the wooden boards. He's wearing a Stetson today, and he shifts it on his head, blue eyes darting left and right. "Owe you an apology."

"Who?" Savage asks.

"Both of you. Savage, I'm sorry I doubted you and made you swear not to go near Hannah," he says. "That wasn't my place. I thought I was protecting my baby sister, when I should've been a better friend to you and helped you work through your shit."

Savage pats him on the shoulder.

"And Hannah," Cash says, glancing back at June who gives him an encouraging smile. She's got her arm around Alex's shoulders, and the pair of them are gossiping, their blonde heads bowed together. They're such a mother-daughter duo it makes my ovaries want to explode.

"Hannah," Cash repeats, and clears his throat. "Shit. Hannah, I'm sorry for the way I've acted. I was too over-protective, but it was because I didn't want to lose you, especially not after what happened with Mom."

"It's okay," I say, and draw him into a hug. "I love you, and I know why you did what you did."

"So, we're good?" he asks.

"We're good." I kiss my brother on the cheek and then return to Savage's waiting arms. I can't keep my hands off him, and his palm pressed to my hip tells me it's the same for him.

"You two are a match made in heaven," June sighs.

I look up at him, this beastly man who I believed had no interest in me, who I obsessed over for years. He's so protective over me, so warm and caring, and determined to do the right thing.

"Mine," he mouths, brushing my hair back from my cheek.

He kisses me gently on the lips. He claims me as his.

And for the first time in my life, I feel free.

Epilogue

SAVAGE

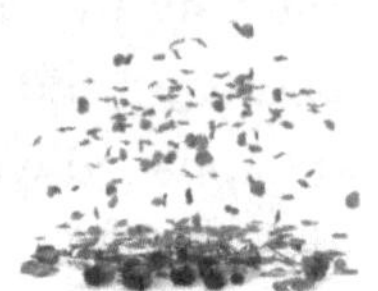

SHE'S LYING in the hospital bed, her hands resting on the cute green covers, the little bassinet next to her.

I stand at her bedside, watching her sleep, exhaustion sitting in my bones. Her exhaustion and mine. But that fatigue is accompanied by comfort, satisfaction, and a happiness that's unparalleled.

Because my baby girl is sleeping in the bassinet beside her mama. She's a tiny little thing, with soft dark hair, her peony blue eyes closed now, as she sleeps, and her little fist, so impossibly small, lifted to her mouth.

My gaze switches out between them, my daughter resting, my wife asleep in the bed, exhausted after giving birth, and I can barely handle it.

Do I deserve to have this much love in my life?

I'll never be sure, but I am selfish enough to never let it go. I will spend my life looking after them.

Hannah's eyes flicker open and connect with mine, and she takes my breath away. I'm fucking instantly choked up, trying to swallow the emotion that's lodged in my throat.

"Hey," she whispers. "There you are. Daddy."

"Daddy?"

"That's what she'll call you. Don't make it weird, Carter."

I let out a low laugh that rumbles through the room. My daughter makes a little whining sigh that's the most impossibly cute thing I've heard in my life.

Hannah shushes me and gestures me closer.

I move in and bend over the bed, kissing her forehead, her nose, her lips. "How are you feeling?" I ask her. "Did you get enough sleep?"

"I have no idea," she says. "But I feel good. Tired but good. She's here. I can't believe she's here."

I sit down on her bed with her, and we both stare at the clear bassinet they've placed her in. She's wrapped in a pink blanket, and she's sleeping peacefully, which I doubt will last long. I wrap my arm around around Hannah's shoulders and enjoy this moment.

"Do you think we'll be good enough?" Hannah whispers. "You know, as parents?"

"Maybe," I say. "We can work on it."

"There are like fifty parenting books in my wishlist," she whispers. "It's funny, when you're getting ready for the baby to come, you read so much about having the baby and being pregnant that you kind of forget the other stuff."

"We're going to do this together," I whisper. "We'll take shifts sleeping."

"That sounds sweet, but I'm the one with the milk."

"True." I kiss her forehead. "Look, we're going to do

the best we can, and we're going to make sure that she has the best life possible. That she always has us to turn to when she needs someone. That we're patient and kind."

"Why are you so perfect?" Hannah rests her head against my chest. "I swear, I didn't stand a chance when I first laid eyes on you."

"You're stealing my lines," I say, and kiss the top of her head. "What do you want to call her?"

We're both silent for a while.

The baby shifts and mewls in her bassinet, and I get up and carefully remove her from it. She's sniffling and seeking with her mouth. I brush my fingers over her soft forehead then hand her Hannah.

She shifts our baby girl's weight in her arms, and undoes her nursing bra. I help her position the baby so that her little mouth can latch over Hannah's nipple. Breastfeeding is something we researched and read about a lot. We're hoping Hannah will be able to breastfeed, but we're prepared if that's not a possibility.

Our daughter settles against her breast, suckling quietly, her fist resting against Hannah's skin. The little baby noises are adorable. Hannah's eyes are filled with unshed tears, and she wears a smile as she looks up at me.

"I think I know what we should call her," she whispers.

I sit down next to her again, staying on the edge of the bed so she has room to feed. "What is it, Princess?"

"Rose," she whispers. "We should name her Rose."

"That's perfect." I press a kiss to Hannah's forehead, then place a protective arm around her shoulders again. I've encircled my little family with love. As we sit there together, there is nothing I wouldn't do for them. For both of them.

I would fight for them. Stand for them. Even let them go, if it was what they wanted.

Hannah and Rose. They've taught me the meaning of love again, and it's not a cloying desperation or a need for control, or the burden of responsibility and the pain of loss.

It's freedom.

And I will love them until my last breath.

Want to read more Hannah and Savage? Read their epilogue by signing up for Bailey's newsletter.

Belle and Leo's steamy, off-limits story is next. Read END GAME LOVE by scanning the QR CODE.

Bailey's Babes

Come join Bailey in the Facebook Group and hang out with other romance babes just like you! You'll get sneak peeks from new books, access to giveaways, and bookish conversations that will make your reader heart sing.

Acknowledgments

This has been my favorite book to write so far. I'm probably going to say that about every story in *the Heatstroke Hearts series*, but Savage and Hannah will always be top spot for me. Just the way he loves and protects her… Ugh.

I need to thank my husband and my son, because I wouldn't be writing without them. They're my reason.

To Claire, my assistant, I literally can't imagine how these books would turn out without your valuable insight. You've helped me become a better writer.

My Betas! You ladies have been so patient with me throughout this process. Your comments made me giggle, gave me insight, and helped me turn this book into what it is. Thank you to Megan, Cal, and Celeste. I love you, ladies!

To the influencers on my influencer team. You have put a smile on m face every single day since the launch of my debut novels. I'm so lucky to have you. Thank you Teodora, Nettie, Nay, Alexandraa, Monica, Sydney B, Amila, Paige, Brit, Fatima, Alex, Brittany, Megan, Bella, and all the other ladies who have been so supportive.

To my ARC readers! Thank you for reading Hannah and Savage's story. I hope you loved it. This book emotionally wrung me out, and I hope it does that to you too (evil laughter).

And to my readers. Every book is meant for you. I hope it has found you exactly when you needed to read it.

FYI My favorite scene in this book is when Savage finally says the magical words… "Fuck it."

Bailey Hart writes small town swoonworthy romance that leaves readers with all the tingly feels. She loves wearing her nails long, eating Mexican food, and dancing like nobody's watching. When she's not writing, she's at dance class, spending time with her son and husband, or daydreaming about her next story idea—spicy scenes included. She lives in Cape Town, South Africa, and desperately wants a cat in the near future.

Come visit her at www.baileyhartromance.com